Strange things happe
The residents have gr

The isolated Australian harbour town of Gulpepper is not like other places. Some maps don't even show it. And only outsiders use the full name. Everyone who lives there calls it The Gulp. The place has a habit of swallowing people.

A truck driver thinks the stories about The Gulp are made up to scare him. Until he gets there.
Teenage siblings try to cover up the death of their mother, but their plans go drastically awry.
A rock band invite four backpackers to a party at their house, where things get dangerously out of hand.

A young man loses a drug shipment and his boss gives him 48 hours to make good on his mistake.
Under the blinking eye of the old lighthouse, a rock fisher makes the strangest catch of his life.

Five novellas. Five descents into darkness.
Welcome to The Gulp, where nothing is as it seems.

PRAISE FOR ALAN BAXTER

"Alan Baxter is an accomplished storyteller who ably evokes magic and menace."
 – *Laird Barron*, *author of Swift to Chase*

"Baxter delivers the horror goods."
 – *Paul Tremblay*, *author of The Cabin at the End of the World*

"Step into the ring with Alan Baxter, I dare you. He writes with the grace, precision, and swift brutality of a prizefighter."
 – *Christopher Golden*, *NYT bestselling author of Ararat and The Pandora Room*

"Alan Baxter's fiction is dark, disturbing, hard-hitting and heart-breakingly honest. He reflects on worlds known and unknown with compassion, and demonstrates an almost second-sight into human behaviour."
 – *Kaaron Warren*, *Shirley Jackson Award-winner and author of The Grief Hole*

"...if Stephen King and Jim Butcher ever had a love child then it would be Alan Baxter."
 – *Smash Dragons*

"Baxter draws you along a knife's edge of tension from the first page to the last, leaving your heart thumping and sweat on your brow."
 – *Midwest Book Review*

THE

GULP

Five Tales of Horror

ALAN

BAXTER

THE GULP
ISBN-13: 978-098-057-8294
ISBN-10: 098-057-8294
13th DRAGON BOOKS

First Trade Paperback Edition – January 2021
Copyright © 2021 Alan Baxter

Cover Art "Warning Sign" (oil on canvas) © 2012
Halinka Orszulok
Cover Design © Alan Baxter
Edited by Mallory Wiper
Internal layout by David Wood

Alan Baxter
www.alanbaxter.com.au

*This book is dedicated to
every creepy town
and every creepy resident therein...*

Table of Contents

Please note that this book is written in Australian English, using Australian spelling and terminology. A short glossary at the back might help with some of the slang in these stories.

Out on a Rim

Out on a Rim

Richard Blake's day had been deceptively boring. Tall, pale gum trees lined either side of the road, and spread thickly back into shadow. Late afternoon sun occasionally lanced through a rare gap in the canopy that closed over high above. Rich sat quiet in the passenger seat as George Grayson drove the Woolworths big rig along the single lane highway.

"It's like a tunnel," Rich said eventually, leaning forward to peer out the windscreen. The road freaked him out. "Kinda claustrophobic."

George laughed. "You haven't seen anything yet. It's like this for nearly twenty minutes from Enden until the Gulpepper turnoff. It's another twenty minutes from the turnoff on the other side too, until you get to Monkton."

"Nothing in between?"

"Only bush and Gulpepper. And that's ten minutes from the turnoff through nothing but more bush until you reach the coast." He nodded out the other side of the cab. "That way is thick all the way to the freeway that bypasses all of this."

"It's the only town there? No other villages or anything along the coast?"

"Not between Enden and Monkton, nah. Just Gulpepper. A kind of big, natural bay with high cliffs either side. It's quite a big town, but there's fuck all else for miles around except bush and ocean." George frowned out the side window towards the lowering sun. "We're running too late. That traffic jam in Enden fucked up our schedule."

"Does it matter?" Rich asked the question despite George's obvious discomfort. What was the problem, other than being a little late home?

George glanced at the young man beside him and sighed. "I don't want to be in Gulpepper at night. Listen, there's some stuff you should know. You're a good kid, you'll be a good driver. I'm just sorry you're inheriting this fucken route offa me. I'm glad as hell to be retiring, I tell you that. Pretty much everything about this gig is just fine, except once a week when you hafta come to this freaky fucken town. There's one road in and out of Gulpepper. I hate driving down it and can't wait to come back the other way."

Rich smiled. Old George reminded him of the conspiracy theory nuts who thought mobile phone towers were transmitting mind control. Rich didn't buy into all that hokum.

"I see you fucken grinnin'," George said. "Trust me, you get in, make your delivery, and get right back out again. Once I stopped for lunch there. Never again."

"Why, what happened?"

George frowned, swallowed. "I don't wanna talk about it. Gulpepper is just... different, that's all. And only outsiders use that name. Everyone who lives there calls it The Gulp." He shot a sideways look at Rich again. "The place has a habit of swallowing people."

Rich laughed. "That what they tell you?" It's not like Australia wasn't riddled with remote towns. George was trying to scare him.

"Mark my words, son, make this stop your quickest of the week."

They fell into silence as the gum trees blurred by on either side and the sun got lower. After the bustle of Enden, especially with the added excitement of the traffic accident, the empty, gloomy road seemed preternaturally quiet. It was ten minutes before another car passed them going the other way, the face behind the wheel a pale moon in the low light, staring dead ahead with intense concentration. Eventually George slowed, leaning forward over the big wheel.

"Junction's coming up," he said to Rich's questioning look. "And nowhere to turn a truck, so if you miss it, you have to go all the way to the outskirts of Monkton to turn around, which adds nearly an hour to your trip by the time you've finished fucking around."

"Seriously?"

"I told you, son, there's nothing good about this place."

George pointed ahead. "See the memorial?"

Rich saw a white cross at the side of the road, a faded wreathe of plastic flowers hanging on it. Painted on the crossbar was *Wayno*. Right behind the cross a large gum tree had a huge scar in its pale bark. His stomach soured. Memories of watching Grant's last drive were still fresh after all these years. His old school friend had a memorial like this on a road heading out of Sydney. They'd been racing, Grant was winning, until he misjudged the bend. Rich thought he'd never shake off the guilt. The image of Grant's car disintegrating as Rich stood on his car's brakes would never fade. "Yeah, I see it."

"It's a good one to look out for. The turnoff is only a few hundred metres past."

Rich nodded. "Okay, good to know."

"Poor old Wayno. Probably aimed his car at a tree rather than have to go back to The Gulp." Before Rich could address that particularly dark assessment, George pointed again. "See the sign?"

On the other side of the narrow highway was a small green sign, pointing across the road.

Gulpepper Road
(Gulpepper 11km)

"Is that a skull hanging off it?" Rich asked as George slowed to make the turn.

"Or a shrunken head. Kids, probably, mucking about with Halloween props. But with this town, you never know."

Rich laughed. The old man was laying it on a bit thick. He realised this was probably like when Rich got his first job out of school, at a factory in Bankstown.

First day, the foreman sent him to the office to ask the manager for a long weight. The manager smiled and nodded, said, *Sit there, son*, and Rich was left for an hour. Eventually the manager came back out and said, *Long enough? Off you go then!* Rich went back to the factory floor among gales of laughter. But fair enough, he'd play along.

The road into town was indistinguishable from the highway running between Enden and Monkton. One lane each way, thick bush either side. But even gloomier now, the sun behind them about to drop below the tree line.

"We've left this much too late," George muttered, almost to himself.

Rich smiled.

After a while the gum trees began to thin and a few farms appeared on either side. The houses were old, tin roofs and weatherboard walls, a lot of them with peeling paint and rust encroaching from all sides above. Tractors and box-back trucks were parked around, most of them at least twenty years old. Dogs ran up dirt driveways, barking at the large green and white Woolworths 18-wheeler as it bulled past.

Another few minutes and regular houses began to dot the sides. Plenty of bush still around, but lawns with fences, trampolines and cubby houses, family cars. Then the side streets began, more houses with smaller plots of land. They passed a large building, lit up with neon, a big *Tooheys New* sign glowing out front. Illuminated letters above the double glass doors proclaimed, *Gulpepper Bowlo*.

"Is there a town anywhere in Australia without a lawn bowls club?" Rich asked with a grin.

"If there is, I haven't been there," George said, but his face was set. Normally the man had a good humour about him, crass and rough sometimes, but he was in his late 60s and that was only to be expected. Now though, he seemed entirely dour. Perhaps he really didn't like this place.

Either that or he was playing his role in this particular hazing with great skill. The road opened out and they came to the main street leading into town. A roundabout at the top of a hill had three other exits, one to the right was signposted to a leisure centre, to the left went towards more housing, and one dead ahead. They went straight across. The road sloped downhill towards the ocean that lay dark and grey across the horizon. From their high vantage point the town lay to either side in undulating waves of steep hills, covered in houses and shops, an industrial looking set of units off to the left. Rich caught a glimpse of the harbour, a small forest of white masts and all manner of fishing and leisure boats, then the road led down and he lost perspective on it. Far to the north and south the land rose steeply to cliffs thickly covered with gum trees and banksia.

"If there was a bush fire, this place would be entirely cut off," Rich mused.

"It's happened once or twice apparently. But given how often the rest of the country burns, this place has been pretty lucky." George nodded ahead as he spoke. "Here we are."

They came to a large area on the left with a car park, half full of cars, and a big shopping complex behind. The huge Woolworths supermarket took up one end of the complex, and Rich spotted a baker, a reject shop, and a couple of other things on the far side. But George turned into the loading bay before the car park, leading him to the back of the supermarket. There was a big turning space and he nosed the truck in, then backed slowly and expertly along the narrow cement apron to big double roller doors at the supermarket's rear warehouse. A few young people in Woollies uniforms stood waiting on the raised dock, looking bored.

"Saw us coming," George said. "Get this stuff inside and we'll be out of here in under half an hour, we're lucky." He killed the engine and jumped down from the cab.

Rich joined him at the back and they opened up the trailer. The teenagers and one grizzled older man began walking manual hand-held pallet jacks back and forth, ferrying all manner of grocery store items from the truck into the big warehouse. George leaned against the wall off to one side, squinting up into the darkening sky. It was indigo out over the water, pale grey and pink to the west over the bushland.

"If this lot pull their collective finger out, we'll be back towards the highway before the streetlights come on," George said.

"What happens when the streetlights come on?"

George sneered. "This place is weird enough in daytime. I don't wanna know what comes out at night."

"It's just a harbour town," Rich said with a laugh. "Tourist town."

"You see any tourists?"

Rich grinned. Next week George would be retired and this route would be his. He'd have to do his best to make good time and take the opportunity to stick around for an hour or two after the goods were delivered, have a proper look at the place.

At twenty-seven, Rich had started to feel like maybe he needed to broaden his horizons. He'd grown up in Sydney, but hadn't been out of New South Wales except for one high school camping trip to Queensland. He became estranged from indifferent parents right around the time school finished and figured it was no great loss. He'd largely looked after himself since the start of high school anyway. University didn't suit him, and after Grant died he decided to go somewhere else, forge his own way. The factory job didn't last long, still too close to home, so heading south down the coast a few hours seemed like a good idea.

He'd done a few different things over the years, mostly drinking his weekly pay cheque from various blue-collar jobs. He was happy enough for a while. He found a job at meat packing plant and thought it would do for a time until he saw a divorced workmate of only forty-two keel over dead from a heart attack. It was like a flare going off in his mind, seeing himself heading for the cold cement just like that poor bastard. So he decided to shake things up, look to a further horizon. He moved another hour south, studied and passed for his HGV licence, and got the job with Woollies. Better pay than the meat plant and cheaper rent too. Save up enough over the next few years, he'd decided, then leave not only the state, but the entire Australian continent behind, see the world. In the meantime, keep painting. He loved to make his small artworks, weird landscapes in oils on miniature canvases. It calmed him. A workmate in his last job had said he should get an Etsy shop or something, try to make some money from it. Maybe he would.

"Stop daydreaming," George said, punching Rich lightly on the arm. "Let's get outta here."

He slammed the trailer shut, dropped the locking bar in place, then went back around to the cab. They headed away from the loading dock, and George made a sound of disgust.

"This fucken dickhead!"

A large white panel van was parked right in the entrance to the loading bay, blocking half the road. The gap it left was enough for most vehicles to get around, but not a truck the size of theirs. George blasted the horn a couple of times, several pedestrians turning with startled expressions.

Rich leaned forward to peer at the van. "No one in it," he said.

"Fuck me dead."

George sat there a moment, knuckles white on the wheel. He blatted the horn again, this time drawing some shaken fists and choice curses from passers-by.

"He surely hasn't just left it there."

"Give it a minute," Rich said. "He'll probably come back."

"Fuck this." George revved up the truck and crept slowly forward.

"You won't squeeze through there," Rich said. His training and licence test were all still fresh. Widths and heights, load limits and speed limits, it was all branded on his forebrain.

"Watch me."

"Nah, George, you'll hit the van."

"Fuck him, shouldn'ta parked there."

"Don't give yourself an insurance nightmare the week you retire, mate. You want a clean getaway don't you? Just wait, he surely won't be long."

George grunted in annoyance and edged the truck a little to the right. "I'll get through."

Before Rich could say anything there was a bump and grinding crunch.

"Fuck it!" George snapped. The cab tilted a little to one side, then bumped back down. "Fucken kerb. I didn't see that."

They jumped out and saw the front right wheel had ground into the apex of a shallow cement curve, and the tyre was already half-flat.

"Ah, shit. I done a fucken rim!" George said.

Rich crouched for a better look. Sure enough, the wheel rim had bent up and out where it had pressed into the cement, the entire weight of the cab on top of it. Only a little, but enough for air to hiss from the gap it made.

"There's no driving on that," Rich said. "We'll have to call out for a new wheel."

"No shit, Richard! You think I was born yesterday?"

Rich frowned at the man's vehemence, but George was already looking nervously at the sky, then down along the main street. He pulled out his phone and rang a number. At least there was reception here. Rich checked his phone and frowned. He had no service at all. George must be on a better provider.

"Nah, gotta be now. Can't you send someone in from Monkton or Enden?" George's voice was angry, but it was higher in pitch too. Scared? "Then what are we supposed to fucken do? Fuck! All right."

He hung up and the eyes he turned to Rich were haunted. "No one coming until the morning."

Rich's eyebrows rose. "Overnight in The Gulp then?" It didn't bother him, he had no one waiting for him. "Better ring your wife."

"I'm gonna back it up before all the air is gone." George got back into the cab and lined the truck up along the left side of the loading bay, as neatly tucked against the supermarket as he could make it, leaving the damaged front right wheel easily accessible. He didn't get out of the cab.

Rich walked over, looked up as George wound down the window. "Where we gonna stay then? You know anywhere? Motel or something?"

George barked a laugh. "Right here." He held up an empty plastic two litre Solo bottle. The man chugged the stuff all day long. "I'll piss in this and sleep where I sit. I suggest you do the same."

"I'm not sharing a fucking cab with you overnight, much less a bloody piss bottle, mate!" Rich gestured behind himself. "There's a whole town out there. It'll have pubs and motels and shit. Let's have a feed, get pissed. Enjoy ourselves."

"Nah, no chance. I'm staying right here. You should do the same."

"You're taking all this a bit far, George. I get it, I'm the new boy, wind me up. But this? It's a bit much."

"You can do whatever you want, son. But I strongly advise you stay in here with me."

"No way, mate. I'll find somewhere to stay in town. What time are they sending out a wheel?"

"Said someone would be here by eight."

Rich nodded. "I'll be back by eight then."

"If you're not here by ten, I'm leaving without you. I've put in years and this is my last week. My last run to this place. I'm not being swallowed by The Gulp three days before I quit."

Rich laughed, twisted his face into something sardonic and said in a bad American accent, "I was three days from retirement, dammit!"

"I am not kidding, Richard. Ten a.m. I leave, with or without you. Then I do my last two days of deliveries and I'm a retired old cunt with nothing but drinkin' and moanin' to do for the rest of my life."

Rich frowned, looking up at George, the sky above him darkening into night. "All right, mate. Whatever you reckon. I'll be here by eight."

George nodded once, but his face was resigned, like Rich had suddenly become his biggest disappointment. Then he rolled up the window and was lost behind its dark mirror as a streetlight buzzed on and made a pool of weak yellow glow.

"Crazy old man," Rich said with a laugh. He turned and headed out of the loading bay, then turned left towards the harbour.

The streets were wide, forty-five-degree angle parking bays along both sides, with deep stone gutters. It was relatively quiet, a handful of pedestrians wandering around, a few cars crawling by in the speed-restricted local traffic zone. Rich passed a Chinese restaurant, empty of customers, and a Leagues club that seemed quite busy, and crossed the road beside another roundabout, a neat circular bed of flowers in the centre. He entered the main street proper, surf shops and pharmacies, a Salvation Army thrift store, kebab shop, banks and a doctor's surgery, a second-hand bookstore. The place was pretty nice, he decided, the architecture old-fashioned like so many country towns in Australia. There was a heavy air of colonial settlement in the style, the white man's boot print heavy on the landscape. Again, like so many Australian towns. All of them, if he was honest about it.

He came to a large park on his left, a big war memorial arch standing white and stark against the shadowy green grass. He frowned at a couple of piles of mushrooms, or were they toadstools? Normally you'd find wreathes of flowers placed against a war memorial, but this was the first time he'd seen fungus. And so deliberately placed. He laughed, kept walking. A children's playground sat far back from the street in the middle of the park. It looked to be in pretty good condition, bright colours in hard plastic, rubberised crash matting underneath. Certainly the most modern thing he'd seen thus far in town. Streetlights beside a community centre next to the playground cast a wan orange glow across the play equipment, and Rich startled when he realised four people were sitting on the large double-sided metal seesaw. They were almost solid silhouettes with the weak light behind them, but they were clearly all watching him go by. He was a good fifty metres away, on the footpath raised a little higher than the park, but they stared up the slope at him with a strange intensity. Grown-ups too, not kids.

Well, Rich told himself, *teenagers more likely*. There wasn't much to do in country towns and kids tended to hang out in public places until they were old enough to drink, then they'd hang out in the pub. Rich was well past the hanging out stage of his life and most certainly headed for a pub. There had to be one. And it would hopefully have a bistro too. He was starved.

He tore his eyes away from the curious teenagers and skipped sideways as a man with a dog walked right at him. "Scuse me," Rich said, even though the man had made no effort to avoid a collision.

He wore a heavy woollen coat, down to his knees, despite the late summer warmth. Rich was comfortable in cargo pants and a t-shirt, a light denim jacket clutched in one hand in case it got colder later. The dogwalker had a dark hat, a trilby or something like it, pressed down low on his brow, his face a dark shadow. His dog was a golden retriever, glossy in the streetlight, face split in a guileless grin.

As they were almost side by side, Rich paused. "Actually, mate, sorry to bother you."

The man stopped and turned, streetlight splashing across his face under the brim of the hat. He had no nose, just two dark, vertical holes beneath his eyes. "What?"

Rich swallowed, determined not to be spun out by the unexpected deformity. But George's words slid across his hindbrain.

Gulpepper is just... different, that's all.

"Well?" the man demanded. "I've got to be home, can't be out when... got to be home."

His dog sniffed wetly at Rich's hand and Rich absent-mindedly patted his golden head. It was damp, a little sticky feeling. He grimaced, pulled his hand away. "I was wondering if you could tell me where the nearest pub is?"

"The Gulp's got two. *Gulpepper Inn* about a hundred metres further along here on the other side, corner of Shellhaven Street. *The Victorian Hotel* is on the same block, diagonally opposite, corner of Tanning and Kurrajong Street."

Rich opened his mouth to says thanks, but didn't get a chance as the man put his head down and walked quickly away. He was stocky and seemed to fill his coat strangely as he ambled off at speed.

Rich walked on. After he passed the park he came to a large sandstone building, an old hall of some kind, now a museum. *History of The Gulp* was stencilled on the door. He might try to find time to spend in there when it was open, he decided. This place was certainly piquing his interest. And not in entirely good ways, but curiosity was a valuable trait, he'd learned. It tended to allay fears. Knowledge was power and all that.

He looked over when he came to a crossroads,

Shellhaven Street heading off up a fairly steep hill and whatever street this was continuing on further towards the harbour. Sure enough, across the road was the *Gulpepper Inn*, the name carved into the plaster façade of the second storey. Maybe they had rooms too. A sign in gold letters across the doors said *Welcome to Clooney's*. Schizophrenic pub? A big sign in another window said *Harbour Bistro*. He imagined a line of sight right through the large block to the other pub the old man had mentioned and decided not to bother. No point in walking further when there was beer and food right here.

Clooney's, if that was its name, was a classic seaside town pub. Busy but not packed, a long bar all the way down one side with sets of beer taps at regular intervals. Shelves of spirits covered the wall behind the bar, a huge plastic marlin mounted above. No stools at the bar, but high tables with tall stools around them at the front, plenty of regular tables and chairs scattered around the back half of the long room, again a little more old-fashioned than might be expected in a city pub. All manner of fish and fishing paraphernalia adorned the walls, a huge net hung across the ceiling in the front corner opposite the door, filled with faded plastic fish and crabs. A few photos, some old black and whites, others in colour, showed locals with particularly memorable catches. A few sharks, some big fish Rich would never identify. One showed a young man with a lobster nearly as big as he was, but kind of wide and flat. Surely that was a fake.

People stood around the pub in groups or sat at tables, most of them young to middle-aged, a fair mix of men and women. A few older people here and there, most notably a table of six grey-haired women who must have averaged at least 80 years old. They were raucous, laughing and rocking back and forth in their chairs, wine glasses in hand. A general hubbub filled the place, the murmur of conversation, music coming from somewhere, but Rich couldn't see a jukebox. Eighties classic "Love is a Battlefield", he realised after a moment.

Deeper in was a corridor with toilet doors on one side, then a back door leading out to a courtyard and more tables and chairs. Smokers were busy drinking and filling their lungs out there.

Rich went up to the bar, an older man and a younger woman serving behind it. The man ignored him and the young woman came over. She was beautiful, with a killer figure and long dark hair tied back in a loose ponytail. Maybe mid- to late-20s, perhaps a year or so younger than him. Rich threw his best casual, disinterested smile at her. "How ya goin'?"

"What can I get you?" she asked. Cold, clearly not interested in a chat or telling him how she was.

Never mind, he'd play nice and friendly and see if she thawed. Would be great to get laid tonight, an unexpected bonus to the night's weirdness. "Schooner of Lashes, thanks."

She poured the pale ale and he handed over ten bucks. When she came back with the change he said, "It's my first time here and I need a feed. Any recommendations?"

She looked at him for a moment with a strange hardness in her eyes. "I recommend you check the menu and pick something you like." She smiled then, and there was a hint of genuine humour in it.

He couldn't help his own smile spreading and opened his mouth to say more but she turned away. Not to serve someone else, she simply turned and moved a couple of metres off and stood looking out over the bar. *Well, all right then*, Rich thought.

The food service area was at the end of the bar and he went along to look over the menu. All the usual culprits, schnitty and chips, steak, chicken parma, salt and pepper squid.

"Anything but the seafood," a voice said.

He turned to look and one of the old women from the group up the back was moving past, heading to get a drink. It could only have been her who spoke, but she didn't even glance back. He decided to take her advice anyway.

The man from behind the bar approached this time.

"What'll you have?"

"Steak, chips and salad, thanks. Sirloin, medium rare."

"Sauce?"

"Pepper?"

"Yep."

"Thanks."

The man rang it up and Rich paid, watching the fluorescent light reflect off the guy's head through a wisp of thinning hair. He was a big fella, maybe only an inch or two taller than Rich's six foot, but he was wide and looked fat at first. Closer inspection revealed barely an inch of fat over thick rolling muscle. He reminded Rich of the powerful dudes he'd seen in World's Strongest Man contests on TV, genetic mutants who seem to naturally grow massive. He probably carried beer kegs around like it was no big thing. He held out a number on a metal stand in one meaty paw and Rich took it. Number 13. He nodded his thanks and turned away.

He pulled out a chair and sat at an unoccupied table towards the back, stood the number in the centre, looked around at the varied clientele. It all seemed pretty normal to him.

"You're a fucken idiot!" one of four young men at the next table said suddenly, leaning back with laughter. His three friends laughed along, one looking a little chagrined as well. No doubt he was the idiot.

The accuser glanced over and saw Rich looking. Rich nodded.

"How ya goin'?" the man said through his nose.

All four were maybe early- to mid-20s, jeans and

work boots, t-shirts, drinking schooners of beer.

"Pretty good, thanks," Rich said. "You?"

"Nice night for it."

Rich wasn't sure what *it* might be, but he nodded again. "Sure is."

The guy kept staring, his face entirely neutral. His three friends watched too. After a couple of seconds the weight of their collective expressionless gaze became uncomfortable.

"The steaks any good here?" Rich asked, grasping for anything to say to break the moment.

"Better than the Vic but it's a harbour town. You should eat the fucken seafood, hey."

"Didn't think of it like that."

"See any fucken cows on your way in?" another of the group said.

"Can't say I did. Saw a few farms, but not what was, you know, on them."

"Fucken great ocean out there full of good tucker. No point eating shit that has to be shipped in from elsewhere." The guy said *elsewhere* like it was a disease.

"Good point." Rich smiled. "I'll try the seafood next time."

The four of them stared again, clearly happy to peruse without conversation. Rich began to feel like a museum exhibit. "You guys fish?" he asked.

"Course." The man gestured around the table. "The four of us here are the best rock fishers in town."

This elicited waves of laughter and guffaws around the table and a few choice comments from other patrons nearby.

"Couldn't catch a disease if he licked a dead hobo's arsehole," one older guy said. He was probably late-50s, iron grey curly hair and corded muscle along his forearms. "Hey? Who're ya kidding, Troy?"

"Fuck ya, Trev!" Troy said, but he laughed along.

"Couldn't catch a train at a single-platform station," one of his mates said.

"Couldn't catch crabs in a one-woman town," said another mate.

Laughter ran long and loud, including Troy. He seemed like a good sport.

"Where do you fish?" Rich asked, as the laughter faded.

The four around the table fell suddenly serious, all the others around quietening down. The man with the grey hair tutted loudly.

"Tryin' a steal our spots, mate?" Troy said.

Rich had never fished in his life, had no idea what it even involved beyond a rod, a hook, and water. "Nah, nah. Just making conversation."

The expressionless gazes from before, which had become full of mirth, were now steely and hard, eyes narrowed. Rich swallowed.

"Thirteen?" a voice said beside him.

He jumped and looked up, saw a thin woman in the black and whites of a chef, long dark hair pulled into a greasy ponytail. She held out a plate.

"Yes, thanks!"

He took the plate, grateful for the distraction. The woman snatched up his number and walked away. The group of keen rock fishers were leaning into each other across their table again, talking quietly. The man with the curly grey hair had his back turned.

Jesus, Rich thought.

He kept his eyes down, concentrated on his dinner, which turned out to be really good. Except the dressing on the salad that seemed strangely bitter, with a tang he couldn't quite place. Not unpleasant, just unusual. He cleaned his plate and felt a lot better for the feed. He drained the last of his beer and went back to the bar.

"Same again?" the girl asked.

"Yeah, thanks. I'm Rich."

"Are ya? Maybe I should marry ya. Then kill you for the money."

He laughed, but her face was a little too intense for

his liking. "Short for Richard. I'm a truck driver, so my wealth is not extensive, sadly."

"Your wealth is not extensive?" She laughed. "Fucken hark at 'im and his fancy talk."

She poured the beer and took his money, but didn't walk away this time.

"I wasn't expecting to stay overnight, but turns out I need a bed," he said.

"It won't be mine, cowboy."

"No, that's not what I meant." He hoped, but it wasn't what he'd meant. "Can you recommend somewhere? Are there rooms here? Nice harbour town like this must get a lot of tourists, yeah? So I figure there's plenty of places to stay."

"Tourists? Nah, not really. Not the sort of place folks pass through and no one comes to The Gulp for fun."

"They don't? Why not?"

She smiled a little crookedly. "They just don't. Some maps don't even show us being here."

"Seems a little weird."

"The Gulp is a weird place. Blackfellas had the right idea."

"What?"

"They wouldn't settle here. One of the few places white settlers really did find empty, but for wildlife."

"Is that right?"

She tipped her head a little to one side. "You walk down the main street to get here?"

"Yeah, I was delivering to Woollies, but the truck... broke down. So I have to stay till morning."

"So you walked past the museum?"

"Yeah, I saw that. It was closed."

"You're so interested in The Gulp, you should go in."

Rich nodded. "Okay, I'll do that."

"Ocean Blue."

"What?"

"Motel. Up the top end of Tanning Street. We don't

have much call for accommodation, but there are a couple of motels, and a campsite with a caravan park. All of 'em spend most of their time empty. You could take your pick of any, but Ocean Blue is probably best."

"Right, okay, thanks. Why that one?"

She shrugged. "Just probably best, that's all."

"Do you have a number? Should I ring ahead?"

She barked a laugh. "You'll probably be the only cunt there. Just show up, Donny'll give you a room. He's in the office twenty-four seven. He lives there. Just ring the bell by the door."

"Okay, great. Tanning Street?" He'd heard that before, when the noseless man had told him about the two pubs.

"When you leave here, turn right out the door. Get to the roundabout, big post office on the corner, turn right again, that's Tanning. Long walk, it'll take you probably fifteen minutes, but just keep going. You'll pass the primary school on your left, then Ocean Blue is a bit further along on the same side. If you reach the servo you missed it."

"Easy as," Rich said. "So what do you do when you're not working here."

"Fuck's sake," she said, and for a moment he thought he'd annoyed her, then realised she was looking over his shoulder.

He glanced around as a crash caught everyone's attention, glasses shattering on the floor as a table went over. Two men, somewhere in their forties with beer bellies and chequered flannies, pushed and shoved at each other. One swung a fist in a haymaker that only skimmed the other man's head from luck. That one grunted, staggered two steps sideways, then came right back, dukes up like a mockery of Queensbury Rules. The other one had his elbows out to either side, fists clenched in front of his chest, and they circled each other, work boots crunching on the broken glass.

"Barry, Mark, will you two cut it out!" the bar girl

yelled. "Or take it outside, at least."

They ignored her. The one with his dukes up skipped forward and fired two quick right jabs. The first didn't reach, but the second caught his opponent by surprise. He cried out as scarlet flooded his face from a busted nose. That one swung haymakers again, from both sides. The rest of the pub had all turned to look. People jeered and cheered, elbowing each other and laughing, like they were making bets, all moving back to give the brawlers room.

The bar girl stood with fists on her hips, scowling. "You're paying for any damage, fuckers!"

The men closed again, each throwing useless punches, then clinched and stumbled around in a clumsy wrestle. They bumped into the table Rich had been sitting at, and the four rock fishers at the next table jumped up, saving their beers, laughing as they sidled around to keep watching.

"Chrissy?" the big barman asked.

The bar girl shook her head, watching, scowling. Rich assumed she was the manager, given the big man's deference to her opinion.

The fighting men broke apart and the one with a crushed nose swung another huge haymaker. It missed by half a metre and he spun around a full three-sixty from the momentum. He was only saved from going down by his shoulder crashing into a column holding the roof beams up. A roar of laughter exploded. The other man tried to take advantage, skipping in again and raining rabbit blows all over the bleeding man's head and shoulders.

"Here she comes!" someone near Rich said, and he turned to see one of the old ladies from the group at the back striding across the pub like a woman half her apparent age. She held a wine bottle like a club, knuckles white around its neck.

Just as Rich started thinking, *Surely she isn't–* she did.

The old woman brought the wine bottle around in a wide, flat arc and it rang as it clocked off the side of the man's head. He'd had his back to her and it came out of nowhere. Amazingly the bottle didn't break. He staggered sideways, almost falling, but somehow keeping to his feet. The man with the bleeding nose looked up to see where his opponent had gone just as that man turned to face his new attacker.

"Maisie, fuck's sake!" he said, and the woman stepped up to him and brought the wine bottle down in a massive overhand strike, right between his eyes. This time it did break and the big man dropped to his knees, wailing as blood flooded his face.

"Fucking hell!" Rich said aloud.

Cheers and applause exploded, the man with the bleeding nose joining in.

"Greg, get a mop," Chrissy said, and the big barman nodded once and moved away.

The one on his knees had both hands to his face, blood streaming out around his palms.

"You started this," Maisie said to the other combatant. "Put him in your ute and take him to Doc Blaney."

"Aw, Mum!" the man said.

The woman raised the jagged neck of the wine bottle, all that was left of her weapon. "You want this in your balls?"

Mum? Rich thought, stunned.

"Fucken hell." Barry or Mark, whichever he was, lifted his recently felled foe with an arm around the back and walked him out of the pub. The hurt man didn't take his hands from his face the whole time.

He could be lacerated under there, Rich thought to himself. So much blood all down his front, all over the floor. Rich realised he was still holding his second beer, barely touched. He upended it, downing it in one.

Greg appeared with a mop and bucket, started picking up tables and chairs. A couple of people helped by collecting the larger pieces of broken glass. All the other patrons had returned to their drinking and talking like nothing had happened.

"Same again?" Chrissy asked him.

Rich managed a weak laugh. "Nah, thanks. I reckon I'm good." He checked his phone. Still not a skerrick of signal, and the time showed not even eight o'clock yet. He wanted to keep drinking, now more than ever, but he didn't feel like staying in Clooney's, despite the beautiful woman behind the bar. "You do off-sales?" he asked.

"Bottle shop around the back, drive through." Chrissy pointed.

"Okay, thanks."

"See you again, hey?"

He smiled at her, felt his lips tremble slightly as he did so. Violence wasn't something he coped with too well. "Sure. See you again."

He left the pub, thankful for the fresh air, tangy with salt and seaweed. He walked around the Shellhaven Street side of the pub and found the drive-through bottle shop. He bought a six-pack of *One Fifty Lashes* pale ale stubbies and a big bag of salt and vinegar chips, then walked back around the pub heading for the post office and Tanning Street. He was looking forward to the long walk to the Ocean Blue motel.

George lay across the front seats of the truck cab, doing his best to ignore a stabbing pain in his hip and lower back. He thought it likely he wouldn't be getting much sleep. In some ways he was glad young Rich had wandered off into town. It meant he could lay down, rather than try to sleep sitting up. That also meant he could stay hidden from view by the high dashboard and side doors. It made him feel safer. He just hoped he saw the new driver again in the morning.

He pushed up onto an elbow and looked out across the dark car park. From his vantage point he could see maybe half the neatly marked parking spaces, and the footpath going along the side. Across the road was a coffee shop and a hairdresser's, closed up and dark. The supermarket closed at 8pm and the last shoppers were straggling out, pushing trolleys or carrying bags. By a quarter past eight, the car park was empty.

The arsehole's van still sat parked at the entrance to the loading bay, though. George lay back down on his side, knees up and crammed against the gearshift because the cab wasn't wide enough for him to stretch out straight. He shifted onto his back, knees up, but that was hell on his neck. He needed a pillow. There was a first aid kit in a padded case under the passenger seat. He sat up and shifted around to get to it. Movement outside caught his eye.

Someone approached the van parked at the loading bay entrance. A tall, gangly fellow, with strangely long arms and fingers, that rippled like white seaweed as he walked. George had never seen such a pale person in his life, the guy was white like marble. Like chalk. He had a long face too, with dark eyes and a mouth that hung half open. He wore overalls, a tatty jumper underneath with voluminous sleeves that didn't reach his thin wrists, and heavy black boots. He slid open the side door of the van then loped away again. George lost sight of him past the bushes and scraggly trees at the kerb where he'd busted his wheel rim.

There was a temptation to hop out and look in the van, but George trembled at the thought of it. Nothing would get him out of this truck cab before dawn lit the sky. Not in this town.

The tall, pale man came back into view, walking backwards. He carried something bulky, a large canvas bag. Another man held the other end. He was entirely normal looking compared to the first guy. This one had dark hair, jeans and jacket, running shoes. His face was twisted in something like disgust and he wouldn't meet the pale man's eye. They turned sideways and hefted the large bag into the van. As they did, it twitched and rippled, like something, or several somethings, were squirming around inside. It flexed and pulsed, then disappeared into the shadowed interior.

The man in the running shoes nodded once, hurried away. The pale man slid the side door of the van closed, then turned and looked directly at George.

George gasped and slumped out of sight behind the dashboard, knees cramped into the steering column. His heart hammered, his palms were cold and sweat-slicked. He licked suddenly dry lips and stayed still, waiting to hear the van start up. It didn't. After several minutes, his lower back began to burn. Nothing for it. He had to move. Surely the guy had gone, maybe locked the van and wandered off again.

George sat up and the pale man was right there, still staring. He hadn't moved a muscle. His half-open mouth gave him the impression of being simple-minded, but his dark eyes were sharp and focussed. That mouth fell open a little wider. *Is that a grin?* George wondered, mesmerised. The man had no teeth.

George nodded once, raised a shaking hand in a weak greeting. The pale man's mouth opened even wider, a black chasm in his white face. Then he turned abruptly to the side and climbed into the cab of the van. George watched as it coughed and rattled twice before firing into life and the pale man backed away from the kerb and drove off.

"This fucken town," George said aloud, and scrunched back onto his side across the seats, pulled his jacket over himself. He squeezed his eyes shut, but sleep seemed a lifetime away.

Rich walked along Tanning Street, the plastic bag with
his beers and chips bumping against his thigh. The road
was long and straight, rising and falling, heading due
south along the coast. The post office had been pretty
cool, with a clock tower and everything. Large
sandstone blocks and interesting architecture. He
lamented they didn't make buildings like that any more.
On the other side as he'd turned the corner was the
harbour, glittering in the moonlight. A large curve of
stony coast with the cement berths and breakwaters
further east as he turned south. He saw a lighthouse on
the end of the furthest promontory of rock, its light
circling, spearing through the night.

He passed a couple of restaurants and takeaways,
most with hardly any patrons. The Victorian pub on the
diagonally opposite corner from Clooney's had seemed
warm and welcoming. More old-fashioned country pub,
less weirdo sea shack. He'd paused briefly, looking in,
part of him wishing he'd gone there instead of
Clooney's. Still, all country pubs were fundamentally
the same under the veneer of their décor. He had his
own beer now, and thought it wise to find somewhere
quiet.

He passed a doctor's surgery on the right and
another park and playground on the left, this one
butting right up to a small beach and the ocean beyond.
Low white caps of surf reflected light from the half
moon. A surf lifesaving club building stood at the south
end of the park, but it looked dilapidated, a couple of
the windows boarded up.

Tanning Street undulated lazily, rising twice to a
roundabout crossroads, descending again in between.
Left off the roundabouts were small headlands with

houses, like the bigger headland that made the south side of the harbour. It seemed The Gulp had numerous small beaches and coves along its coast before the high cliffs to the north and south. The shops and services quickly gave way to houses after the small beach and park. He passed a big primary school on the left, Saint Augustine's.

Most of the houses were single storey, from at least the 70s if not older. A lot of weatherboard, a lot of metal roofs, some tiled. Low garden walls and neat lawns in front. As he approached one he heard a kind of low whistling sound, and lots of scuffling. He frowned, then saw the garden was full of cages. As he leaned closer, he realised the cages were full of whiffling guinea pigs. Dozens of them, at least ten to a cage, crawling over each other in a mess of straw and vegetable scraps. It couldn't be right, keeping them so overcrowded like that. He grimaced and walked on.

He passed a large funeral director's on the right, a low building with a neat drive and well-tended shrubs. *Let Us Care For Your Dead* the sign said and Rich frowned. Hell of a way to phrase it.

A little further on he saw the sign for the Ocean Blue Motel, a large white square lit up inside with fluorescent tubes that flickered slightly. A U-shaped drive had a single story of motel units all around it, twelve in all, with an office at the end. A car park space was painted on the bitumen outside each unit, but none of the spaces were taken and the only lights on were in the office. *Reception*, it said on the door. Rich walked up and peered in through the grimy glass. A rack of postcards and flyers stood just inside to the left, two old vinyl chairs on the other side, and a desk with computer on it against the back wall. A door led away behind the desk but that was closed.

Ring the bell, Chrissy had told him. He looked for a button, then saw a weathered rope hanging down. The rope led up to a small brass bell that made him think of fishing boats. He let out a short laugh. "An actual fucking bell," he muttered, and pulled the rope.

The bell swung in its mounting and the high brassy ring was strident in the otherwise quiet night. Rich winced, glanced around. Not really anyone to disturb, he supposed. The nearest house was on the other side of the office and the motel seemed unoccupied.

He waited, reluctant to ring again, despite the lack of people. He was also reluctant to try anywhere else. He'd had enough walking and needed a quiet spot. After the weirdness and mayhem of the pub he just wanted to be on his own and drink his beers. He raised a hand to knock when the door behind the desk popped open. He jumped, then gathered himself. A young-ish man came out, maybe mid-30s. He had on striped pyjamas and a black woollen beanie, oversized ugg boots on his feet. His hair hung long and greasy in brown and blond strands around a narrow face with the most hooked nose Rich had ever seen and a strangely prominent Adam's apple. He smiled and nodded, pointed to his desk. Rich waited. Donny, Chrissy had called the proprietor.

Donny dug in a desk drawer, then came up with a bunch of keys and unlocked the office door.

"How are ya?"

Rich smiled. "Pretty good, thanks. Donny is it? I'm Rich. Chrissy at the pub said you'd be able to fix me up with a room for the night?"

"You're rich? Maybe I should charge ya double, hey?" Donny *hyucked* a laugh.

Why was everyone making the same joke, had they never met a Rich before? "It's Richard, and I only have a card to pay with. No cash."

"That's all right, we're not entirely medieval here." Donny leaned out the door and looked left and right, sizing up his motel. "Number six, hey?"

Rich shrugged. "Sure, I'm easy."

Donny gestured inside and went back to his desk.

He pulled out a large book and opened it. "Sign-in details here, please."

The page was otherwise blank, so Rich filled in the top line with his name, address and mobile number. He chose not to include his email address. He pointed at what he'd written. "My phone gets no service here." He pulled it out to check again and it still had no signal. "Yep, not a thing."

Donny grinned, pulling the book back across the desk. "Only a couple of providers get any signal in The Gulp. The cliffs either side put the whole town in a kind of bowl. Don't worry about it, just a formality. I won't be calling you for a date or anything. What brings you here then? No bags?"

"Unexpected stopover. Truck broke down, waiting for a repair in the morning."

"Right. Pain in the arse, hey?"

"Yeah, I guess. Still, it's given me a chance to check out Gulpepper. I've never been before."

Donny looked up from under the rolled over wool of his beanie, eyes narrowed. He licked his lips and nodded once, then turned his attention back to the book. What was he looking at for so long? There were only ten or so words written there. Donny sniffed suddenly and put the book away, then rummaged in the drawer. He pulled out a key on a ridiculously large wooden tag, shaped like a dolphin. It had *SIX 6* burned into both sides.

"Eighty-five bucks a night and we put a deposit of another hundred bucks on your card. That'll get credited back right away assuming there's no damage when you leave. Just one night?"

"Yes, thanks."

Rich tapped his card, waited for the beep, then Donny handed him a receipt and his giant key fob.

"No car?"

"No, I walked up here. Truck broke down?"

"Yeah, that's right."

Donny sat, smiling up at Rich. His two front teeth crossed ever so slightly, making a slight ridge that pushed his top lip forward under his weirdly large nose.

"Okay," Rich said. "Thanks very much. I'll, errr..." He gestured back over his shoulder.

"Right-o," Donny said.

Rich turned away and was halfway out the door when Donny said, "How hot is Chrissy, hey?"

Rich looked back. "She's really good-looking, yeah."

"Good-looking? She's a fucken cracker, that one. I'd love to..." Donny rocked in his chair, like he was trying to thrust his hips while sitting down. The chair creaked.

"Ha. Yeah, I get that. Night then." Rich hurried out and closed the door before Donny could share any other thoughts of what he'd like to do.

The room smelled of dust and damp when he opened the door, a slightly off, briny smell no doubt from being so close to the sea. But it was clean enough, simply furnished. A double bed, desk and chair, small bar fridge in one corner with a microwave, kettle, tea and coffee stuff on it. A wardrobe with sliding mirror doors in one corner reflected Rich back at himself. He looked into the bathroom at the back. It had a sink, toilet and glassed-in shower cubicle. Simple and clean enough.

"This'll do fine," he muttered and went back to close the unit door. He locked it and hung the chain up inside. An immense sense of relief fell over him once he felt enclosed and safe in his own space. George had been right, this was a weird town. But it was only isolated country people, nothing more than that. He went to the big front window and drew the curtains across. A large white van drove slowly up the hill outside, exhaust sputtering dark and smoky behind it.

A small TV was mounted on the wall above the desk. He turned it on and was pleased to see it did get reception, albeit it grainy with a slight hiss to the sound. He tried other channels, but only the one working was

ABC2, showing a British cosy mystery.

"Good enough," he said.

He kicked his shoes off and sat on the bed. He opened the chips and a beer, leaning back against piled pillows that were ever so slightly damp to the touch, and watched the village drama unfold on the small screen.

Five out of six beers and a couple more shows later and Rich was pleasantly drunk and overcome with fatigue. He staggered to use the bathroom, wishing he could brush his teeth. His breath would fell cattle in the morning. He stripped down to his boxer shorts and t-shirt and climbed into the bed. When he turned out the light, the room plunged into pitch darkness, the heavy curtains almost entirely blocking the watery glow of the streetlight and motel sign outside. It was wholly quiet. Alcohol helped sleep overcome him in no time.

He walked along a dark street, gentle rain misting the air. Shadows moved across a green area where a swing set creaked, the seats penduluming with no one on them. A dog barked and a man with no nose leaned in close and whispered something. His breath reeked of fish but his words were unclear.

"What did you say?"

The noseless man spoke again, his voice a stinking hiss, the words still unintelligible.

"I don't understand!"

A dog barked again, something cold and slippery pressed up into his palm. Why was the dog slimy? He looked down but there was no dog. The noseless man had gone. No one at all shared the street with him, all the buildings along one side were dark, the park on the other side empty. The swings went back and forth, back and forth, creaking. The rain became heavier, it hissed like the noseless man's voice. A bell rang, repeatedly like a ship rocking on a rough sea, its brass clanging against the mast. He slipped and looked down to see slick seaweed underfoot, black and greasy. It smelled like rotten flesh and stuck to his shoes. The rain became heavier, soaking him, plastering his hair flat. He looked up and saw the ocean roiling, waves tumbling over each other, spray carried on a strong wind that blew the rain into his face. He turned and there was nothing but ocean and beach, littered with rotten weed, and seemingly endless bush behind. Tall gum trees, twisted banksia, thick undergrowth. He tried to move along the beach but slipped and slid on the fetid weed. He went down, landing heavily on his hands and knees. The stink of rotten flesh grew stronger as wetness splashed up into his face. He cried out, staggered to his feet, hands slicked with foul blackness that dripped from his fingertips. The smell made him gag and he turned, saw something huge rise and shift far back in the trees. It seemed to unfurl, arching up above the tree line like a whale's back in the ocean, then sank away again out of sight. He turned a full circle, nothing but a rocky beach rising into high cliffs at either end, the impenetrable bush behind. "Where am I?" he yelled, but his voice came out like a seal's bark, whipped away by the wind, lost in the rain and sea spray. Thick black clouds hung low and pendulous over the water, a deep crimson glow across the far distance like a giant wound in the sky. Things with wavering limbs tumbled from clouds, splashing into the waves, from nearby to far away on the horizon.

"Got to be home," a voice said. The noseless man stood there, looking up at him from under the brim of his trilby hat. His dog ran and jumped in the waves, barking at the falling creatures. "Got to be home!" the man said again, urgency in his voice. "I want to go home!" he suddenly yelled up at the night sky.

Rich jerked awake in the motel bed, heart racing, gasping like he'd sprinted a mile.

"Fuck me dead," he muttered, trembles setting in throughout his body. He was damp with sweat, the sheets clinging to him. A desperate urge to piss became suddenly evident and he lurched up.

As he came back from the bathroom, the dream fading, he saw a weak orange light behind the microwave. He frowned. That hadn't been there when he went to bed, he remembered noticing how dark it was. His head was thick with the beer, that halfway state between still drunk and the possibility of a hangover. He went back to the bathroom and downed a tumbler of water. Then another. He came back and the light was still there, a soft glow. He moved nearer, leaned over the microwave to see, wondering if perhaps some light had activated on the back of the thing. Maybe he could unplug it.

The light came through a small hole in the wall, a centimetre or so in diameter. Did that mean there was something in the wall or someone in the room next door? Rich stared for a moment, then curiosity overcame him. He pulled the plug out and lifted the microwave aside as quietly as he could, placed it gently on the floor. Then he crouched to peek through. There was a corner of white linen obscuring about a third of the hole. He realised that was a pillow on the bed next door. A similar bar fridge with a microwave on it sat against the far wall, the entire room an exact replica of his. He assumed all the rooms were largely identical. A man walked past the end of the bed and Rich startled backwards, then slowly looked again. The man headed to bathroom, a tap ran, the clink of a glass, sounds of drinking. The walls were thin, sound carried clearly. The man returned and sat heavily on the end of the bed. He was not especially tall, but he was broad, a blue King Gee work shirt stretched taut across his back and rounded shoulders. He sat there, elbows on his knees, unmoving. Was he waiting for something?

Rich crept back to his bedside table and checked his phone. 2.10 a.m. Maybe the man had just got off a long shift and was doing that thing where the mind flatlines and you have to sit motionless, too tired to even go to bed. He wished the man well and started to climb back into bed when car tyres scrunched on the gravel of the drive outside and a bead of light briefly lit the edge of his curtains, then winked out. Car doors opened and slammed, several footsteps sounded, then the door to the next room opened and shut. Muffled voices came through the thin walls, talking low and somehow menacing. Then one cut through, louder, panicked.

"I wouldn't, Mr Carter! You know I wouldn't!"

There was a sharp slap and Rich immediately saw an open palm meeting a cheek in his mind's eye. That sound couldn't be anything else.

Go to bed, Rich, he told himself. *Leave the light off, get into bed, ignore everything.*

"Mr Carter, please!" Another slap, this one meatier followed by a rush of exhalation. Gasping sobs, more menacing voices, too muffled by the walls to make out clearly.

Despite himself, Rich crept forward on hands and knees, then straightened enough to lean against the fridge and look through the small hole.

"Get a chair for Daniel, please, Stephen."

The broad man in the King Gee dragged out the chair from under the desk and a young man, surely not older than 20, was sat heavily into it. He had shoulder-length dark hair and wild eyes, his cheeks wet with tears. He looked up in terror at someone Rich couldn't see.

"Mr Carter, please!"

"Please what, Daniel?"

The man moved into view. He was probably somewhere in his late-forties, maybe fifty, heavyset, but not bulky, black hair slicked back like a 50s rocker. He wore jeans and a black shirt with mother-of-pearl press stud buttons and metal tips on the collar. His face was hard, icy blue eyes over a lantern jaw. He held an old, stained Akubra in one hand. He leaned down to stare hard at Daniel.

"Please what?" he asked again.

"Please don't hurt me, Mr Carter, I done nothing wrong, I promise."

"That so? Then why were you seen drinking with the Stinson brothers?"

Stephen pulled the young man's arms back and used zip ties around his wrists, securing them behind the chair. *Are they going to rough him up?* Rich wondered. *I shouldn't watch. Go to bed.* But he kept looking.

"Not drinking *with* them, Mr Carter. Same pub is all. I don't usually go in the Vic, but Sal wanted a steak and says Clooney's steaks are shithouse and insisted on the Vic and I thought it meant no harm so said yeah. We had dinner there and the Stinsons was in there, yeah, sure, they were, and I said hello, of course I did. Just courtesy. But I wasn't *with* them, not drinking with them."

"But you stayed after your steak, didn't you? You and Sal."

"Yeah, a little while, had a couple more beers, usual thing, you know same as Clooney's only Sal insisted on the Vic this time."

"You're beginning to repeat yourself, mate."

Daniel dragged in a ragged breath, staring up at Mr Carter, seemingly lost for words. Carter stared back. Stephen moved around the other side of Daniel's chair and Rich saw his face. Eyes too wide apart, broken nose, flattened like a career boxer's, dark stubble up almost under his eyes. He lifted the King Gee work shirt and unbuckled his belt. Daniel became suddenly aware of his presence and turned to look as the big man slid his belt from the loops on his waistband.

Carter grabbed Daniel's chin, twisted his face back, his fingertips making white circles, he was gripping so hard. "Never mind Stephen, son."

Rich grimaced, swallowing hard. What was Stephen going to do? Rich leaned back, started to turn away, but couldn't tear his eyes from the scene. He slowly drifted close again as Carter said, "Those Stinson cunts have cost me dear, more than once. You know that."

"I do, Mr Carter, of course—"

"Shut the fuck up. The thing is, I have reason not to trust you. I haven't forgotten New Year's before last. No, I said shut the fuck up, we're not talking about that now, I'm simply illustrating a point. I wanted to trust you, Daniel, I really did. You seemed to be doing so well. Then you're drinking with the fucking Stinsons in the Vic like you're a wet-behind-the-ears fucking teenager. You should know better."

"I wasn't drinking *with* them, Mr. Carter, just in the same pub. I told Sal we shouldn't but she kept on about the Clooney's steaks being crap."

"I suggest you stop bad-mouthing Clooney's, Daniel."

The steak was pretty good, Rich thought absently. Maybe this Sal wanted to get Daniel into trouble. He half-smiled. This was better than the British cosy mystery he'd watched earlier. Was that big fella, Stephen, going to whip Daniel with his belt?

Carter put his hat on the desk and pulled out a knife. Daniel stiffened. All good humour drained from Rich in an icy torrent. Stephen stepped behind the chair and his belt went over Daniel's forehead. He pulled it taut above Daniel's eyebrows and hauled back, the young man's head pressed into Stephen's large but incredibly solid-looking belly.

"I suggest you hold very still," Carter said, leaning forward.

"No, no, no, please, Mr Carter!"

The knife had a 10cm or so blade, sharpened on one side, and a bright green plastic handle.

"I said hold still!"

Carter put his free hand to Daniel's throat and squeezed. Daniel gasped and gagged, eyes bugging. Carter put the point of the knife to Daniel's left eye, just below the brow, and drove it in. Bile shot up into Rich's throat, sour, as he watched. Daniel screamed, high and shrill. Carter dug with the knife, his expression one of concentration as blood sluiced down Daniel's cheek. He thrashed and writhed in the chair, heels drumming against the tiled floor, as Carter drew the knife around, the young man's head the only still part of him, locked into place as it was, his arms secured to the back of the chair.

Carter popped Daniel's eye out onto the palm of his hand, released the young man's throat, and stood up, smiling. Stephen stepped back, began threading his belt back into his waistband. Daniel wailed, whipping his head left and right as blood poured from his ruined eye socket.

"Let's have a look then," Carter said.

With Daniel's eyeball resting on one palm, he handed the knife to Stephen and then stuck the thumb of his free hand into Daniel's empty, gore-soaked socket. As Daniel screamed, Carter tossed the young man's eye into his mouth. He tipped his head back, chewing, swilling the contents around his mouth like a sommelier experiencing a particularly decent vintage. Daniel howled, Stephen held his head steady with one meaty palm, Carter's thumb buried to the second knuckle. Rich shook all over, his skin wet and cold with sweat, bile burning his throat, threatening to burst forth.

"I see," Carter said, slurred slightly by his mouthful. Jelly leaked over his bottom lip. His head was still tipped back, eyes closed, thumb shifting about in Daniel's face. "You went out into the courtyard for a cigarette and *that's* where you had your conversation. A shame there's no sound with this show, eh? But I see it all. I see you taking the money from Craig Stinson." He shifted the chewed eye in his mouth, sucking it back and forth across his front teeth. "I see the younger Stinson cunt, William. What's he giving you there, eh? Wrapped up pretty well, isn't it. Looks interesting, Daniel. Very interesting."

Carter smacked his lips and swallowed, opened his eyes to look down at the bloody-faced youth. He pulled his thumb free with a wet slurp. "What was in the parcel, Daniel?"

Daniel shuddered and tipped sideways, taking the chair over with him.

"Out cold," Carter said. "Not to worry, we'll bring him to the farm anyway. I'll put him in the car." He turned and pointed straight at Rich. "You go and get that one."

Rich stumbled back from the hole with a gasp, heart hammering. He turned to one side and vomited, but was already up and moving, the puke catching along his arm and left foot. He grabbed his cargo pants off the back of the chair. An identical chair to the one he'd just watched Daniel tortured in. Surely that fucking guy couldn't see what Daniel had seen, what the fuck? Doesn't matter, pants on, grab the phone and fucking run!

He got both legs into his pants and snatched his phone off the bedside table. He jammed it into his pocket as his unit door crashed inwards, splitting right through the middle and breaking in half. The top half swung hectically from a bent hinge.

"Fuck!" Rich yelled.

The big silhouette of Stephen filled the doorway. He was a similar height to Rich, but twice as wide. Rich turned, ran to the back of the room, but it was just a wall. He pushed into the bathroom. There was a tiny window with sliding panes of frosted glass. He wasn't sure he could fit through, but he was going to try. He stood up on the toilet and hauled back a fist to punch the window out, heedless of any cuts he might get, but Stephen was already there. One thick arm went around Rich's waist and pulled him back.

Rich slammed left and right with his elbows and fists, fighting like a man possessed. Every glancing blow he got to Stephen's blocky head was like hitting a rock.

Stephen planted him on his feet, spun him around, and slapped him hard across the face. Blackness whined in from the edges of Rich's vision, stars sparkled all around. The world tilted sideways as Stephen picked him up. He tried to struggle, but his body was loose, unresponsive. His head throbbed. He smelled oil and dirt a moment before something hard slammed into him and he realised he'd been thrown into the boot of a car. The lid slammed down, plunging him into darkness.

George twisted around in the front seat of the truck cab, trying to align his dick with the neck of the two-litre plastic bottle. Why did something so simple in principle prove to be so difficult in practice? He'd put it off as long as possible, but the need was too great to ignore any longer. He finally managed to get things lined up, using the wrist of the hand holding his dick to press his gut out of the way so he could see the bottle he held in the other hand. It took a few seconds to relax enough for the flow to start and his knob immediately skipped in his hand as it did so, the firehose stream of piss shooting right over the neck of the bottle and soaking hand, his pants leg, the floor of the cab.

"Fucken shit and fucken!"

He clamped tight inside, wincing as he held back the flow. With an incoherent curse, he unlocked and opened the door and half fell out to the cement below, damp trousers around his ankles. Regardless of spying eyes, he turned his back to the road and pissed with abandon, head tipped back, sighing as he painted the road of the loading dock.

When he finished, relief a warm glow through his abdomen, he pulled his pants back up. They were wet, but not as soaked as he'd feared, mainly one patch the size of his palm. He looked into the truck and the puddle on the vinyl matting was already spreading out and he decided to ignore that. He held up his wet hand and looked at it. There should be a service tap somewhere around, but he couldn't see one. And he wasn't about to go searching around in the dark. He already felt vulnerable, simply being out of the cab. He had some baby wipes in the glove box and he climbed back in, found them, wiped his hands, had a half-arsed go at the floor, then threw the handful of wipes out the window.

Once everything was closed and locked up again, he felt secure once more. His watch said two-forty a.m. and he was fairly sure he was yet to sleep a wink. Fatigue hung off him like weights, though, and perhaps if he lay down again... At least he wasn't busting for a piss any more.

He had a bad feeling about the kid, imagined Rich somewhere out there in The Gulp. Where was he? What was he doing? George didn't hold much truck with psychics or any of that malarkey, but he felt deep in his gut that something was wrong.

He curled on his side across the seats and dragged the coat back over himself, praying for unconsciousness until dawn.

Rich blinked as the boot was opened, a porch light of some kind directly above him. His head swam. Stephen reached in, grabbed his upper arm in an iron grip and hauled him out. The man's strength was insane, made Rich feel like a child.

The drive had been only about ten minutes or so,

smooth at first with a few turns Rich had quickly lost track of, then boneshakingly rough, an unsealed road that seemed to travel up quite steeply, switching back on itself a couple of times. As Stephen planted Rich on his feet he saw back down the long dirt road, white-fenced paddocks on either side, the town of Gulpepper a blanket of undulating lights down below. The view from so high was wild, over the paddocks and thick bushland the ocean glittered in the light of the half-moon. A naturally level area of land, it had the look of somewhere that had been farmed for generations. The bush rose steeply behind against the night sky thick with stars.

Stephen turned him and pushed, made him stagger past the car which he'd parked in a car port next to a large federation-style farmhouse. White painted weatherboard, russet-painted metal roof, stained glass panels in the old-fashioned windows. A deck ran all around the building. Beyond it were a variety of sheds and barns, tractors and threshers and other equipment scattered about. A Toyota Hilux crew cab ute was parked just beside the car port. Carter climbed out, then opened the back door and dragged Daniel off the seat. The young man hit the dirt with a grunt and rolled up onto his hands and knees. Blood dripped heavily from his face.

"I won't tell anyone anything," Rich said, appalled at the slur in his voice. The after-effects of the beers combined with the mighty slap from Stephen had left him thick-headed.

"Course you won't," Carter said. "Bring him." He dragged Daniel up with a hand under one arm and pushed him ahead as he walked past the Toyota.

Stephen's hand on Rich's right shoulder was a painful clamp the big man used to guide him. Wearing nothing but cargo pants and t-shirt, the cool night air made his skin stipple with gooseflesh. He needed to find a way out of this, any way, it didn't matter. Just get out.

He'd make a bolt for the bush if the chance arose, take his shot there. The reassuring pressure of the phone in his pocket gave him some hope. With any luck they wouldn't notice he had it, and maybe up here he'd catch a signal when he got the opportunity to try. Comply in the meantime, he told himself. Be compliant, let them concentrate on Daniel, the poor bastard.

They walked past a double garage filled with a mystifying array of tools and an old ute up on blocks, then between two open-front hay sheds into a wide field with fencing in the distance. This seemed to be a pretty big property, the bush cleared for several acres in every direction. Cattle, black and white Fresians and a few Jerseys, stood around in the paddock off to the right and Rich thought he saw the silhouettes of horses far to the left. The field they walked across was empty, sloping gently upwards, with thick bush on the far side that rose steeply to a ridge line, black against the sky.

The moonlight held back the darkness enough, Rich's eyes adjusting to see where he walked. The stars were a thick blanket, not an artificial light source for kilometres around to dim them, just the speckles of light down in the town below.

Then he saw the large hole in the dirt.

Ice chilled his veins. The hole was about two metres long and one wide, a perfect black rectangle in the grass. A pile of dirt stood in a mound beside it with a shovel stuck in the top. A large wooden board lay beside the dirt.

"Mr Carter, don't, please," Daniel said, voice half lost in sobs. He'd been quietly stumbling along until that moment, but now he became animated, struggled against Carter's grip. "What do you want, Mr Carter? Hey? Anything you want, Mr Carter, I'll do it. Anything!"

"What I want, Daniel, is a more peaceful life. What I want is people I can rely on. What I *want* you fucking cunt, is people who don't blab and deal with the fucking Stinsons!"

"Mr Carter, please, I–"

Daniel's sentence was lost in a cry of alarm as Carter shoved him forward and he staggered and fell into the hole. Stephen held Rich firmly, a few feet back. The hole wasn't as deep as Rich had thought, Daniel finding his feet and standing up, the edge of the hole at his chest. He put both palms on the damp grass and made to push himself up, but Carter swung a booted foot and clipped him under the chin. Daniel yelped and went back down. He moaned weakly, out of sight.

Carter walked around the hole and picked up the large piece of wood. Several planks fixed together with crossbars, Rich noticed. A lid. A coffin lid.

"You disappoint me greatly, Daniel," Carter said and dropped the lid down into the hole. He took the spade and began shovelling dirt in. It thumped onto the wood, the sound more muffled each time. Then a banging started, Daniel yelling, calling out Carter's name over and over again, begging please, please, please. But the dirt kept going in, the sounds more muted by the minute.

Rich stood stock still, aware his mouth hung open in a gape, his knees weak. But he didn't dare make a sound. Stephen's vice-like grip never left his shoulder. It took about ten minutes for Carter to refill the hole completely, then he walked back and forth over the dirt, pressing it down, sweat sparkling on his brow. Daniel's muffled cries still came faintly from below, punctuated by weak blows against the wood.

Carter finally looked at Rich, for the first time. He smiled warmly, gestured back towards the farmhouse. "Shall we?"

Stephen turned him and they walked back, Rich's legs rubbery.

"Did you enjoy what you saw at the motel?" Carter asked as they walked.

"No, Sir, I did not."

"Why's that?"

Rich licked dry lips, lost for words. He shook his head. "I won't tell a soul," he said eventually. "I promise."

"You had so many choices," Carter said. "So *many* chances. You could have ignored the light. You could have gone to bed. So many times you could have turned away, but you didn't."

How did he know?

"Why didn't you turn your back, hmm?"

"I... I didn't know," Rich said weakly. "I couldn't believe it."

Carter sucked his teeth, let out a sigh. "Such is life, hey? So many don't believe. Too many people have lost touch with the old ways. Everything so modern." He turned and pinned Rich with his icy blue gaze. "No respect for the numinous any more."

Carter couldn't have seen what Daniel saw. Someone in the pub saw, told him about it. He tortured Daniel to scare him. But why? He brought Daniel to the farm and obviously planned to let him die anyway.

Carter led Rich back between the hay sheds as another car pulled up along the dirt road. A small hatchback. It parked, the engine went off and the headlights with it. A woman got out.

"Hello, darling," Carter said.

Chrissy walked into the light of the car port, came to meet them. She wore the same clothes she'd had on in the pub, but her hair wasn't tied back any more. It hung over her shoulders in a wave that shone with reflected light. "Worked out all right then?" she said.

Carter laughed. "Yep. Donny put him in room six like you told him to, and the poor lad couldn't help himself. Curious as the proverbial cat."

Chrissy smiled, wide and filled with teeth. "I thought it too good an opportunity to pass up." She moved to Carter and they embraced, kissed long and deep. The man had to be at least twice her age, Rich thought numbly. He tried to swallow, but his throat was thick with fear.

"Daniel?" Chrissy asked, once their sensuous kiss finally ended.

"Dealt with," Carter said. He turned his attention back to Rich. "You're new here." Statement, not a question or guess. "But why did you come, hmm? No one passes through The Gulp. You *came* here."

"I'm a truck driver. I deliver to Woollies. The truck broke down–"

"It didn't break down, your friend fucked it."

How did he know that?

"But that's not what I meant. Why did you come *here*, hmm? At *this* time? Wheels and machinations, son. There are *reasons*."

"It's a new job, that's all. I'm in training, to take over George's routes. The last couple of weeks he's been showing me the..." Rich's voice petered out under Carter's witheringly disdainful gaze.

"You won't let it in, will you." Statement again.

"Let what in?"

"You dreamed of it. The before time. Everyone who sleeps in The Gulp dreams of when they fell at least once." Carter moved to put an arm across Rich's shoulders. Stephen let go at last, the skin burning where the pressure was finally released. Carter turned Rich to face out over the view of the town below. "You have to embrace The Gulp. You do what it wants or it swallows you. What's your name?"

"Rich. Richard Blake."

"You can call me Mr Carter. You've already met Chrissy."

"Let me go, please! I won't tell anyone anything."

"You will though, won't you?"

"No! I won't–"

"Oh, you might not tell any authorities. But you'll tell the story. People always tell stories."

"Fuck you, man! Let me go!"

"Let's not be unpleasant to each other. You're with me now."

"What do you mean I'm with you? I'm not with you! You have to let me go!"

Carter tipped his head to one side. "Do I though?"

"Please!" Rich said, hating the plaintive tone in his voice.

"There's some better manners already." Carter took out a cigar, lit it from a brass Zippo, then slipped the lighter away into his shirt pocket as he puffed acrid smoke into the air. "Now then, let me give you your choices. For one, I can dig another hole next to Daniel. He'll go quiet soon. So that's one choice. The other is that you work for me. You do as I say, and make yourself useful. Accept the fact you're in The Gulp now. We could develop a wonderful working relationship together, you and I. There is great potential in you, I see it. You came here for a reason. And I am, as you know, in need of a new employee."

"I don't want to!" Rich internally cursed the tears rolling over his cheeks, but he couldn't stop them. "I want to go home. I'll never come here again, I won't tell a soul anything. I'll quit the job, never drive another truck for the rest of my life! Please, just let me go."

Carter sighed, shook his head. "I gave you your choices." He puffed on the cigar, then smiled again. "Your personal life, family situation, it's suited to The Gulp finding you, no?"

Rich swallowed, mind adrift, desperate for purchase. "What?" he managed.

"You have your choices. I'll give you some time to think about it." Carter smiled. "Welcome to The Gulp, Richard Blake."

Rich flinched as something sharp scratched his neck. He looked to the side to see Chrissy step away, a syringe in one hand. She wiggled the fingers of her other hand in a wave as Rich's vision closed in from all sides. His tongue felt suddenly swollen, then everything went black.

George's head pounded from lack of sleep. He'd maybe caught an hour or two of fitful dozing here and there, but it amounted to nothing really. He was too damn old to stay up all night any more. He remembered the long benders of his youth, all that drinking, carousing, womanising. He didn't miss those days, if he was honest. They had been where he'd found his wife. He couldn't wait to see her again.

The day was bright, harsh against his gritty eyes as he sipped the coffee and ate a croissant from the bakers. The Woollies precinct opened at eight, allowing him a leisurely piss into an actual urinal, rather than the debacle of the night before. His body ached in every place he put his mind to, but the night had passed. That was the main thing. Still no sign of Rich though. Until ten, he'd told the kid. He intended to stick to his promise. He would wait, but he'd leave without Rich if necessary. A big tow truck pulled into the loading bay, gleaming chrome and bright decals. The driver gave George a wave.

It took over an hour, disengaging the trailer, jacking up the cab, changing the wheel, putting it all back together again. But it was finally done by 9.15. George went inside for another coffee and then sat in the cab drinking it. The minutes ticked slowly by.

"Come on, kid," he muttered aloud.

It was ten minutes past ten when he finally called it time to keep his promise. He rang in the problem, told the office the new driver had gone out on the town and not come back. They told him to try ringing the kid, which he had about nine o'clock, then again at nine-thirty, but it went straight to voicemail.

"He said he had no signal in this arse-end-a-nowhere town," George told his supervisor.

"Can you wait for him?"

"Already did. I told him last night I'd wait until ten, he said he'd be here by eight. Still no sign, though."

"Give it a bit longer?"

"And then what?"

There was a pause, muffled conversation, then the supervisor came back on. "Look, we'll try to raise him too, see if he catches some reception. Can you wait a little longer? If he's not there by eleven, head out and the fool will have to hitch out to Monkton or Enden or something when he wakes up."

George looked at his watch. Forty-five minutes more in The Gulp. He sighed. "Okay, I'll give it until eleven, then I'm out."

He stayed in the cab until a few minutes past eleven, then started up the truck. Still no sign of Rich. George shook his head, easing the big rig out of the loading bay and turning right to head for the main road back to Enden.

"What the hell did you get up to, kid?" he said as he went around the roundabout by the leisure centre. "Or what the hell got to you, eh?"

He didn't look in the rear view mirror once until he turned right onto the highway, thankful to be leaving The Gulp for the last time.

Mother
in Bloom

Mother in Bloom

"We need to air this place out," Maddy said, face scrunched in disgust under her strawberry blonde hair.

Zack turned from the bed to look back at her. "You gonna finally come in?"

"Nah."

"She's dead now. You can come in."

"Fucking stinks, Zack."

Her brother shrugged. "That's death for you."

"Just open the window at least."

Zack sighed and moved around the bed, pulled open the curtains and unlatched the window, swung it wide. As daylight flooded in, the cadaver that was their mother took on super-real details.

"Doesn't even look like her any more," Maddy said. She leaned a little into the room, wincing against the stench. It was sickly and thick, sweet and harsh at the same time, laced with shit and antiseptic. She'd only been dead a few hours. It would get worse quickly.

"You're a year older than me," Zack said. "You're supposed to be the responsible one."

"Am I really?"

"You're eighteen soon!"

"Another six months. Zack, I'm no more an adult than you are. Don't try to pull that shit. I'm the one said we should shut the bedroom door and leave her to it. You insisted on caring for her. Just cos she died now, doesn't make it suddenly my problem."

"She cared for us–"

Maddy shot one hand up, palm out. "When did she ever fucking care for us? She kept us alive when we were babies, that's it. I been taking care of myself *and* you since I was five. You looked after yourself enough too. Daddy helped until he disappeared, and I was only nine then. We been on our own our whole lives, Zack. Fuck her. I'm glad she's finally dead."

"You think he really left us?" Zack asked. "You always say disappeared and vanished and shit. Never left."

"I'm not having this conversation again. Who knows? This town, anything is possible."

Zack looked down at the skeletal woman in the foul, stained bed. Maddy couldn't help looking too. Their mother's skin was patched ochre and pale browns where it had once been creamy, her lips cracked, eyes and cheekbones bulging from a sallow face that was mostly skull. Her mouth hung slightly open, tips of yellowed teeth showing. Zack sniffed, wincing against the smell, then nodded. "Yeah, me too."

"What?"

"I'm glad she's dead."

"Yeah."

"But we owe her something."

"Do we?"

Zack looked up, eyes flashing anger. "What do we do with her?"

"Harbour?"

Zack pursed his lips, shook his head. "I'm worried she'll float or something. Be found."

"We can't risk the house, Zack." Maddy looked around, glanced back over her shoulder. "I mean, shitty as it is, it's finally ours. We get to relax and enjoy it at last."

"I know. That's all okay. I have the login details for Centrelink, all the benefits and pensions and shit. We're well-prepared. We just need to make sure no one knows she's dead. But every time I bring up what to do with her, you change the subject. Well, time's up. Now we *have* to decide. So what do we do with her?"

"Dump her in the bush?"

"What if someone finds her? Or an animal drags her back or some shit?"

"Bury her in the bush?"

Zack stared at his mother, lips pursed. "Would take

a bit of effort, and we'd have to park up somewhere on the road out of town, then carry her in. Might get seen at any point. We have to be absolutely safe, Maddy. No one can know."

"Whatever we do with her is going to be risky." Maddy took a step back. "I can't stand this stench any more, Zack. Leave the window open but shut the door. Let's talk about this somewhere else."

They sat in the lounge room, Zack on the threadbare couch, Maddy in one of the armchairs. The other armchair, their mother's spot, hadn't been sat in since she'd gone to bed about three months prior and stayed put. She'd lay there, making demands of Zack, getting sicker and sicker, wasting away, wallowing in her own filth. How Zack stood to go in Maddy would never know. They should have let her die weeks ago, but Zack kept her going until last night.

For months before that, she'd shuffled around the house, getting sicker and sicker, refusing to accept help. She knew she was dying and welcomed it, was Maddy's opinion. Happy to waste away right in front of her kids. On a good day, when Maddy was feeling charitable, she wondered if perhaps their mother recognised the benefit of her dying in secrecy so Zack and Maddy would have the best chance on their own. No interference from DoCS, or the Department of Communities and Justice, as the fuckers called themselves now. Busybodies is what they were. But with the welfare still coming in, Zack and Maddy had a chance at a peaceful life. It was their grandfather's house, after all, bought and paid for, the only thing of any value the family had ever owned, now in their mother's name. Of course, it was in The Gulp, so what was it really worth? But it was a home.

Most days, though, Maddy wasn't charitable at all and knew their mother was too damned selfish to even consider the possibility. She made constant demands, probably too stupid to realise there might be consequences for anyone else. Maybe she was so selfish she imagined the whole world ending when she did, so no one else mattered. No one else ever mattered with her.

"How's your mum?" friends and neighbours would ask.

"Oh, she's okay," Maddy would reply. "Just prefers to stay in. You know how she is. We take care of her."

"You're good kids."

Yeah, Maddy thought. Real good. Agoraphobic was a word she'd learned, and it came in handy. Their mother had a lot of issues, they told everyone, including germaphobia, agoraphobia, diabetes and asthma. They'd been laying the groundwork for their reclusive mother for the last couple of years. The woman was only forty-six. Would only ever be forty-six now, but that gave them decades of living at home, ostensibly caring for the strange old lady who never went out while they collected her welfare. It was sort of perfect, really, if they could get away with this last bit. If they were caught disposing of the body, that would be a problem. A real problem.

"So what do we do?" Zack asked again.

The TV was on, but muted. Some game show where idiots grinned at each other and answered questions on their specialist subject. Maddy stared at it, thinking. "I don't know," she said at last. "I'm scared, Zack."

"Me too."

They were quiet for a while. Maddy felt like a little kid, trembling and nervous. This was what they'd wanted, wasn't it? What they whispered about while their mother wasted away in her bedroom. Now it had come about, there was a kind of finality to it that made Maddy feel hollow inside. The bitch was one of the most awful people Maddy had ever known – and in The Gulp, you met a lot of awful people – but she was their mother too. Some bullshit chemical or emotional power consistently worked on Maddy's insides, made her care.

Only a few weeks ago she'd tried to score some of

her mother's approval. Working at Woollies full-time since she quit school at the end of year 10 some three or four months prior, had been thankless enough, but it was work and it was hers. She'd worked there part-time to supplement the welfare for a couple of years already. But scoring an Employee of the Month certificate had been one of the few things Maddy had been genuinely proud of in recent memory. She'd braved the sickly-sweet miasma of her mother's room, squinted to blur the image of the woman emaciated and wheezing on the pile of pillows, and held up the certificate for her to see.

"What do you think of that, Mum?"

"I 'spect everyone gets one. Like a rota," her mother had croaked, chest whispering with phlegm. "You'll get another in a few months."

"I fucking earned that!" Maddy had shouted, and stormed from the room. The stench had trailed with her, like a cloak lifting in the wind of her passage. She'd run to the bathroom and vomited, got puke on the certificate and screwed it up into a ball as tight as her rage. She threw it away and that was the last time she'd gone into her mother's death chamber. The last words they'd spoken.

When Zack had called out earlier that day to say the woman's breaths were stretching further and further apart, Maddy had said, "So what?"

"Last chance," Zack had called from the gloomy, stinking room. "You want to say goodbye?"

"Fuck no. She's not even conscious, hasn't been for two days."

"I know. I told *you* that. But maybe she can still hear us."

"Then tell her to go to hell."

Yet here she sat now, an empty ache in her gut. Her mother was dead. Her useless, selfish, mean mother was dead, and she cared. Regardless, now they were alone. Her and Zack against the world. They had the house, the welfare, she had her job, Zack would quit school at the end of the year and get a job of his own. He had an apprenticeship lined up. The future was bright, by the standards of any future in The Gulp. One last hurdle to leap, getting rid of the body.

"Bury her in the back yard?" Zack said.

Maddy jumped slightly, looked up, torn from her thoughts. "First place they'll look if they suspect foul play."

"I know how to lay cement. Been helping Brian out for a while now. How about I make us a new patio?"

Maddy shook her head. "They'll smash it and pull it up. Anyway, a new cement deck is pretty fucking suspicious on its own, right?"

"I guess. So what do we do?"

Maddy looked at her phone. "It's nearly four. I have to go out."

"Where?"

"Just friends. Let's think on this a bit, yeah? Another day or two won't make any difference."

Zack grimaced and shook his head. "I dunno. I mean, I know she's foul in there already, but I was reading up on some of this stuff online. Dead bodies start to putrefy really quickly and... What?"

Maddy could feel how wide her eyes had gone. Ice trickled around her gut. "What the fuck have you been looking up online? What if someone searches your internet history?"

"I've been careful, Mads! Proxies and shit. I'm not an idiot. Besides, it's nothing specific or incriminating."

"Jesus, I hope not."

"Trust me! Anyway, all I'm saying is we need to decide. We can't leave it much longer."

Maddy stood. She needed to be out of the house. Away from... all this. "Until morning, Zack, okay? Let's decide in the morning."

"We have to make a decision, Sis. We've been going around and around this subject for weeks now. It's the one thing you'll never make a choice about. Everything else is done, why is this the one thing?"

"I don't know. It's too big, too weird. The rest is fucking admin, you know? It's stories and lies, and we're good at that. This part, it's physical. In the morning, I promise. Before you go to school we'll decide. When you're home from school, we'll *do* whatever we decide. Yeah?"

Zack nodded. "Okay."

"I might stay out. You okay for dinner?"

"Yeah. Probably go over to Josh's anyway, play Xbox. Charm his mum into letting me stay for dinner."

Maddy drew in a deep breath, then blew it out. "Okay, good. I'm working tomorrow, so I'll wake you when I get up. We'll decide over breakfast."

Zack nodded, lips a flat line. His eyes were wet, red underneath. Maddy swallowed. He was just a kid. They were both just kids, no matter how grown up they'd had to become. They would take care of each other, but she resented the need. No wonder Zack hung out with Josh so much. Josh was everything Zack wished for – loved, cared for, he had a mum and dad who were around plenty, a nice clean house. She went over and leaned down, kissed the top of his head.

"Love you, Zackattack."

He smiled up at her. "Love you too, Mad As Hell."

They grinned at each other. "We'll be okay," she said at last.

He nodded. "We will now."

"If I don't see you later, I'll wake you tomorrow."

She left the house, the late summer air fresh and fragrant with the salt of the ocean only a few blocks over from their place. "We'll be okay," she said again, to herself.

"Let's go to the Vic," Dylan said. "Get pissed."

Maddy pursed her lips, shook her head. "Can't afford it. What about some takeaway grog from Clooney's drive-through and come back here?"

They sat on a bench on the footpath, looking out over Carlton Beach, The Gulp's only easily accessible beach, just south of the harbour, all blackened volcanic sand and gravel. The dilapidated surf lifesaving club off to their right, the playground quiet, devoid of activity, behind them. They had the whole park and beach to themselves. For the moment, at least. Maddy was enjoying the fresh air, salt spray, quiet of the night, though it was barely eight o'clock. She didn't want to go home. Didn't want to go to the pub. They knew she was underage, but didn't care. Dylan was twenty-two and he always went to the bar, whether it was to spend his own money or hers. But she just didn't want the people.

"Come on," Dylan said. "Just for a couple, game of pool, see who's there? We can get takeout beers and come back here later."

Mum's dead. Really dead. It kept going around and around in her mind. It filled her thoughts, pushed against her brain like it needed to get out. The massive relief. The fear of what came next. The immediate concerns of what to do with the bitch's carcass.

"Maddy?"

He'd been talking again, she realised. "Sorry, what?"

"You're not yourself tonight. You okay?"

She looked up at Dylan's kind eyes. He was a funny-looking fucker, everyone said so. Gangly and tall, wide apart eyes, a pointed chin. Far from classically handsome, but he had an intriguing look as far as Maddy was concerned. But more than that, he was kind, respectful. That went a long way beyond what someone looked like.

"I'm okay," she said. "Bit distracted, sorry."

"Home stuff? Your mum?"

"Yeah, the usual." She forced a smile. Maybe distraction was what she needed after all. "Let's go the Vic."

He grinned and took her hand. They walked the few hundred metres down Tanning Street to the Victorian Hotel. It was bustling inside, busy for a weeknight. Maddy frowned as they went in and Dylan pointed to a sign by the door.

New Wednesday Special – Trivia Night!
How smart are you?
Register a team now.
Starts 7pm

Maddy groaned. "Sounds awful."

"Right? They must be between rounds. Let's get a beer and head out the back before they start again."

One end of the main bar had a stage where bands sometimes played and a drop-down screen in front of it, where they often showed boxing matches, the UFC, some of the bigger footy games. A middle-aged woman Maddy didn't recognise had a table set up there with a laptop, the big screen showing a PUB TRIVIA logo. The woman had a microphone in hand and stood grinning out at the busy room.

"Five minutes!" she said, as Maddy and Dylan reached the bar.

He bought the drinks, she took hers and followed him out the back into the bistro and pool area. Two big rooms, one with tables and chairs and the kitchen where food could be ordered and collected, the other with two tatty pool tables, surrounded by the usual motley array of patrons. A door behind the second table led out to the courtyard and several picnic bench and table combos dotted with smokers.

Dylan looked around the pool room, spotted a

couple of mates. They headed over, raising their glasses in greeting. Three burley bearded guys with denim and leather, arms full of tattoos, long beards and hard eyes, had colonised the nearest pool table and their friends looked a bit pissed off about it.

Maddy glanced over, saw Desert Ghost MC patches on their backs. *Arseholes*, she thought, but didn't say aloud. They always made trouble when they came into town. Their bikes would be parked around the side, big Harleys with ape-hanger bars and fancy airbrushed paintwork of flames and skulls.

"They'll only play for money," Dave said, nodding at the bikers. "And they're bloody good, so always win."

"Hustlers," Dylan said, as if this were some pearl of wisdom.

"Exactly." Dave reached out and clinked glasses with Dylan, then Maddy.

They fell to chatting and drinking, ignoring the bikers and their pool table dominion, not bothering to move around to the other table where people scowled and muttered about the interlopers. The bikers loved it, of course, half the reason they stuck around was to annoy the locals. The other reason was to fleece them, and they'd probably round out the night by picking a fight.

The distraction worked partially, but Maddy still couldn't get the image of her mother's wasted body from her mind, finally devoid of life. Dylan's brother worked on one of the farms out on the Gulpepper Road leading to the highway. Did they have pigs? She'd seen shows where gangsters got rid of bodies by feeding them to pigs. Maybe she and Zack could cut up their mother, take her bit by bit to the farm and drop the bits in the pig pen.

She shuddered. What the hell was she thinking? Apart from trying to conceal body parts from the farmers, as if she would be able to chop up her mother. Maybe Zack's idea of the harbour was a good one. But she had another thought. They could rent a dinghy for the day, say they were going out fishing. If they could somehow get the body into the dinghy, wrapped up and weighed down with rocks or something, they could dump it much further out than the harbour. But how would she get it there?

Her mum's car sat in the garage at home. Maddy had been learning to drive, was still on her Ls, but could do all that was required. If they put the body in the back of the car, then backed it up to the harbour as if they were loading supplies for a day's fishing... It could work. Especially if they started really early before many people were about. And there were never cops in The Gulp, so no one would pull her over if she only drove around town. Hell, if you *needed* cops and rang triple-0 it was always at least an hour before someone came from Enden or Monkton. If they came at all.

Their mother had been a small woman in life, barely over five feet tall, and she was wasted away to little more than bones now. They could surely wrap her up tight in something, maybe an old doona cover, rope it all together with weights inside. She wouldn't make too big a parcel, they could flip her straight out of the boot of the little Toyota hatchback into the dinghy. If they picked their moment, no one would see a thing. They could take her from the bedroom to the car through the kitchen, so no one would see that. She'd only be out for a second while they dumped her in the boat, then they'd take her out as far as they dared and sink the bitch. Let the snails and worms of the seabed have her. If they wrapped her up enough, tied weights to her limbs tightly enough, she'd never surface again.

"What are you smiling about?" Dylan half-smiled himself in anticipation of her answer as he held out a fresh beer.

She didn't realise she'd made any outward indication of her thoughts. "Nothing really," she said quickly. "Just a little drunk, I guess. You want to get out of here?"

"Take outs back to the beach?"

"What about take outs back to your place?" She gave him a sultry look. Dylan had his own place, a rented flat that was barely more than a studio, but it was private. He kept trying to convince her to move in with him, but she wasn't taking their relationship nearly as seriously as he was. One day she would have to let him down, she had no intention of staying with him long term, but for now it was fun.

He grinned. "Better skull these then."

"Race ya!" She upended the schooner and downed the beer, Dylan grunting in surprise and trying to catch up, but she had him beat.

They both laughed, gasping as they caught their breath. Maddy's head swam a little from the sudden impact of alcohol. She took his hand and they left the pub.

"More cordial, boys?"

"Muuu-uuum! I said before we're fine, thanks!"

Josh's mother made a roll-eyes face at Zack as Josh concentrated on the videogame, hunched forward over the controller. Zack grinned. A mother who cared enough to keep offering was one of the reasons he loved coming over here as much as he did. She was everything his mother wasn't – kind, caring, well-fed. Alive. She had motherly curves and full curly hair, sparkling green eyes. He knew he loved her a little bit.

"We're fine, thank you, Mrs Brady," he said.

"Well, you holler if you need anything else. Want a snack?"

"Mum!"

"No, I'm so full from dinner. Your lasagne is..." Zack made a chef's kiss gesture and grinned again.

"Oh, you!"

Mrs Brady ducked out, pulling Josh's bedroom door almost but not quite closed. Zack stared at where she'd been for a moment, then turned his attention back to the game just as Josh died again.

"Dammit!" he snapped, and held the controller out to Zack.

"Why don't we go two-player?"

"Nah, I want to get through these levels single-player. God, my mum is so annoying."

Zack restarted the level. "She's kinda cool, really."

Josh looked at him with his eyebrows almost vanishing into his hair. "Cool? My mum? Earth to Zack, what have you been smoking?"

"I know she's a dork, but you should appreciate all she does for you. And you've got a dad around who gives a shit. Don't take that stuff for granted, man."

Josh smiled. "Yeah, I guess it's easy for me. You should have the same."

"I do. I have it here. That's why I'm always coming over."

"For my parents?"

"Well, not just your parents. Your Xbox too."

"Fuck you!" Josh slammed a good set of knuckles into Zack's arm and Zack cried out, laughing through the pain as he desperately kept the character moving on screen.

"Also, your sister is *hot*! So it's sweet when she's home from uni."

"You want me to hit you again?"

Zack laughed and shook his head. "No, don't! I can barely feel my right hand as it is!"

"You know, your sister is pretty hot too," Josh said, turning back to look at the screen. "If she wasn't so... I dunno, angry all the time."

"Angry all the time?"

"Always scowling."

"I guess she does it tough, looking after Mum and all that."

"I thought you said you did most of it," Josh said.

"Yeah, well, we both do. Mum has a lot of problems. And Maddy works too."

They fell into silence for a while, except a *Whoop!* when Zack completed the level, comfortable in each other's company. Zack took his turns, doing his best not to think about his mum, finally expired in the fetid bed at home. Josh's house was so clean and bright compared to his own. It smelled so fresh. Even the air at home seemed dirty, notwithstanding the stench. Once they got rid of Mum, he planned to make sure Maddy helped him clean the place from top to bottom and back again. He wanted to scrub and polish everything, maybe even repaint. The house was finally theirs and he wanted to make it more like Josh's. This was what a family home was supposed to be like.

Get rid of Mum. That was the tricky bit. His stomach started to go watery again at the thought. If they were caught, it would destroy everything. DoCS would come in, they'd be carted off somewhere, lose the house. He didn't even know if they had extended family. His mum had talked about useless cousins in Bega, but what did that even mean?

He felt panic welling up again at the thought. *Please, Maddy*, he silently begged. *Please have a plan by the morning.*

"School night," came a gruff but kind voice from the door.

They turned to see Josh's dad, short hair, neat beard, still wearing the slacks and white shirt from his suit and tie office work combo. He was an accountant in Enden, or something like that. Advisor of something or other. He was just as kind as Mrs Brady. He smiled and nodded at Zack. "How are ya, mate?"

"Good, thanks."

"And your mum?"

Zack made a face, shrugged. "She's doing okay."

"You know, if you ever need any help..."

"I know, Mr Brady, thanks."

"Another half hour, Dad?"

"School night, Josh. It's already getting late."

Zack got up from the floor, grabbed his hoodie. "It is getting on," he said. "Mum'll be worried. I'd better go."

Josh nodded, turning back to his game. "Until next time then, loser."

"Which will be school tomorrow, friend of losers."

Mr Brady stepped back to let Zack out of the room, then followed him down the hallway towards the front door. The well-lit hallway, with family photos on the walls. All that was on the walls in Zack's house were flower-shaped mould stains.

"Seeya, champ!"

"Seeya, Mr Brady. Thanks!"

"Any time."

He jogged the five hundred metres or so home, up the hill from Josh's place near the beach to his own where the houses got smaller and closer together. He let himself in and stood in the dark hallway as the door clicked shut behind him. He could replace that blown light bulb if nothing else, that had been out for weeks. Tomorrow, he decided. He wouldn't start until they'd done whatever they were going to do with Mum. Let it mark the beginning of a new era for him and Maddy. A free era.

He walked along and stared at the closed door of his mother's room. The cloying stink reached his nostrils even here, creeping under the door like a mist. He'd left the window open and had a moment of panic that the neighbours might notice. Her room was at the back of the house, her window overlooking the scrappy patch of lawn and flowerbeds gone to seed. It was a half-decent size for a back yard in town, maybe twenty metres to a side, two-metre high wooden fence all around. No one could see in, all the neighbours yards backing onto each other. Someone would have to climb up onto the fence to see, and even then they wouldn't get much of a view into the house. The curtains were drawn again even though the window was open. He shook his head. No, no one would see her. But would they smell her? Maybe when she started to really rot, that kind of stink was epic. You could smell a dead roo on the roadside even as you drove past at eighty Ks an hour. But they'd be rid of her before that happened.

Come and help me, son.

Zack jumped. He must have imagined it, but the voice of his mother had been all too real. Stress maybe. She was dead. Really dead at last. He can't have heard her.

Unable to help himself, he drew a deep breath in, held it, then opened her door for a look. The breath escaped him in a rush, his eyes going wide. He scrabbled his hand around for the light switch, not believing what he saw in the low light coming from the kitchen behind him.

The room burst into light as he flicked the switch, and he stared. What the hell was growing all over her?

Maddy crept in a little after 2 a.m., closing the front door and leaning against it for a moment. Physically satisfied – for a funny-looking fucker, Dylan knew what do with his gangly body – she was still mentally antsy. She was also pretty drunk.

A bead of light glowed from under the closed door to her mother's room. She frowned. Zack must have turned it on, but she wondered why. Maybe he'd gone in again to look at her. This must be hard for him. He always kept some part of his heart open to some essential goodness he saw in their mother. Or believed in, even if he never saw it. It showed what a good person he was, but he suffered for it. Maddy had long-since locked away every part of her heart where their mother was concerned.

Well, she could lay there dead with the light on. Maddy wasn't about to crack open that stench, even to flick the light off. She went and looked into Zack's room and he was curled up under the doona, snoring softly.

She suppressed the urge to go in and kiss his forehead. Only thirteen months apart, it was ridiculous how much of an older sister she felt sometimes. Girls mature faster than boys and all that shit, maybe. With a sigh, she went to the bathroom, brushed her teeth and washed her face, then headed into her bedroom, stripped to her undies and pulled her current sleeping t-shirt on. It was a gift from Dylan, a *Bullet For My Valentine* tour shirt. She kind of loved it. Poor Dylan, he was a good person too, and she hated the thought of breaking his heart. She'd have to do it soon, it wasn't fair on him to drag things out. She wasn't the sort to settle down, certainly not now, and hopefully never.

She fell into bed and sleep swept over her.

The alarm woke her at seven and it didn't feel like she'd moved a muscle since she hit the sheets. With a groan, lamenting the background pounding of her head from last night's beer, she stumbled up and went into the bathroom to piss. On the way back she leaned into Zack's room to call him awake, but frowned. The lump wasn't under the doona any more.

"Zack?" Jesus, her voice sounded like a sixty-a-day smoker's croak. Should have drunk some water in the bathroom.

She went into the kitchen, planning to drink a big old glass of water before calling for Zack again. He was already in there, dressed in his school uniform. His eyes were haunted.

"You have to look at Mum."

Maddy swallowed, went to get water and it was nectar on her parched throat. She turned and leaned back against the sink. "What?"

"You have to look at Mum."

"What do you mean. Are you okay?"

"Please. Just go and look at her."

She stared at him a moment longer and his steady gaze discomforted her. With a frown, she downed the rest of the water, put the glass down and went back along the hall to their mother's room. She stood a moment, gathering herself, took a few steadying breaths. Then she held the last breath and opened the door.

The held breath rushed out of her along with her voice. "The fuck?"

The light was on still, the thin curtain shifted in the breeze of the open window. Her mother was in the bed, propped on the pillows exactly like the day before, but she was covered in... something. Maddy leaned forward, trying to see better without going in. The bedclothes were rumpled, stained near her mother's corpse with yellowing patches. Her mother had on a t-shirt that before had clung to her bony frame like a rag, but now stood taller, as if the woman had gained weight overnight. Her bare arms lay either side of her torso, her scrawny neck emerged from the shirt, her skull face staring sightlessly up at the ceiling, but all that exposed skin had pale lumps over it. Rounded and smooth, white as alabaster, like half-ping pong balls dotted all over her. There were barely a centimetre or two of skin between each of them. One covered her left eye, her right eye down in a hollow between two others. One pushed from the side of her nose, another forced her mouth open in a silent scream. Several made a range of rounded hills out of her neck, more on her shoulders under the shirt. Her forearms were covered in them, the back of her hands. Her fingers were splayed as the smooth white half-orbs grew between them. In some cases, the lumps seemed to encircle her fingers completely.

"What's happening to her?"

Maddy startled at Zack's voice right behind her as he looked in over her shoulder. When did he get so tall? "What is it?" she asked.

"They're like mushrooms. They feel soft."

"You touched her?" The horror was clear in her sharp tone.

"Not with my finger! I poked one with that straw from the water glass by her bed. It's soft like a fresh mushroom."

Maddy shook her head. "Is she going mouldy?"

"They were half that size when I got in last night."

"What?"

"I looked in when I got back from Josh's. She was covered in them like that, but they were further apart, smaller, sort of like marbles. You weren't here, I didn't know what to do. I shut the door and went to bed. Didn't sleep well, couldn't stop thinking about it. I got up about dawn, came to see again and they were bigger, like that."

"Jesus, Zack, this isn't normal. This isn't what happens to dead bodies."

"Is it because of her sickness. She said it was nothing, we knew it was cancer, but maybe it wasn't."

Maddy ran a hand over her head, tucked her hair behind her ears. "I don't know any sickness that would result in... that!"

"Looks like it's all over her body."

"Have you checked?"

"No!"

Maddy nodded, chewed her lower lip. "We need to check."

"Why?"

"We have to move her. We need to figure out if

that's safe. I don't want to get that stuff on me!"

"It doesn't smell so bad," Zack said.

"What?"

"Sniff. It's covering the stink."

Maddy allowed herself a slow breath in through her nose and he was right. The sick, cloying aroma of sickness and death was still there, but vastly reduced. Unpleasant, but not appalling like it had been. "Get the big scissors from the kitchen," she said.

Zack said nothing but she felt him move away from her. Reluctantly she went into the bedroom and took another steadying breath, then lifted the bedclothes away. The stick thin remains of her mother lay in a shallow hollow on the mattress. The sheets beneath her were dark and sticky, some foul combination of blood and shit that had leaked out of her. Zack had tried to keep her clean, but admitted he'd stopped in the last week or so before she died, unable to bear it any longer.

"She shits this black stuff that stinks so bad," he'd said. "It just pours out of her."

The mattress would be soaked with it. Maddy crouched, looked under the bed. Sure enough, the stains had gone right through, a patch on the floorboards where it had dripped and spattered.

"Fuck me."

Her mother's legs were barely more than bones, the skin browned like leather except where it was red with lesions and sores. But those things were only partially visible now under the numerous smooth white blobs growing out of her. They pushed her toes apart, grew out from the soles of her feet. Zack held out the scissors beside her. She took them.

The white stuff seemed fused with the sheets where her body lay against them, like it grew from the gross stains as well. Maddy lifted the bottom hem of the shirt and began cutting up towards the neck. She peeled the two halves apart and made a quiet noise of distress. Zack bolted from her side and vomited noisily somewhere down the hall. She heard the splatter of water and hoped that meant he'd made it to the toilet.

These... things... Maddy paused, dragged in a ragged breath. Mushrooms, she decided. For the sake of argument, let's call them mushrooms. They were bigger on her mother's torso, and the skin around them had split, stark red like fresh steak. One bulged from between her labia, streaked with a viscous fluid tinged with blood. The growths covered her, went around her sides to connect her to the bed where she met the mattress.

Maddy opened the scissors and pressed a point into one of the larger growths on her mother's stomach. The surface was tough, but there was give in it. She pressed a little harder, the point of the scissor blade dimpling in. Then it punctured through and the mushroom hissed as it flattened slightly. Maddy cried out and jumped back.

The mushroom leaked a dark, red-brown fluid, that trickled over the half-deflated side and pooled at the base where it fused with her mother's sallow skin.

"What the fuck, Mads?"

She turned, saw Zack standing in the doorway, eyes red and wet with tears. "I don't know. I just don't know."

She went over and took him in a hug, then turned and pulled the bedroom door closed, guided him back into the kitchen.

"This is so fucked up," Zack said quietly. "Not even just... that. Fucking everything. She was awful and now she's dead and now this. What do we do, Mads?"

"I don't know. I need to think. I don't want to move her, you saw what happened when I... that stuff came out."

"Is it eating her?"

Maddy swallowed. "I don't know. Maybe. Perhaps that's a good thing? Like, if that fungus or whatever it is eats her up there's nothing for us to move. Maybe it's a good thing?"

Zack burst out a bark of genuine mirth. "What luck! Mum died and now she's getting eaten by mushrooms!"

Maddy grinned and for a moment they both devolved into uncontrollable laughter, a relief valve blowing through the insanity. "Jesus fuck, Zack," Maddy said as the laughs reduced to giggles. "What the hell is happening?"

"I had lasagne at Josh's last night. It was so normal!"

"Sounds amazing." She hugged him again, then stepped back to look at him. "Go to school, yeah? I have to go to work. I'm only on a short shift though, eight till two, so I'll be back when you get home. There's no need to decide anything right now. Things have changed, hey. I have to get ready or I'll be late."

"I'm going to Josh's, see if he wants to walk to school together. I don't want to be here now."

Maddy smiled. "Don't blame you. We'll sort this out. Not much longer, then the house is ours and we can be normal too."

He looked at her, a little blankly.

"Okay?" she said.

He nodded. "Yeah. Okay."

The day at work crawled by even though it was a short shift. Maddy couldn't get the image of that mushroom popping and leaking from her mind. Or the image of her mother's body covered in the pure white growths, the ichor streaked white swelling out from between her legs. On several occasions bile would burn up into her throat and she'd brace, thinking she would need to rush for the bathroom to vomit, but managed to swallow it down each time.

She had a break at eleven and realised she had

eaten nothing since before she'd started drinking the night before, and that was only a serve of hot chips shared with Dylan. She went to the bakery out the front of Woollies and bought a bread roll and a can of coke, ate the bread dry, drank the soda. It was all she could face, but she felt immeasurably better after it hit her stomach.

"You right?" Wendy Callow asked as Maddy went back into the supermarket. Wendy was just heading out, presumably on her break.

Wendy was a year older than Maddy, and a bit weird. Most people uncharitably suggested some kind of impairment, but Maddy had come to know the girl and decided Wendy was actually quite smart. She was also intentionally cruel. She made racist remarks frequently, joked about kicking her stepfather's dog, stuff like that. People didn't like Wendy Callow for a reason. "I'm fine," Maddy said.

"Sure? You look like cold shit warmed up."

"Gee, thanks. Just drank too much last night."

"With Dylan?"

Maddy sighed. Wendy was hot for Dylan's mate, James. Maddy wasn't about to be a matchmaker though. "Yeah, with Dyl. I gotta get back."

She pushed past, heard Wendy mutter "Stuck up bitch" under her breath but ignored it. Not worth the mental anguish. Strengthened by the food and sugar from the soda, she got back to work.

When she came out again just after two, Dylan was loitering against one of the columns near the entrance. He grinned stupidly when she emerged and she frowned.

"What are you doing here?"

His face fell. "Last night we arranged to meet up. You said you finished at two. We're gonna drive to Enden and hit some shops, maybe eat there and catch up with..." He petered out, frown deepening at her expression. "You forgot? You weren't that drunk were you?"

"Shit, Dylan, I'm really sorry. I did forget." Maybe she'd been more drunk than she realised. She had some recollection of talking about heading to Enden, but didn't remember planning it for this afternoon. "But something's come up. Have to rain check?"

He nodded, eyes sad. "Sure, I guess. Everything okay?"

He was such a good guy. Some dudes would get angry, offended and offensive. Dylan was better than that, and she felt bad. "It's just a thing with Mum. I'm sorry."

"She's hard work for you, huh? And Zack. Need help?"

"Thanks, but nah. We'll be okay. We'll do the Enden thing another time, yeah?"

"Sure. I'll call you later?"

She stepped up and kissed him quickly. "Maybe tomorrow?"

"Blind Eye Moon are playing the Vic tomorrow. Wanna go?"

"Yeah, maybe. If... you know, if things are okay with Mum. Give me a call tomorrow arvo and we'll see, yeah?"

"Okay."

She gave his hand a squeeze and hurried away. She didn't dare glance back, knowing he'd be watching her go, hangdog eyes and a slight rounded curve to his shoulders. He would have to fortify and deal with it, she had more pressing concerns.

When she got home the house seemed quieter than it had ever been, still and somehow extra empty. She went around and opened all the curtains, made sure light flooded every room, opened all the windows too and let the late summer breeze blow through. She'd get the vacuum-cleaner out and go over every floor before dinner.

Then she stood outside the only door in the house

still closed.

Twice she reached for the door handle but chickened out. Her fingers shook.

"Come on, Madeleine," she told herself.

She clenched her teeth, building up her courage. She didn't want to know, wished she could just walk away from it all. No one should have to deal with any of this. But that wasn't an option, this was her life right now, and she had to live it. She blew out a quick breath, then swung the door open before she could stop herself.

"Fuck me!"

The fungus covering her mother had grown exponentially. None of the woman's body was visible any more, just a rolling, undulating mass of huge rounded mushrooms in a vaguely human shape filling more than half the old double bed. It was so white, such pure, unblemished paleness.

Maddy crept forward, sniffed tentatively. The stink of sickness and death was almost non-existent, but it had been replaced with an earthy, fungal scent. Not entirely unpleasant, but also not entirely natural. Or perhaps super-natural, like an artificially created facsimile of what a mushroom should smell like. Super-real.

On the old armchair in the corner of the room, a wire coat hanger lay atop a pile of clothes her mother would never wear again. Maddy took it and used one rounded end to prod at the nearest bulge of fungus, her mother's right foot buried somewhere deep within. That same tough but pliant exterior, the same cushioned softness under pressure. She didn't dare push hard enough to split the skin of it again.

"What is happening?" she whispered to herself.

The whole mass shivered.

Maddy squealed and ran backwards, bumped into the wall. It shivered again, a vibration rippling through, then it settled. Maddy's body shook with horror, imagining the whole thing splitting open like one of those puffball mushrooms she'd seen on a nature doco, a dusty cloud of spores bursting from it.

She felt behind herself for the door as she sidled along the wall, not taking her eyes from the corpulent white mass. She slipped out of the room and closed the door.

When Zack got home a little while later, she was sitting on the sofa staring at some rubbish commercial television show. She genuinely had no idea what it was, what it was even about. She'd been in some kind of fugue state, just waiting.

Zack dropped his bag in the hallway by his bedroom door then came to join her, sitting on the edge of the armchair. "Haven't stopped thinking about it all day."

She laughed softly. "Me either. It's worse."

"Worse?"

"Or better, maybe. Depending how you look at it."

They opened the door, shoulder to shoulder to see in. The mass had pushed the bedclothes aside as it grew, a parody of a cloud sat atop the mattress. It covered two-thirds of the bed, vaguely ovoid with an undulating surface. The light above reflected off it, so bright, so white.

"It looks so..." Zack frowned, searching for a word. "Clean," he said eventually.

"What's happening to her in there?" Maddy said. "That's what I can't stop thinking about. Like, is it consuming her flesh? Will there be nothing but polished bones inside eventually? Or will it take the bones too? And then what?" The memory of her previous thoughts came back to her. The idea had been haunting her since the thing shivered so suddenly. "Will it fucking spore?"

"Fungi are eukaryotic organisms," Zack said, monotone like a newsreader.

"What?"

"I've spent all afternoon in the school library, reading, memorising. Fungi are eukaryotic organisms such as yeasts, moulds, and mushrooms. Some fungi are multicellular, while others, such as yeasts, are unicellular. Most fungi are microscopic, but many produce the visible fruitbodies we call mushrooms."

"Fruitbodies?"

Zack pointed at the bed. "That's what it is. Growing out of her, that's the fruitbody of the fungus. And it's what produces the spores." His voice dropped into the reciting tone again. "Unlike plants, fungi can't produce their own food and have to feed like animals, by sourcing their own nutrients."

"Jesus, Zack, you're not helping." He'd always been able to read and recite like this. It was funny sometimes. Now it was decidedly creepy. "So some microscopic fungus found her and fruited while feeding on her? I guess we kinda figured that already. So what?"

Zack shook his head. "I don't know. I thought learning about it might help, but you're right. So what? It'll spore by bursting or scattering in some way, some use animals to carry the spore, most use the wind. I guess what I'm thinking is that maybe it'll feed on Mum until there's nothing left and then it'll wither and die or something, and it may or may not spore in the meantime. But I think we should just leave it alone. Shut the door. Maybe block the gap at the bottom with a towel or something and leave the window open."

"And then what?"

"Just fucking forget about it, Mads. For, like, a week or something. We can always go around the back, I suppose, peek in at the window, but I don't know if I dare. Maybe give it a month, then check? Perhaps everything will be over then, and she'll be gone. Or just bones and we can think of a way to bag them up and get rid of them."

Maddy thought of her fishing boat idea again. It would be even easier if it was just the woman's bones. Stack them in an esky and carry it to the harbour. Easy. She reached in and turned out the bedroom light, dropping the room into gloom broken only by the wan glow through the thin curtain. The fungal mass on the bed was still bright, almost luminescent it was so pale.

She looked at Zack and he nodded, so she closed the door. Zack turned to the hallway cupboard, rummaged in the bottom for one of the old towels and rolled it up into a snake that he pressed against the bottom of the door.

"So that's it?" Maddy asked.

"I reckon. Just forget about it now. For a while."

Maddy glanced at the closed door. "Is there anything in there we need?"

"Nah. I took it all weeks ago. Got all the paperwork, her few bits of jewellery, all that stuff is in my room. All that's in there are her clothes. And some books."

Maddy nodded. "Okay then. So that's that. For now."

"For now," he agreed.

"I want to clean the house," Maddy said.

Zack smiled. "I was thinking the same thing. Three bedrooms, bathroom, lounge, kitchen, hall. It's not much." He went to his bag, reached inside and pulled out a large blue plastic bottle, held it up. "Sugar soap. Mix it with a bucket of water to clean the walls. Cuts through grease and grime, and it's got a mould protection in it too."

"That seems definitely worthwhile right now." They laughed nervously, then Maddy said, "But two bedrooms. For now. We're leaving hers alone, remember."

"Yeah."

"Okay, I'll vacuum and dust, wipe all the surfaces. There's bleach under the sink. You do the walls."

"Gonna do the ceilings too. With a mop."

Maddy gave her brother a crooked smile. "Fucking look at us, eh?"

They busted their arses for hours, taking turns to crank music from their phones through Maddy's

Bluetooth JBL speaker. The focus seemed to be something they both needed, the physical labour of it taking up the nervous energy they'd been carrying. Maddy thought maybe the tensions and anxieties had been building for weeks, as their mother's illness quickly deteriorated from ongoing sickness to terminal decline. Then the actual death and rapid-fire shocks since had left them both shaken. Working hard, taking control of something, was like medicine.

It was nearly 9 p.m. when they both collapsed onto the couch, sweaty and dishevelled, and absolutely spent. Zack ordered in pizza with their mother's credit card, and they stared at the TV until it arrived. Starving, they devoured it in minutes, then watched more TV without talking. There was nothing to say, no need to plan or discuss. They were simply getting on with it. Maddy had some reservations, wondering if it was entirely wise to ignore the thing growing on their mother. She had occasional visions of it blooming to fill the room, bulge against the door until it burst, billowing in great rolls out the open window.

But she shook those thoughts away. It wouldn't come to that. If it did need more attention, maybe in a week or two, they'd decide then. Not now. They'd done enough for the time being. Their mother had just died, after all. Let them enjoy that for a while first.

She noticed Zack nodding off, chin on his chest, and gave him a prod. "Let's go to bed. School tomorrow. And I'm working eight till six."

He nodded and dragged himself off. The house gleamed, it almost looked like they'd redecorated more than cleaned it. The mould stains and scuff marks were gone, the floor was free of lint and grit and all manner of small detritus that had gathered. It smelled fresh, slightly lemon-scented from the cleaner Maddy had used on all the benches and tables tops.

Zack hugged her and went into his room and she went into hers. It felt like a new start.

They got up the next morning and it was like a house transformed. Zack looked with pride at the clean walls and ceilings. They were still old, paint peeled in places, but the blooms of black, spotted mould were gone. The cobwebs and various unidentified marks were gone. Dust and dirt had been vacuumed from the corners and edges. With late summer sunlight coming in through all the windows, the place gleamed. The windows were grimy though.

"We got any Windex?" he asked Maddy as they ate breakfast.

"Under the sink."

"Cool. After school, I'm going to clean all the windows too. And on the weekend, let's tidy up the garden. Shall we make a couple of veggie beds?"

Maddy laughed. "Sure, why not!"

He did his best not to think about the closed room. He especially tried not to think about the sensation of a whispering voice that had seemed to drift from that room while he tried to sleep the night before. He'd been bone-tired from all the housework, his mind abuzz with missing his mother, so surely it was just his tired brain freaking out a bit. He was glad she was gone at last but couldn't help grieving for the mother she could have been. Imagine if she'd been even ten percent the mother Mrs Brady was. Josh had no idea how lucky he had it.

But he still heard her voice.

Help me, Zacky.

And

I need something, Zacky-boy.

Like it was coming through the wall from her room to his. Cajoling, that familiar edge of demand to it as always. Perhaps he should tell Maddy he could hear her. But she'd think he was mad.

Zack left the house and headed down the hill, then left and right onto Tanning Street. Josh was waiting for him at the usual spot and they fell into step together heading up Tanning towards the servo, then right to the high school at the top of the hill.

"What's new?" Josh said after a few minutes of companionable silence.

"Same old," Zack said.

"Your mum any better?"

"Nah, she won't get any better." Zack paused, licked his lips. "I think me and Maddy'll be looking after her forever."

"Well, not forever," Josh said. "Parents get old and die."

"I guess. Seems like forever, that's all."

A few more minutes of silence passed as they scuffed along, then Josh said, "My dad asked me to ask you something." He sounded uncomfortable.

"Yeah?"

"Said did you want him or mum to come over? Talk to your mum?"

Zack startled, but quickly gathered himself. "Nah, man. What for? Talk about what?"

Josh made patting motions with both hands. "It's all good, dude. I told them it was a stupid idea, but they insisted I ask you."

"But talk about what?"

"I think they wonder if your mum needs any help or anything. Like, grown-up help."

Zack laughed, tried to make light of it. "We're not kids any more, mate. Tell 'em it's all fine, we'll be good. She's getting help anyway. Doctors and shit." His mother had refused to ever see a doctor, but Josh didn't know that. Or need to know.

"I'll tell them."

They walked on, got to school, went through the

drudgery of high school bullshit. But Zack spent the whole time concerned about how much interference there might be from Mr and Mrs Brady. He decided they needed a contingency story. He'd talk to Maddy about it later. Those useless cousins in Bega his mum sometimes talked about might need to become a little more involved. Nobody else knew his mum hated them. Zack himself didn't even know if they were real, but that didn't matter. The concept was useful. If the Brady's, or anyone else, came sniffing around, he and Maddy could say their mum had gone to see her cousins for a few days.

At lunch when he was allowed to take his phone out of his locker, he sent a garbled message about it to Maddy. She replied, *What?* He texted, *Talk about it later*

An hour after Maddy got the text from Zack she realised what he meant. Her brother was rubbish at expressing himself. But yes, having a ready-made story about their mum away visiting cousins in case people came around was a good idea. It was a little disturbing how easily they were slipping into the new role they'd made for themselves. Except for the white mass blooming in the bedroom. Try as she might, Maddy couldn't get it out of her mind.

She was tired after work and though Dylan rang and asked her if she still wanted to go see Blind Eye Moon at the Vic, she blew him off. She apologised, and she meant it, but she needed to start distancing herself. And she genuinely wanted to spend time with Zack in the new clean house that was finally theirs. She went home and Zack wasn't there. She texted and he said he'd gone to Josh's after school but would come home for dinner. He hadn't done the windows after all, but would do it on the weekend. She smiled. The great fervour to clean and take over the house had burned out as quickly as it had ignited, but that was okay. They'd done enough for now.

An hour later they made dinner together and talked about the visiting cousins in Bega story. It came together easily, really not much detail required. Then they watched movies on Netflix and drank from a bottle of Kraken rum Maddy had bought from the bottle shop behind Clooney's on her way home. Zack even did the dishes before he went to bed, and they both crashed out about midnight, both more than a little drunk, both giggling.

Life, Maddy ruminated as she lay in her clean sheets, freshly laundered, was actually not so bad at last.

Don't think about that pale thing in the bed...

The booze helped sleep along and she sank into blissful ignorance of the world.

The next day was Saturday and Maddy had one Saturday in four off. This was one of them. A rare alignment of planets where her two days off were actually the weekend and she could hang out with all her other working mates, and the few still in high school heading towards their HSC. Maybe even heading towards university and a ticket out of The Gulp.

Dylan rang and said two carloads were heading into Monkton, going to the Plaza to shop and goof off, probably stay for the evening and a movie. Did she want to tag along? She said she did and it was a good day. Fun was had, there were enough other mates around that she could keep Dylan a little bit at arm's length without it seeming weird. The movie was rubbish, but that didn't really matter. Late, after the film and a couple of drinks at the Monkton Tavern, where most of them got carded, but thankfully not Maddy, Dylan drove her, Pete and Jonathan home. Pete and

Jonathan sat in the back canoodling, and Maddy sat in the front passenger seat, watching the trees flicker by in the moonlight. The other four had elected to stay longer, drink more. They'd probably drag themselves home in the shameful light of dawn and have ribald tales to tell. Maddy wasn't in the mood.

Pete and Jonathan wanted to get back to Pete's place for obvious reasons, and she thought Dylan was probably entertaining similar ideas. Once he'd dropped the two blokes off, he turned to Maddy and grinned, soppy and kinda goofy.

"My place?"

She smiled, but shook her head. "Not tonight. I'm really tired. Can you drop me home?"

He visibly deflated, but tried to put a brave face on it. "Sure." He paused a moment, then said, "Is everything all right? With you... With us?"

Break up with him, her mind said firmly. *Do the right thing. Look at him, poor fucker. Don't be mean and drag it out. Like ripping off a Band-Aid, short term pain then it's all over and everyone is okay.* Though by the look in his eyes, he would not be okay.

"Maddy? Are we okay?"

She nodded. "Sure, of course. I'm just really tired and... well, Mum has been kinda hard work lately. It'll ease off soon, I know it will, but I don't want to leave it all for Zack, you know?" *You chickenshit loser*, she told herself.

He smiled, clearly relieved. "Well, of course. That makes sense."

Poor bastard, she thought. *So trusting.*

"You want me to help?" he asked. "Anything I can do? I could come around and, I don't know. Help. I've never been inside your place."

And you never will, sweet Dylan. "No, really, it's fine. Mum's going to visit her cousins soon anyway, the break will do her good and it'll be nice for me and Zack to have a break."

Dylan frowned. "I thought she was aggro... something phobic... too scared to leave the house."

"Agoraphobic. Yeah, she is. Which is why we're not pushing but slowly convincing her to go on this trip. Her cousin will come to pick her up and everything. Hopefully. We'll be okay. Just drop me home, yeah?"

"Okay."

Zack was asleep in bed when she crept in about 1 a.m. and Maddy was soon pulling the covers over herself. She couldn't have been asleep more than a few minutes it seemed, when something jerked her awake. Disoriented, in that place between states, brain circling looking for a landing spot, it took a moment to realise what had woken her.

She blinked when she saw light pouring in through her bedroom door. She normally closed it at night but had inadvertently left it half-open. Maybe a by-product of relaxing now her mother had died. The light came from across the hall. And she heard a soft voice, whispering.

Nerves rippled across Maddy's skin and she moved silently along the bed. Kneeling on the end of it she leaned forward and looked through the small gap between door and frame, across the hallway to their mother's room. She suppressed a gasp. The smooth white fungus had grown again, so bright, clean and rounded in the light from the bedroom fixture directly above the bed. It covered the whole mattress now and hung in pendulous bulges down either side. The bed had a wooden headboard and footboard, both of which stood a half metre or so above the mattress. Both were buried in rolls of pure white. The rounded centre of the thing bulged up more than a metre above the mattress.

She saw it all because her mother's door was wide open and Zack stood at the foot of the bed, his head tipped to one side. Maddy had the impression he was listening.

"I don't know, Mum," he said softly. "But why?" He

paused to listen again. "Are you sure?"

Maddy chewed her lower lip. This wasn't good. Maybe he was sleepwalking, having some kind of weird lucid dream. Enough for him to get up, open their mother's door, turn her light on, start a conversation? It seemed unlikely.

"I don't want to, Mum!" He sounded more sad than defiant.

He took a step back and shook his head. "Let me think about it."

He reached back for the light switch, starting to turn, and Maddy ducked back out of sight. The light clicked off as she pulled the covers over herself and heard Zack trudge back down the hallway, then his bedroom door *thunked* shut.

"What the fuck was that about?" she whispered to herself.

The next morning she woke a bit after nine and crawled from bed, but Zack had yet to emerge. It was more than an hour later when he slumped into the lounge, hair in disarray, carrying a bowl of cereal.

"Yo," he said, and sat down, flicked on the TV.

Maddy looked up from her phone. "Yo yourself. Going all right?"

"Yeah, why?"

"No reason. Sleep okay?"

"Yeah." He shovelled cereal.

Maddy sighed. She'd have to come right out with it. "You remember getting up in the night?"

"What do you mean?"

"What do you mean, what do I mean? You got up in the night, like 2 a.m. or something. You don't remember?"

He looked at her over his bowl, eyebrows crunched together. He opened his mouth to speak, then seemed to think better of it. He paused. Then, "No I didn't."

Was it worse if he didn't remember or he was lying? Maybe he'd been sleepwalking after all. But he looked disturbed.

"Are you right?" he asked, sounding sarcastic. His eyes looked haunted, one squinted slightly like he was trying to remember something.

Maddy laughed it off, looked back at her phone. "Yeah, all good."

Zack stared at the TV, partly enjoying the time alone, partly wanting to go to Josh's house. Maddy was off with her mates again and it was a novelty to have the place to himself. No scratchy-throated mother calling out to him, or ringing that little fucking bell he'd given her when she got really weak. Calling him to give her water, to wipe where she'd shit herself, just to see him, her little man. He shuddered, thankful it was all over.

But it wasn't over. She was still in there, under that stuff. He wanted to go to Josh's, forget it all and play games, but was also cautious not to push his luck. He couldn't spend every minute over there, even though he wanted to. Maybe sometime soon he could invite Josh over instead. If that fungus did get rid of the body he could call Josh, say his mum was at her cousins in Bega. Having a friend over to the house seemed both audacious and exotic. He'd never done it before.

Bring him to me.

Zack stiffened in the chair, refused to accept he'd heard her.

Bring him.

"No, Mum!"

The whispering voice was muffled by the closed bedroom door, but still clear enough. He didn't want to admit he'd known what Maddy was talking about earlier. He'd thought it was a dream. He'd *dreamed* that he'd been woken in the night by sounds of water, rain and waves, and by distant screams. He'd got up, looked out his bedroom window, and seen creatures falling from thick and pendulous clouds, limbs writhing as they tumbled through the rain to land with distant splashes in the ocean. Some far out near the horizon, others closer to the beach. What should have been sand was slick and shiny with some dark ooze. Between his bedroom window and the sea was nothing but thick, verdant bush, battered by incessant rain.

But he knew it was a dream. He couldn't see the ocean from his window. He only saw the street outside, other houses, cars, whatever. Maybe if there were no houses between theirs and the beach he might catch a glimpse, but not this clear a view, as if from high above, looking out over the vast expanse of roiling sea as the creatures fell.

Then he'd heard a voice, whispering, calling him. It was still the dream, it had to be, because it was his mother's voice. He went to her room, turned on the light, and the bulbous white fungus that covered her, bigger than ever, had shivered and her voice drifted from it.

Bring people to see me, she had said.

He told her he didn't want to, but she begged him. She cajoled and whined and said it was so important, that she'd finally be able to be a proper mother to him. He'd told her to let him think about it, everything hyper-real in that dream state super-clarity. And he'd gone back to bed.

In the morning, he remembered the dream. When Maddy asked if he remembered being up in the night he said no, because it was a dream. Wasn't it? So how did she know? But he definitely wasn't dreaming now. And his mother was talking to him again.

He got up, knees trembling, and opened her bedroom door. The swollen whiteness reached the floor on either side of the bed, bulged up almost to touch the light fitting above.

Bring Joshy to me!

"No, Mum! No way." How could she be talking to him? He was going mad, that had to be it. Was it guilt? Fear of being caught in their lie? Surely they deserved their shot at living alone. Living free.

Bring someone. Zacky, I need someone.

"What for?"

To help me.

"To help you what?"

Come back.

"You're dead!" he shouted and slammed the door shut. He ran back to the lounge, fell onto the couch, and turned the TV up loud.

He decided he'd hold out through the morning, then call Josh after lunch. But not go over to the house, he didn't want to lie to Mr and Mrs Brady again, not yet. He'd invite Josh to the skate park.

It was almost noon when a knock at the door startled him.

Standing on the porch was a middle-aged woman in jeans and a red jumper. She had long hair tied back and sneakers on, but they looked brand new, completely free of dirt. Behind her, Zack saw a small Volkswagen parked at the kerb.

"Yeah?"

"You must be Zachary Taylor?"

"Who are you?"

The woman smiled and held up a small plastic wallet hanging on a lanyard from a belt loop of her jeans. She said aloud what was written on it. "I'm Stephanie Belcher, from the Department of Communities and Justice."

Zack's heart hammered and his skin went cold. "DoCS?"

She smiled again. "That's what we used to be called, yes. Is your mother home?"

"Why?"

"I'd just like to have a chat, that's all." She looked over his shoulder into the house as she spoke. "Can I come in?"

Zack's mind raced. Should he use the story about visiting her cousins now?

Bring her to me!

Zack jumped, looking quickly at the woman's face. She gave no indication that she'd heard his mother's voice.

"Are you okay?" Belcher asked.

"Yeah, I'm fine."

Bring her to me!

His mother's voice was insistent. Desperate. Something dragged hard at Zack's chest, seemed to haul at his insides.

Bring her! Let me fix it!

He stepped back from the door. "Come in. Mum's in bed. She's not been well."

"I'm sorry to hear that."

"She's agoraphobic. Never goes out."

Belcher smiled. "Yes, that's in your file. Must be tough on you, huh? And your sister?"

"I guess. We're okay. You really don't need to see her, we're all just fine."

"I'm sure that's true, but this is standard procedure."

Zack noticed their neighbour, Jack Parsons, standing on the far side of his car where it was parked on the driveway. He looked over the roof at them, ducked away and got into the car when he caught Zack's eye. The man had to be ninety years old, a real busybody. He'd always been old and grumpy Zack's whole life.

"Which is your mum's room?"

Zack jumped slightly, and quickly closed the front door.

Bring her! Bring her!

Zack's whole body shook, his mouth was dry. He walked around Belcher and pointed to the bedroom door, then stood slightly aside. He knocked, hoped the woman couldn't see his hand trembling. "Mum, someone to see you." His voice wavered and he cursed it.

Belcher didn't seem to notice. She smiled, raised her eyebrows.

Zack shrugged, gestured to the door. "After you?"

Belcher turned the handle and pushed open the door. "Mrs Taylor, I'm sorry to disturb you... What the hell?"

The social worker had taken one step into the room and stood staring in shock at the voluminous white fungus that obscured the entire bed. The light was pushed slightly to one side by its highest bulge.

Give her to me!

His mother's voice was high, desperate, commanding. With a cry of fear and revulsion, Zack stepped forward, put both hands against Stephanie Belcher's upper back, and shoved. She yelped in surprise and staggered forward, raising her hands to stop her fall. Her palms hit the front of the pure white curve and immediately hissed, smoke pouring up off them. Belcher screamed as her hands sank in, her arms swallowed into the stuff up to her elbows. More smoke roiled up, Belcher's throat tearing with the pitch of her cries, her eyes wide in agony. Nothing could stop her forward motion as her arms went deeper and she managed a high, terrified, "NO!" which cut off instantly as her face slammed into the fungal mass. She twisted her head to the side and Zack caught for an instant her mouth stretched in horror, her eyes desperate and beseeching, as her skin bubbled and smoke obscured her.

The smoke reached him and it had a terrible smell, both earthy and like burning meat. Belcher's entire upper body sank into the fungal mass, bending forward at the hip, until just her butt and legs showed, feet still flat on the floor. Where the front of her legs touched the stuff, the jeans seemed to fuse and sink slowly. Only where the fungus touched bare skin did the sizzling and melting occur. But Zack thought maybe the material protection wouldn't last long.

He turned and ran for the bathroom where he vomited noisily. Again. It seemed not so long ago that he'd done the same thing, but then he could never have imagined things progressing to this.

He came back to close the bedroom door, saw the social worker sinking slowly into the mass covering his mother's body. He saw something in her back pocket and gasped, a series of realisations flooding over him. He darted forward, holding his breath, and plucked the keyring from her pocket. A bunch with a variety of different keys on it, but one clearly for her car. The VW logo glittered silver.

He closed the bedroom door and stood in the hallway, taking deep breaths to compose himself. His mind raced, making plans. After a moment he nodded to himself, went to the front door. Peeking out he saw Jack Parsons's car had gone. How the ancient old fart was still driving was a mystery, but it served his purposes now.

Zack unlocked Belcher's car and got in, started it up. He saw her bag on the passenger seat, a phone in the front pocket. The edge of a wallet poked up too. Ignore it all, he told himself. He saw a pack of wet wipes in the centre console and smiled. Good, he could use those.

He pulled the hood of his sweater up and low over his eyes, started the car and drove away from his house. He wasn't a great driver, but he knew the basics. All he lacked was experience, really. He'd driven enough to safely stick to the limits, obey the traffic signs, and thirty minutes later he pulled up on a quiet back street on the outskirts of Monkton. He grabbed the wipes and judiciously cleaned everything he'd touched – wheel, gear shift, handbrake, door handle. He wiped the keys and left them in the ignition, then got out and surreptitiously wiped the handle on the outside too. He pocketed the wipes, kept his head down and his hood up, and walked quickly away.

He was pretty certain there were no cameras anywhere around this part of Monkton, but he took no chances and stayed hidden inside his hood until he was all the way inside Monkton Plaza, a few kilometres from the abandoned car. He checked the time on his phone. Nearly 1 p.m. He was reluctant to go home. Who knew what might be happening in his mother's bedroom.

He texted Maddy.

if docs call say yeah the woman saw mum then left again all good. explain later

Maddy messaged right back.

What?

docs came, saw mum, all good. you weren't home i was. explain later

His phone started to ring immediately, *Maddy calling...*

The last thing he wanted to do was talk about it over the phone. He rejected the call then messaged.

TALK LATER! when you home?

I don't know. Should I come now?

nah come later

About 6 then?

okay

He switched his phone off and went to watch a movie. It was rubbish, but took his mind off stuff. About four he started walking the main road out of Monkton, thumbing for a lift. He walked a good twenty minutes, then a truck picked him up and dropped him at the Gulpepper turnoff. He thought he'd end up walking all the way back from there, but about halfway along a car slowed. It was a local he'd seen around but had no idea who it was. They were kind enough, didn't talk much, and that suited him. They dropped him by the harbour just after five and he walked home. He slumped onto the couch, turned on the TV and waited for Maddy. He didn't dare even look at his mother's bedroom door, let alone open it.

Maddy stared at a pair of pristine blue and white Nike sneakers sticking out of the massive, bulbous whiteness. The soles were barely even scuffed. Every other part of the woman was consumed. Vomit threatened to burst forth at any moment. "What the *fuck*, Zack?"

"Mum told me to."

"What do you mean? Mum's dead!"

"But she talks to me, I think maybe she's in there, like, transforming or something?"

"Into what, Zack, Optimus fucking Prime? She's dead, this is fucked up. You killed that woman!"

"No, I didn't. Mum told me to give the woman to her, so I did. It's okay, it's all good now."

Maddy took a deep breath, swallowed down bile. "All good? Are you insane? What about when she doesn't report back? What about when they send someone else?"

Zack pushed gently against her, moved her out of

the room and shut the door. "Come on, I'll explain all that happened."

By the time he'd finished his story, as they sat across from each other at the kitchen table, Maddy's hands had mostly stopped shaking. "Did anyone see you leave the car in Monkton?"

"Nope. And if they did, they wouldn't have seen my face. And that hoodie I had on was an old one, I've already thrown it away."

Maddy nodded, thinking, chewing her lower lip. "So no one saw anything? If they call or send someone else around, we can tell them the woman never even came here?"

"Yeah, we could, actually. And when they find her car in Monkton, they'll assume that's as far as she went and the search will be focused all the way over there."

"So we just need some plan for when the next one comes around."

"By then, the fungus will hopefully be done," Zack said.

"What do you mean, done?"

"I don't know, finished its lifecycle kinda thing? And Mum's body will be gone and we can use the story about visiting her cousins. It's only another year, less than a year, until you're a legal adult. Not much longer for me. Then we're free. We claim the house, say Mum fucked off to Bega and we've lost touch, whatever. They can search all they like, but they'll never prove anything, right?"

"Why did you push her in, Zack? Why didn't you use the cousins story today?"

Zack looked down at the table, at his hands, picking at his nails. "Partly I panicked. But also, Mum said to give the woman to her."

"It's not really Mum, you know that, right? I can't be."

Zack nodded, picking at his thumbnail until a bead of blood sprang up.

Maddy reached over, put her hand over his. "Zack? It's okay. We'll be okay. But we have to be smarter."

The next morning, Maddy got up early because sleep had been elusive since dawn. She made coffee, tried to eat breakfast, but had no appetite. At seven she opened Zack's door and called in.

"Monday morning, school."

He made muffled noises of annoyance and consent and turned over. Maddy stared at the lump of doona for a while, then left. She'd give him another ten minutes. Poor kid, all this was pretty tough. Kid! Why did she have to be the responsible one all the time? She remembered being five when Zack was four and her mother going out and saying, "Watch your brother. Any trouble when I get back and you'll get the hiding of your life!"

"Fuck you," she spat at her mother's bedroom door as she went past.

A hissing came from the other side.

Maddy jumped and stopped, turned to look back at the closed door. Another hiss, like a snake under a rock disturbed by movement. She reached out, put a hand to the door handle, then shook her head and walked away.

She was surprised when Zack scuffed into the kitchen a few minutes later, eyes bleary. "It's smaller."

"What?"

"Come and look."

Reluctantly she got up and followed her brother back to their mother's room. The fungus was as smooth and white and rounded as ever, and there was no trace whatsoever of the social worker. But Zack was right. While the pale thing covering the bed was about the same shape, it was smaller. Shrunk back away from the light fitting, the bulbous edges a little off the floor.

"Maybe it'll shrink away to nothing soon, yeah?"

"Maybe." What was the hissing she'd heard? Was the thing deflating somehow?

The curtains shifted in the soft breeze, a little cooler today as autumn approached. Maddy watched the soft undulations for a moment, mesmerised by it, then shook herself and closed the door.

"I have to go to work. Don't be late for school, Zack."

"Yeah, yeah."

When Maddy stepped out the front door, grumpy Jack Parsons was shuffling along his driveway towards the letter box, a grubby dressing gown hanging on his skeletal frame, tatty ugg boots on his feet.

He glanced up and Maddy forced a smile, and a nod.

"Social worker, was it?" Parsons said.

Maddy's heart pulsed once extra hard. "What's that?"

"Yesterday. Nice looking lady came by, hadn't seen her before. Didn't see her leave though."

"You didn't see her leave?"

"Went to see my sister across town. I still drive, you know."

Maddy nodded. "Right. You went out."

"That's what I said, are you deaf? I'm the old one. She come to see about your mother, did she?" The old man gave a crooked half-smile as he asked, something glinted in his eye.

You fucker! Maddy thought. *You called DoCS on us.* "Just routine, I guess," she said. "I wasn't in, but she had a chat to Mum then left again."

"Don't see your mum much these days. Used to chat over the fence quite often, good to have a yarn, eh?"

"She's sick. Doesn't like to go outside any more, not even the garden."

Parsons nodded, mouth hanging slightly open. Maddy heard his rasping breath as he stared at her. She quickly patted her pockets, then said, "Damn it, forgot my phone."

"You young people and those things!" Parsons said.

She flashed him a forced smile and ran back inside. She hadn't forgotten her phone at all, but it was the first excuse that came to mind. "Zack, for fuck's sake!"

He looked up from his bowl of cereal, milk dripping off the spoon. "What?"

"Jack Parsons saw the social worker arrive!"

Zack's eyebrows climbed into his hair. "Oh yeah! Nosey bastard was getting in his car."

"You have to be more careful. If he saw her arrive, maybe others did. Are you sure no one saw you get into her car and drive it away?"

"Pretty sure, yeah."

"Pretty sure?"

"I'm sure!" Zack's eyebrows slammed back down, drawing together. "What are you, the fucking police?"

Maddy took a deep breath, decided to calm things down. "No, but they might come around. More importantly, we can't say she never came here. We'll have to say she came in, had a chat with Mum, then left again. That's what I just told Parsons."

"Okay. That's what I was going to say in the first place. Easy as."

She stared at him. Easy as. Was he really so blasé about the whole thing? Maybe it was a defence mechanism. The phone on the kitchen counter rang. Their mother's phone. Maddy always left it plugged in there. She went over and looked at it, but didn't recognise the number.

"Might be DoCS," Zack said.

She glared at him.

He shrugged. "Might be. Answer it. You be Mum. Put them off."

"Fuck!" She snatched up the phone and answered. "Hello?" She made her voice a little weak, a little croaky. This was far from the first time she'd impersonated her mother. But it was the first time she'd impersonated her *dead* mother.

"I'm after Mrs Claire Taylor." The woman on the

other end was kind-sounding, her voice soft with a slight accent Maddy couldn't place.

"Speaking."

"Ah, good morning, Mrs Taylor. I'm Hilary Wong from the Department of Communities and Justice."

That's right, Maddy thought. *That's what they're calling the welfare these days.* "We just saw you lot yesterday," she said, in her mother's snappy tone.

"That's what I was ringing about, actually. You say you saw someone yesterday?"

Zack held up his phone, where he'd typed *stefanee belcher* into a text message.

"That's right," Maddy said. "Woman called Stephanie something-or-other. Beacher? Beacham?"

"Stephanie Belcher."

"If you say so."

"Yes, right. So she came to see you?"

"Yes. Unusual to come on a weekend, I thought."

"Well, our staff tend to try to find times best suited to families," Wong said. "So she came about what time?"

What time? Maddy mouthed at Zack.

"Lunchtime," he whispered. "About twelve?"

"Sometime in the middle of the day," Maddy croaked, then turned her head only slightly from the phone and coughed raucously. She imagined poor Hilary Wong wincing at the other end, but it was the kind of awful thing her mother did all the time. Zack grinned.

"And you all had a chat and then she left again?" Wong asked.

"Yes. I didn't invite her to stay the night or anything. Honestly, why even send her when you can just email or call or something? It's an invasion of privacy, you know!"

"What time did Ms Belcher leave, Mrs Taylor?"

"She was here half an hour or something before I was finally able to shoo her out."

"Did she mention where she was going next?"

"No. Why would I care?"

There was a moment's pause and then Wong said, "Okay, thank you, Mrs Taylor. Sorry to bother your morning."

"Right-o." Maddy hung up the call, then blew out a breath, leaning back against the counter.

"You do such a good Mum!" Zack said.

"Fuck, Zack, that was awful. I have to go to work. You know, it's entirely possible they'll report the woman missing now and then we'll have the police around here too."

"We'll just tell them the same thing, right?"

"Yeah, I guess so. And if anyone else does come asking about anything, Mum has gone to see her cousins in Bega and we don't know when she's coming back. Okay?"

"Okay."

"I have to go to work."

The whole time Maddy was home, Zack had tried to ignore his mother's wheedling voice. It drilled into his brain, but he managed to tune it out most of the time. When Maddy left again, finally going to work at last, he finished his breakfast, then went and got dressed. He put on his school uniform but had no intention of going to class yet. First he forged a note, signed by his mother, explaining he'd had a dental appointment. He'd use that at the office to get a late note when he finally went in. He tucked it into the side pocket of his backpack, then went around next door and rang Jack Parson's bell.

His mother still cajoled in his ears, even from this far away, telling him what to do. It took a few minutes, but he finally saw movement behind the frosted glass panes in Parsons's door. The door opened, then *thunked* against the chain. The old man scowled out at him.

"What?"

"Good morning, Mr Parsons." Zack gave his warmest smile.

"Er... morning. What do you want?"

"Do you think you could come around? My mum wanted to have a chat with you. She said she knows you used to enjoy a chat over the fence, but she's too scared to go out any more. Do you know what agoraphobia is?"

"Of course I do, I'm not an imbecile." Parsons paused, brows creasing. "Is that it? Why I haven't seen her for a while?"

"Yeah, she barely even leaves her room these days. But she was asking after you. I don't know, I think she wants to give you something."

"Give me something?"

"That's what she said."

Parsons stared a moment longer, then nodded once. "Wait a minute."

He shuffled away and through the gap Zack saw him sit on chair by the door and grunt and wheeze as he pulled his shoes on. Then the door closed, the chain snicked free, and it opened again. Parsons gestured for Zack to lead the way.

They went into the house and Parsons looked around, eyes narrowed. He seemed to be assessing the place, maybe judging their cleanliness. Clearly he thought little enough of them that he'd called the welfare.

Bring him!

"Mum's in her room," Zack said, pointing. "This way." He went along the hall and opened the door. "Hey, Mum. Mr Parsons from next door is here." He stepped back and smiled at the old man.

Parsons nodded and turned into the room. "Good

morn– What the hell is that?"

Zack stepped in behind and put one hand on the old man's shoulder, the other on his opposite hip, and walked him hard into the bulging fungus. Parsons cried out as he staggered forward, then screamed as his hands and face planted into the soft white mass and began to immediately hiss and bubble. That acrid smoke rose up again and Parsons vibrated, his scuffed shoes rattling against the floor. His scream became a gargled, strangled sound, then a muffled coughing, then Zack had slammed the door and staggered back to lean against the opposite wall. He stood there, breathing hard, swallowing down bile, waiting for his hammering heart to calm.

Then he pushed himself up, grabbed his school bag, and went out, locking the front door behind himself.

"You did fucking *WHAT*?" Maddy screamed. Her heart seemed to almost block her throat and her hands shook in rage.

"He would have called again! He would have called welfare again, that's what Mum said!"

"And what about when people report *him* missing?" Maddy asked, trying to swallow her anger enough to talk. "What about when the police start asking the neighbours what happened?"

"We tell them we have no idea, haven't seen him for a few days."

"Jesus, Zack."

"I would have told you last night, but you didn't come home."

"I went to Dylan's. I texted you."

"I know, but I wanted to tell you in person."

Maddy nodded, swallowed. "You were already in bed when I got back."

"Come and see."

Zack pulled at Maddy's arm where she sat at the kitchen table. To think she'd been feeling a little better about things. She finished work, Dylan was waiting outside and she'd given in. Went to his place, smoked some weed, had a shag, it was all pretty good. She'd got home and Zack was sleeping, and it felt like they were moving forward. Then he gets up and tells her he fed the old neighbour to the mother-fungus whatever the fuck it was thing in there? "Come and see what?" she asked.

"Just come."

She trailed him down the hall and looked in when he opened their mother's bedroom door. The great swollen thing, pale in the bed, had shrunk again.

"It's going down, see?"

Maddy nodded. "Thank fuck for that. Zack, this has to stop. We need to leave it, let it disappear, whatever. Can you do that?"

"No, you don't understand."

"What don't I understand?"

"She needs more. Just one or two, she says."

"What?" Maddy stared at him, her stomach water.

"Just one or two more and that'll be it, she'll have finished her cycle."

"Zack. Fuck, no. You've killed two people! You can't kill any more!"

Zack licked his lips, looked at the white fungus, then back at Maddy. "We have to. I promised. This is how it works. Then she'll be gone. It will be gone, all of it. And the house will be ours."

Maddy ran shaking hands through her hair. "You'll get caught. *We'll* get caught!"

"I promised Mum."

"It's not Mum!" Maddy yelled. "Whatever the fuck is going on, whatever you think you're hearing, it's not

Mum! How can it be? You saw her die. You saw her body."

Zack stared at her, tears in his eyes. He looked lost, haunted.

"We got away with the Belcher woman, for now, at least. Parsons next door was just some shrivelled old cunt. His sister might miss him or something, but whatever. He was close to dead anyway, I expect. But who's next, Zack? Hmm? Who are you planning to give to it?"

"I don't know. That's what we need to talk about."

"There's no we in this, bro! It's you. It's all you."

Zack shook his head and his eyes hardened. "You're in on it too. If something happens to me, you think anyone will believe you knew nothing about it? You may not have pushed them, but you're part of this too."

"Oh, Zack, what the hell is going on?"

"One or two more, that's all. That what she said. Then it's done. We have to figure out who."

Maddy's head spun, dizziness edging her vision. She pulled the bedroom door closed and pushed Zack back towards the kitchen. "Go to school. I have to go to work. We need to think about this."

Zack picked up his school bag and headed for the front door. "What about Dylan?"

"Jesus, Zack! Go to school! We'll talk when I get back from work. I'll be home by six."

After he left, Maddy went and sat at the kitchen table and drank coffee. She had to end this. By the time the mug was empty, she'd decided to kill the thing. She went out into the back garden and the small tin shed in the corner, and then came back with a square-bladed shovel.

She pushed open the bedroom door and stepped into the room, raised the shovel high overhead, planning to chop it to mincemeat. The fungus began vibrating violently, shaking the whole bed, making it skitter slightly against the floor.

"Fuck!" Maddy brought the shovel down hard into the nearest swollen curve of the thing.

It split open and hissed, and it screamed. Dark brown ichor leaked thickly from the slash she'd put in its tough skin, and the thing wailed in her mind. It seemed to bypass her ears completely, and drill deep into her brain. Maddy dropped the shovel and clapped both palms to either side of her head, crying out in pain. She felt as though her eyes were about to burst. The thing shook and screamed and Maddy's knees weakened. She staggered back from the room and then half ran, half fell down the hallway. The noise from the bedroom slowly eased until the house had sunk back into a tense, eerie silence.

Don't do that again, her mother's voice said, directly into her mind. *Feed me and it'll be done.*

"You're not her!" Maddy shouted back down the hall.

Just feed me!

There was no way Maddy ever wanted to feel pain like that again. Her head throbbed, her muscles were weak, her eyes had sharp spikes of sensation through them, repeating every few seconds.

"Okay," she said at last. "You'll really go? Really leave us be?"

If you feed me.

"One more."

Maybe two.

Maddy began to cry, despite herself. She hated being reduced to tears for any reason but couldn't stop it. "Okay," she said again. She grabbed her bag and left for work.

When Maddy got home, her nerves were frayed. She'd spent all day with her head buzzing about who they could give to the white thing in the bed. How could they make a choice like that? It was straight up murder. She'd considered a few options, like the homeless guy who always hung around near the beach. Or that weird guy without a nose she saw around town all the time. There was the old woman at the harbour everyone called the sea witch, but Maddy kind of liked her. Maybe someone from work, plenty of choices there. Wendy Callow, perhaps, no one liked her anyway. She even thought about Dylan or one of his stoner mates. But every time she considered anyone, the thought would progress to how she would entice the person around, and how she would give them to the fungus, and at that point her bile rose and panic gripped her chest. She derailed the thought again and again, tried to work, until the same process rose in her mind and repeated. Over and over, all day.

The house was still and quiet when she got in. Suspiciously so. Where was Zack? She badly needed a shower and decided if he wasn't back by the time she got out, she'd call him. Ten minutes later she was towelling herself off when the front door clicked and she heard voices.

"Thanks so much for coming over, Mr Brady."

That was Zack's voice. Mr Brady? Josh's dad? Why the hell had Zack brought him over?

"It's no problem," Brady said. "I can't believe you forgot Josh was going to his grandparents for a couple of nights though."

"Oh, I remembered, only I thought it was tomorrow, not today. And I promised Mum I'd help shift this furniture and figured Josh could help. But I really appreciate you stepping in."

"I'm glad you feel you can ask us for help, Zack. This way, is it?"

Maddy had stood frozen in panic for a moment,

then she lunged for the door. She had to stop him. Then she realised she was naked, holding a towel. She dragged on her work pants and shirt again and pulled open the bathroom door just as Mr Brady said, "What the hell is that?"

Then a metallic clang rang out. Maddy ran down the hall to see Zack in the doorway to their mother's room, the shovel she'd dropped earlier in his hands. Mr Brady was face down on the floor, blood pooling from his ear and a gash on the back of his head.

"What the fuck, Zack!"

"Help me get him up. Onto Mum."

"It's not our mum!"

Zack flashed her an angry look. "Whatever it is, help me get him onto it."

"That's your best friend's dad! There's too much connection. Does his mum know he came around here?"

Mr Brady rolled a little on the floor, groaning.

"I'll explain everything. Maddy, they come back!"

"What?"

"Just help me!"

"Fuck!"

Zack moved around and got his hands under Mr Brady's armpits and Maddy had no choice but to grab his legs. They hoisted him up, swung him once, then hefted him onto the fungus. It was much smaller again, Maddy noticed.

Brady immediately thrashed and screamed, but was already stuck, his face and hands bubbling and smoking. The bulbous fungus vibrated, almost like it was shivering with pleasure.

"Jesus!" Maddy said, voice choked like wire in her throat.

"Come on." Zack pulled her from the room and closed the door as Brady's screams became gargles.

They went into the lounge and Maddy collapsed onto the sofa, trembling. They'd blown it. Zack had blown it, there was no coming back from this. Zack sat in the armchair opposite and all she could do was stare at him in shock.

Zack grinned. "So, I remembered Josh was going to his grandparents with his mum. That's all the way up near Cooma. His grandma has to get some minor surgery, so his mum went to help out, took Josh out of school for a visit. They're away until the weekend. I pretended I got the day wrong, but I didn't. I knew Mr Brady would be there alone, and no one saw me go and talk to him. I was really careful. And I told him my mum needed some help. He jumped at the chance."

"Zack..."

He held up a hand to stop her. "No one saw, no one knows he came here. But it doesn't matter anyway. Come and see this."

He jumped up again and headed for the back door from the kitchen. Reluctantly she followed, thinking perhaps her numbness was a kind of shock. Zack led her into the garden and over to the fence. An old milk crate sat there, one his mother used to stand on to see over the fence for a chat. Maddy and Zack crowded onto it and Zack pointed at Jack Parsons's house next door. "Look."

She looked into Parsons's side window. He sat in there, in his lounge room, staring at something. The TV maybe? She couldn't tell from her vantage. "What the hell?"

She climbed down and looked at Zack.

"I don't know exactly," Zack said. "But I saw him earlier, coming back home. Just walking up the street like normal. And that's when I came up with the plan to get Brady over. If they come back, it doesn't matter who, right?"

Maddy shook her head, mind spinning. She couldn't catch hold of a single thought.

"Did you see the thing in there was smaller again?" Zack asked. "Mum said one more, maybe two. Brady is one more. And look here."

He led her over to their mother's bedroom window, still open as it had been all along. There were footprints in the scrubby, patchy flower bed right below the window, and pale white marks on the sill. Maddy leaned forward to look but didn't dare touch.

"They'll remember," she said weakly. "I mean, being pushed in. They'll remember what we did to them."

"I talked to Parsons this afternoon when I saw him. He doesn't remember a thing."

"Was he... I mean, was he normal?"

Zack laughed. "I don't know. What's normal for Parsons?"

The breeze shifted the curtains slightly and Maddy caught a glimpse of Brady, still, sunk half into the fungus. She gasped and looked away. "I can't process this, Zack. I can't... I just can't."

Zack hugged her. "It's okay. I've got this. Brady might be the last. If not, Mum said just one more. We have to decide who."

"Zack..."

"We'll worry about it tomorrow, yeah? For now, it's all done."

Maddy nodded and walked away. She didn't want to think about any of it. A weight of fatigue dragged at her and she wanted only to shut everything out. She went into her room, closed the door, and collapsed onto the bed. She let sleep take her.

The next morning Maddy felt a little better, the shock reduced to a dull sensation of surreality. If they were going to suffer for this, so be it. What was done, was done. But maybe damage control was an option. How the hell was Parsons back? That was the thought that kept circling her mind like a vulture looking for prey.

Zack was still asleep. She opened her mother's door and looked in. The fungus on the bed was reduced again. Down to a small set of undulating white lumps, not much bigger than her mother's body had been before all this madness started. And in a vaguely humanoid shape on the mattress. Would they really be shot of it soon?

One more!

The voice was sudden and harsh, and triggered the spikes behind Maddy's eyes. She shut the door and hurried out. She rang Parsons's doorbell and gripped her hands into fists to hide their shaking. It took a few minutes, but the old man eventually shuffled into view and opened the door.

"Madeleine?"

"Hello."

"What can I do you for?"

He was never this friendly. She'd expected grumpiness from the outset. "I, er... Well, I just wanted to see if you were okay, that's all. My mum said I ought to check on you, living alone as you do."

"Very kind, but no need. I'm fine."

"Okay, that's good to hear."

Parsons's skin looked unnaturally pale, almost alabaster. His eyes were pale grey. She remembered his eyes as being rheumy and bloodshot, but not any more. They were pale, but clear. "So you're feeling okay?"

"Perfectly." He rubbed a hand along the other forearm and his thumbnail snagged a curl of something white off his skin. Without looking he pressed it back down. "What's your mother worried about exactly?"

"Oh, I don't know. You know how mothers are." What did that even mean? She was rambling.

Parsons shook his head. "Not really, no." He frowned a moment, like he was trying to remember something. "We used to talk over the fence, your mother and I. She would stand on something to see over. So would I."

"That's right."

"I haven't seen her in a *long* while." He raised his eyebrows, almost as if he were challenging her to deny the assertion.

"She doesn't really go out any more."

"Maybe I should come and visit sometime? I've never been inside your house, have I." It wasn't a question.

"You haven't?"

"No. *Never.*"

Maddy nodded. "Okay then. Well, as long as you're okay."

"Perfect. You don't need to check on me any more."

"Okay, sure. Have a good day."

"You too." He shut the door and Maddy stood staring at it for a moment, then turned away and went back home.

Zack was up when she went in. "One more then?" he said. "You okay to help me get it organised?"

"Yep. But I have to work." Maddy paused, remembering some of the thoughts she'd had the previous day. "You leave this one to me, yeah?"

"Sure. You got a plan?"

"I have. Make sure you're home by six for when I get back."

"Okay."

She went to work, steeling herself all the way. It took about twenty minutes at a fast clip to get from her house on the hill down to Woollies. In the staff room she saw Wendy Callow sipping a coffee. Mean Wendy Callow, always a bitch to everyone. And so sweet on Dylan's mate, James.

"Morning, Wendy."

"Maddy?"

"Yeah. You okay."

Wendy frowned. "Why do you care?"

Maddy swallowed the retort that came first to mind and said. "Dylan and some mates are coming over to mine tonight, have a few drinks. Mum's away. James asked me if I'd invite you."

Wendy instantly brightened. "James asked you that?"

"Yeah. Don't know why he didn't just invite you himself. I told him to. Chicken, I suppose. You want to come?"

"Sure, why not?" Wendy tried to play it cool, but her expression was an open book. The girl was gleeful.

Maddy nodded. "Cool. You can walk back with me after work. You're finished at six too, yeah?"

"Yep."

"Right."

Conversation was awkward for the long walk home, but Maddy did her best to dissociate from it. *Just doing a job*, she kept telling herself. *Securing our future. This is for me and Zack.*

When they got to the house, Zack was watching YouTube on his phone. He looked up and nodded once, acting completely uninterested.

"Where is everyone then?" Wendy asked.

"They'll be here soon. You want a drink?"

"Sure. You got gin?"

"Yeah. Have a seat."

Wendy sat in the armchair, their mother's armchair they never used any more, and that seemed strangely appropriate. As Maddy headed for the kitchen she caught Zack's eye and he nodded, got up to follow.

"Let's do it quick," Maddy whispered as soon as they were out of the lounge. "Before I lose my nerve."

"Okay. Who is that?"

"Doesn't matter. How do we do it?"

"Get the drinks."

Maddy stared at him for a moment, then turned to the counter. She made three strong gin and tonics, then went back towards the lounge.

"I'll be there in a sec," Zack said.

Maddy handed over the drink, then lifted hers. "Cheers."

Wendy grinned crookedly. "Cheers." She took a big gulp. "Damn, that's strong!"

"Only way to drink 'em, right?"

"I suppose so."

Maddy took another sip, and Wendy matched her, then put the glass down on the small table beside the chair. As Maddy stepped backwards to sit on the sofa, Zack walked back in. He strode directly to Wendy and punched her clean across the point of the jaw.

Maddy yelped in shock as Wendy slumped loosely in the chair. She groaned weakly.

"Let's go," Zack said, grabbing one arm and one leg.

Maddy hurried over, grabbing the other arm and leg, saying, "Fuck, fuck, fuck," over and over again.

Zack had opened their mother's bedroom door and they carried Wendy right in, one either side of the bed, straining under the girl's weight as they had to reach out, dragging her over the remaining fungus. They manoeuvred her into position and then dropped her directly onto it. Wendy cried out in pain and writhed as the skin of her neck, arms and legs below her shorts hissed and smoked.

Zack put one knee on the bed and planted his hands against her shoulders. "Hold her down!" he shouted.

"Fuck!" Maddy said again, and grabbed Wendy's legs, palms over her shins, and pressed them back into the whiteness. The smoke that rose was sharp and acrid, vaguely like a barbecue burning, but thick with something else as well, a cloying, earthy sweetness.

Wendy's eyes opened and rolled, the whites showing all around. "What are you doing?" she cried. "Please, stop! It hurts!"

"Hold her down!" Zack yelled, leaning his weight harder.

Maddy gritted her teeth, clambered onto the bed and pressed as hard as she could, being careful her fingers got nowhere near the fungus. Wendy thrashed and screamed, the bed shook with her efforts. She bucked up, trying to arch her back, but her clothes and skin had already become stuck to the remaining fungus and it stretched as she rose, then she collapsed back down. She howled and sobbed, tipped her head up to look beseechingly at Maddy, and Maddy knew she would never forget the sight of that gaze as long as she lived. The back of Wendy's head stretched like taffy, her hair and skin smoking, bubbling into blisters around the backs of her ears. She sobbed and wailed but her thrashing weakened. Her head fell back, her neck smoking. She gurgled, twitching but no longer fighting.

Zack climbed off the bed and staggered away, face twisted in horror. Maddy stumbled away too. They stood either side of the bed watching as Wendy slowly stilled. Maddy gasped as Wendy's eyes popped open once more, staring crazily, her mouth worked silently, then she fell still.

There was no sound except Zack and Maddy's ragged breathing and a soft hissing from the bed. Without a word, the siblings turned and left, Zack shutting the door. They went into the lounge and swallowed down their drinks, then to the kitchen, made more drinks, and silently swallowed them down too. Then another, and another.

They began to chat quietly about nothing in particular, the booze loosening their shock. By a little after nine they were both thoroughly drunk. Zack passed out on the sofa in the lounge and Maddy crawled to bed.

Sometime in the early hours, head pounding, mouth dry, she woke to sounds of scratching and scraping. Then a clunk. All from her mother's room. She ignored it all.

In the morning, she and Zack stood looking at her mother's bed. It was empty, no trace of anything having been there except the rumpled bedclothes. Even the stains of their mother's illness were gone. They called in sick to work and school, then got busy.

They stripped the bed and rolled up the sheets and doona into garbage bags. Zack got a sledgehammer from the small tin shed and smashed the wooden bedframe to pieces. They dragged the pieces out into the back garden, doused the pile with petrol from the can kept for the mower, and lit it. When the wood was burning well, they dragged the mattress on top and watched that go up. They threw the bedclothes on too. Black, oily smoke from the artificial materials clouded up and they stood downwind and watched until they were sure it was all ignited and burning well.

Back inside, they washed and cleaned the floor, walls, ceiling, like they had the rest of the house before, only with twice the vigour. The stain under the bed took some extra elbow grease, but they scoured it eventually. They packed up half of their mum's clothes and possessions, which was a sadly small collection, into two suitcases and put them in the boot of the car. Maddy knew there were big bins out the back of the industrial area on the south side of town. Mechanics and some kind of metal workshop, a few other businesses, all occupied large metal warehouses up there. The bins were never locked.

They backed the car up, making sure no one was paying much attention, and dumped the suitcases in, dragging cardboard and industrial waste over the top of it all. When they got back home, the bed was nothing more than a scorched mark on the grass with ash and blackened, twisted metal springs atop it. They decided to leave that as it was. Worry about it later. Maddy ordered a new double bed online, to be delivered. Their mother's room would soon look like she'd gone away for a while, expecting to come back. It could stay like that indefinitely.

They went back inside and made more drinks.

"The house is ours now," Zack said, lifting his glass in a toast.

"To the future," Maddy said. Her hands still shook.

Dad's been acting really weird ever since we got back," Josh said on Monday after school.

"Weird how?" Zack asked.

"Dunno. Just not his normal self, you know? He doesn't look well, either. He's so pale."

"Maybe he's sick?"

"He goes out a lot at night. Mum's really upset about it."

"I'm sure he'll be fine. You want to come over to mine instead? My mum's gone to see her cousins in Bega."

Maddy was high from some good weed Dylan had. Maybe he wasn't such a bad guy after all. She might stay with him for a while yet. She was enjoying her walk home in the moonlight, the cool air of approaching autumn invigorating. The streets were quiet. After midnight, The Gulp seemed to slip into a coma. A poster on a telegraph pole caught her eye, photocopied black and white with a picture of a straggly-haired young man. *Have you seen Daniel?* in bold letters across the top. She turned up Tanning Street past the post office and made her way up the shallow hill, then down the other side. She paused as she came by the playground on the opposite side of the street behind the beach. A figure stood just past the park, staring out to sea. They were motionless. Uncannily so.

Maddy frowned, recognising Jack Parsons. As she watched, someone else came wandering up and stood beside him. Wendy Callow. They didn't speak, didn't even acknowledge each other. Just stood there. A moment later, Mr Brady joined them. Maddy walked on, slowly, watching from the corner of her eye, glad of the street and the park between them. The three just stood there, staring at the ocean.

When she reached a patch of deep shade under a fig tree, Maddy paused again. There should be one more. Sure enough, after a moment more, a woman walked slowly across the grass past the play equipment and joined the others. Stephanie Belcher, Maddy presumed. The social worker.

When Belcher reached the group, they all turned as one and walked back across the park and onto Tanning Street. Lurking in the shadows, Maddy watched them head towards the harbour. They walked out of sight, never having said a word to each other.

Part of Maddy wanted to follow, see what they did, but she didn't dare. Her role in all this, whatever it was, had ended. She hoped the promise to leave her and Zack alone would be kept.

The Band Plays On

The Band Plays On

Blind Eye Moon were playing and Patrick had no idea if they were any good. The Monkton Tavern was packed for the Friday night gig, and so many locals had said to check them out it seemed like a necessary part of the trip. Backpacking was all about immersion in the local culture, after all. In Thailand they'd gone trekking into the jungles of the north and visited the Karen hill people. In Malaysia they'd developed a taste for hawker street food. In Darwin they'd been mesmerised by the vast splendour of Kakadu and were keen to learn about the local folks who showed them around there. It was all so far removed from Dublin. Leaving for a one-year trip around the world had been the best decision of his twenty-four-year life. Ciara had needed to cajole and badger him about it for months, sure. He was a creature of habit and took some convincing, but she had been right. He'd told her so and would tell her again. That they travelled so well together was also good evidence a life together would be long and fruitful. But he needed to wait until they got home to Ireland to put that to her. A proposal on the trip would fundamentally change the nature of what they were doing.

Torsten and Simone came back from the bar, carrying beers. The brother and sister had turned out to be excellent travelling companions, the four of them sharing the costs and the driving of a small camper van. It was a little cramped inside, but not too bad. To take a break from the confines they planned to book into a motel for a couple of nights in Monkton. Warm showers, comfortable beds, and other home comforts every few days made the whole thing more bearable. They were backpacking, but not slumming it.

Having driven from Darwin, down through Alice Springs to Adelaide and then along the coast to Melbourne on their own, Patrick and Ciara had welcomed the team up with the German siblings, for financial reasons if nothing else. Two weeks road tripping along the coast from Melbourne to Sydney together was proving to be good fun.

"Took so long to get drinks!" Torsten said, sitting down and sliding a beer across. "They're four or five deep at the bar."

"Lucky we got a table," Patrick said.

Ciara returned from the bathroom, took her seat. The four of them raised their glasses and clinked them together.

"I talked to a girl in the bathroom who said Blind Eye Moon are the best band in the world," Ciara said with a laugh.

"So good we've never heard of them before," Patrick said.

"Maybe big only in Australia?" Simone asked. Her accent was strong, her English not as good as Torsten, who spoke almost fluently.

"Maybe," Ciara said. "But we've been here two months already and never heard of them before. We've been catching as many local acts as possible. Honestly, I think they're something of a local phenomenon with a bit of a cult following. Lots of folks here seem really into them. You see all the t-shirts?"

Patrick nodded, gestured with his glass. "Yeah, look at this place. It's big enough, and heaving, but there can only be, what? Five hundred people, tops? If they were as big as all that, they wouldn't still be playing pub gigs in small towns, would they?"

The Monkton Tavern was a long building with a high A-frame roof and slate floor. Patrick had begun to recognise a few features of Australian architecture and knew this was a little different to anything he'd seen before. It was old, built down near Monkton harbour, in the oldest part of the town, so it had to be colonial. Regardless, it was a good space with a long bar and a raised stage at the far end with an impressive looking

PA stack and light array. For a small town, it seemed the Monkton Tavern was a hub for entertainment. They'd got there early, hence the luck with a table, and were already a few beers deep. The booze buzz was settling in, the crowds were reminding him of Dublin's busier nightspots, and Patrick thought they were in for a good night. At least, they would be if the band were half as good as their numerous groupies seemed to think they were.

"Yo, Monkton!"

The crowd roared and surged forward, the space around the tables opening as people thickened towards the stage. Patrick hopped up, stood on his chair for a better look.

"Stage is still dark," he said.

The instruments were in place, two dull red spotlights reflecting weakly off the polished wood of the guitars and drum kit.

The crowd began to chant. "Blind Eye Moon! Blind Eye Moon!"

"Heeeey, Monkton." The man's voice was cajoling now, full of humour.

"No support band?" Patrick asked, looking down. His friends smiled and shrugged.

The chant grew louder. This band had really ardent fans, Patrick thought. The red spots winked out, plunging the stage into total darkness. The crowd began cheering and baying, feet stamped in a one-two, one-two-three rhythm. People began clapping the same rhythm. Voices rose with it. "Blind Eye! Blind Eye Moon! Blind Eye! Blind Eye Moon!"

A massive distorted guitar chord slammed out through the PA and the crowd exploded. Patrick winced against the combined volume as the stage burst into view from the multicoloured array in the ceiling. Three men stood across the front of the stage, each with a guitar, the one on the left the bass player. All three wore black clothes, black sleeveless t-shirts, their arms a mass of colourful tattoos. Their faces were pale with heavily kohled eyes, long hair, two black, the one in the centre blond. Behind them a woman stood behind her drum kit, also in black, also heavily kohled around her eyes. Her lips were painted blood red and her hair was long and straight as vibrantly scarlet as her lipstick. The guitar chord rang on, then the woman raised her sticks, struck them together one-two-three-four, then attacked her skins. The guitars all kicked in together, tight as hell, and the roaring of the crowd was lost in a powerful, thundering riff, galloping along with double kick drums underneath like a machine gun.

"Holy shit!" Patrick said to himself, dropping back into his seat, nodding his head along with the music. "This is instantly brilliant!"

The riff pounded on for a minute or more, then the blond guy in the centre started to sing over his rhythm guitar. His voice was powerful, reminded Patrick of Layne Staley in tone, but with more gusto. The woman at the drums provided backing vocals, their style something like a super-thrashy Led Zeppelin. Big riffs, complex bass runs, relentless drums. The lead guitarist frequently broke into solos that were intricate but never too long. After the first couple of tracks the band showed some diversity of talent by dropping to a low, slow ballad about the difficulty of love in the modern world. Then the pace increased again.

During a lull between tracks, Ciara said, "I think the locals are right. Blind Eye Moon might be one of the best bands in the world!"

"Are there any out of towners in tonight?" the lead singer called out.

The crowd booed and hissed, and the singer laughed. Ciara stood up, and Patrick grabbed her forearm. "Don't, love! Let's just enjoy the band."

Ciara smiled down at him, began to sit, then the singer said, "I see you up the back there, with the brown hair and red t-shirt! Where are you from?"

"Ireland!" Ciara called out. She pointed to the siblings. "And Germany."

"I can't hear you, what was that?"

Voices rang through the crowd, people passing the message on.

"Ireland and Germany?" the singer said. "Wow, that's a long way from Monkton! Get down here, this next song is for you."

The crowd parted, most people smiling, warm gestures to come on, get forward. Patrick shook his head, embarrassed to look in any eyes, but he enjoyed how excited Ciara was as she bounced up and trotted away.

"Coming?" he asked Torsten and Simone.

"Sure, let's go."

They made their way towards the stage, the crowd patting them on the back and shoulders, laughing and coaxing them along. Right at the front, among a group of sweating, grinning superfans, the lead singer put his guitar around behind his back and crouched to be at eye level with them.

"What are your names, mates?" He held the mic out to Ciara. Patrick noticed his fingernails were painted blood red. In fact, all the band had blood red nails. And the deep black makeup around their eyes wasn't just smudged kohl, but jet black with dozens of thin filaments, like capillaries, spreading out around the orbit of the eye and over the cheekbone. They had to be wearing contacts too, because their irises were all a deep crimson. The overall effect was quite stunning.

"Ciara, Patrick, Torsten and Simone," Ciara said. "We're from Dublin, they're from Frankfurt."

"And don't you both make lovely couples!"

"We're a couple. They're brother and sister."

The crowd laughed and jeered, and the singer grinned. "Sorry, I shouldn't make assumptions. Well, I'm glad you're here tonight. I'm Edgar, on bass is Howard, on lead guitar is Clarke, and our lady of the skins is Shirley." The crowd whooped and cheered again. Edgar stood up, swung his guitar around to the front. "It's good to meet you, Ciara and friends. Enjoying the show so far?"

"Are you kidding?" Ciara said with a laugh. "You guys fucking *rock*!"

Edgar grinned again. He was handsome, beguiling. "Yes," he said. "Yes, we fucking do." He clipped the mic back into its stand. "And this one's for you. It's called Far From Home."

Clarke began a lead guitar melody, haunting in a minor key. The hairs along Patrick's forearms bristled. Shirley tapped a single beat on the closed hi-hat, the effect with the guitar hypnotic. It reminded Patrick of early Metallica, like the opening to a track from *Master of Puppets*. Edgar picked a counter melody, the whole tune rising, swelling. Howard began soft bass runs.

The crowd swayed like ocean seaweed, forcing Patrick and his friends to move with them. The music filled the venue, and Patrick's mind. They were so tight, so technically perfect, yet emotionally charged. The melody ground its way deep under his skin. Then Edgar hit a power chord that thumped into Patrick's chest, made his heart race. Then another, as the melody and the ticking of the hi-hat continued. When Edgar hit the third power chord, Shirley matched her hi-hat with a bass drum, doubled like a heartbeat.

Then Edgar leaned into the mic and roared, " *When you're far from hoooooome!*" and sound exploded like a supernova. The drums were furious, the bass raced, the guitars ground a sonic attack, the best riff Patrick could ever remember hearing. The rest of the words, the song, the rest of the gig, was lost in a maelstrom of powerful music and physical exertion. The four of them stayed at the front, immersed in the crowd, dancing, leaping, sweat-soaked and euphoric.

This is the best gig I have ever been to in my life, Patrick thought to himself as he danced.

And all too soon, it was over. Edgar had announced it was their last song, but Patrick didn't want to believe it. When they finished, thanked the crowd, entreated them to come back again next time, Patrick was devastated. Loss clawed a hole in his chest.

The crowd thinned, but the four of them stayed up near the stage. The house lights went half up and the spell was broken. They were in a pub in a country town, somewhere on the south coast of New South Wales, miles from anywhere.

Edgar grinned at them as he put his guitar into a case, handed it to a roadie. "You have fun?"

Patrick could only nod, but Ciara couldn't stop talking. She told them how much she loved the music, their energy, the lyrics were just so *true*, such universal truths.

"I love your accent," Edgar said, head tilted to one side. "Hey, you want to come back to the Manor?"

"What's the Manor?" Patrick asked.

"It's our place. We have a little party there after gigs. In The Gulp."

"In the what?"

"The Gulp."

Patrick grinned, shrugged.

Edgar laughed. "I forgot, you're not from around here. Next town up the coast, it's called Gulpepper. But everyone calls it The Gulp. We live there."

Patrick checked his watch. "It's nearly midnight. Probably a little late—"

"Pat, are you mad?" Ciara said. "What, you have to get up early? Let's go and party!"

"We've all been drinking. Who can drive?"

"You can drive," Edgar said. "You want to know how many cops there are around here at this time?" He held up his thumb and forefinger to make a zero, and grinned.

"Is it far?"

"It's about a thirty-minute drive. Everywhere is far

around here, but thirty minutes is nothing by our reckoning."

Ciara punched his arm. "Let's go, Pat!"

Patrick looked at Torsten and Simone and they both nodded, smiling. It did sound kinda fun, and there wasn't much more of a local cultural experience than a house party. He noticed the rest of the band chatting to a few of the other fans, people nodding, bumping fists, heading off.

"There'll be a bunch of people there," Edgar said. "But we don't invite everybody. Our van is parked in the alley outside. Why don't you go and get your car, then pull up behind us. You can follow us back."

"We'll know which is your van?"

Edgar laughed. "It's the only one with Blind Eye Moon painted on the sides."

Twenty minutes later they followed a large black van out of Monkton. It had a beautifully air-brushed band logo of a red eye superimposed over a full moon on the side, set against stormy clouds in a night sky. They took the main road to the north, but instead of joining the main freeway, signposted to Enden and other places, including Sydney a ridiculous number of kilometres further on, Edgar pointed the van down a narrow turnoff from a roundabout that looked like it wouldn't go anywhere much at all. The sign only had two names on it: Gulpepper and Enden.

A little buzzed from the beers, a lot buzzed from the gig, Patrick drove with a grin on his face. He felt like a naughty kid, staying out late, sticking it to the man, hanging with a real life rock'n'roll band. It was mystifying that Blind Eye Moon played such parochial venues.

The small road led past an industrial area on the edge of Monkton, large metal sheds and cement loading bays, then became a straight line, one lane each way through thick vegetation that came right up to the road on either side. Sometimes the tops of the trees met above the bitumen.

"This is old forest," Torsten said from behind. He and Simone sat at the campervan's small table in the back, while Patrick drove, Ciara beside him in the passenger seat.

Patrick glanced into the rear view mirror, saw Torsten looking out the side window, nose pressed to the glass. "Old?"

"Yeah, I've studied a bit."

"He's a tree nerd," Simone said with a laugh.

"Hey, I like nature. Australia has what they call old growth forest, but not much left. Mostly in Tasmania, I think? Not sure. Anyway, this region is supposed to be dry sclerophyll forest, but here it looks way older than most of the coast around."

"Dry what now?" Ciara asked.

"Sclerophyll. Wait a minute, I can't remember the details."

Patrick glanced up again, saw Torsten tapping at his phone. "Here it is. Dry sclerophyll forests are characterised by their scenic landscapes and diverse flora and represent south-east Australia's last remaining areas of wilderness. Typically eucalypts, wattles and banksias... associated with low soil fertility... blah blah blah. Low fertility also makes soils undesirable for agriculture and native vegetation has, therefore, remained relatively intact." He looked out of the window again and shook his head. "But this seems much older than dry sclerophyll should look." He scrolled his phone again and read aloud. "Plants grow slowly in nutrient-deficient conditions and some species have developed symbiotic relationships with nutrient-fixing bacteria and fungi to enhance nutrient availability."

"Booooring!" Simone said.

"Bushfires play a vital role in regeneration of dry sclerophyll forests. Many species are able to resprout from buds protected beneath soils or within the trunk or branches. Other species have seeds that are protected by a hard seed-coat or woody fruit, which are stimulated to open or germinate by fire." Torsten stopped, eyes scanning. "Let me just look... oh."

"What is it?" Ciara asked.

Torsten looked up with a shrug and a smile. "No more signal, must be a dead spot for reception."

"Thanks fuck for this, yes?" Simone said.

"So whatever," Patrick said, laughing along. "It's old and weird looking. We don't need Google to know that. Look how dense it is! And this place, Gulpepper, must be miles from anywhere. How much further, you think?"

"Everyone calls it The Gulp, remember?" Ciara said.

"Yeah. Sounds delightful."

After twenty minutes along the straight road through strangely old and thick bush, Edgar indicated and they turned right onto Gulpepper Road. Another ten minutes and they started to see farms and other properties, then came over a hill to a large roundabout and a decent sized town spread out before them.

"Jaysus, I didn't expect that," Patrick said.

"There's a harbour and everything," Ciara pointed, then the view was lost as they descended the other side of the hill.

"The sign said 'Gulpepper, population 8,000'," Torsten said. "That's not a tiny hamlet."

"Did you saw the bit underneath?" Simone asked. "Someone writed it on."

"What bit?"

"It said 'But the dead outnumber the living'."

Patrick laughed. "Well, isn't that cheery."

They drove on, past a large Woolworths supermarket on the left, lit up white and green, and then Edgar indicated again and turned right up a steep hill. They followed, engine whining. Houses lined either side, some clearly older, with more modern buildings in between. Patrick imagined the place when it was first settled and everyone had plenty of space, until they began selling the land, subdividing as the town grew. They reached the top of the large hill, the town spread out below them, then went around a tight S-bend and along further. More houses, these a little more spaced out, and then a huge building on a corner block.

The block was thick with old trees, huge with high, wavy buttress roots, and well-established garden beds of shrubs and flowers. A stone wall stood all around it, and in the middle a large two-storey stone block house. Big bay windows, verandas with curlicued metal fencing all around both floors, a steep tiled roof with intricate chimney stacks. Behind the house, on the far side of the big garden, was nothing but bush. The road turned left and went back down the other side of the hill. More houses lined that street. Edgar drove his black van into the driveway of the big house. A stone sign carved with the words "The Manor" marked the entrance to the driveway.

"Far out," Patrick said. "He wasn't joking."

The driveway curved around behind the house, several other cars already there. Some were empty, others had people inside, waiting. Edgar drove the van past them all and into a large three car garage, the door on the left open to receive him. Patrick parked up behind the other cars. When the band emerged, people poured out of their vehicles and crowded around.

"Time to party!" Edgar said, and everyone cheered.

There were ten or twelve others, all chatting with the comfort of familiarity. Patrick and his friends loitered back a little and let everyone else enter first. The band still wore their black clothes and makeup as they led the group into a huge sitting room with a massive bay window. All manner of couches and armchairs were dotted around, a few low tables, a giant television in one corner. Paintings hung on the walls, mostly portraits but a few landscapes, all quite old-looking. An ostentatious chandelier hung glittering from the twenty-foot-high ceiling, and Edgar flicked a switch to turn it on, then used a dimmer switch to set the brightness low. Shirley went to a computer on a desk in the corner and started some music, old school Pantera, Patrick realised. There had to be speakers all around the large room, as "Mouth For War" seemed to blare from every side, every corner.

People sat themselves around, flopping comfortably into chairs and couches, chatting and laughing. Patrick and his friends stood slightly awkwardly just inside the door.

Edgar appeared beside them, swept his long, blond hair back behind his ears with a grin. "Welcome to the Manor! Make yourselves at home."

"Maybe we could pop into town or something?" Patrick said. "Get a case of beers or..."

Edgar laughed. "There's nothing open in The Gulp after nine o'clock. But don't worry, we have plenty of grog." He pointed to a corner where a large fridge was plugged in and beside it a dresser covered with a forest of spirit bottles. "Me cassa, you cassa, mates!"

"Thanks!"

"This house is amazing," Ciara said.

"Isn't it? Built in 1862. Home of Governor Charles Gulpepper, the colonial arsehole who decided to make this little bit of paradise his own. He established a colony here and this was one of the first permanent buildings to go up. Oyster farming mostly, at first. Then other fishing too and the town grew, but it was all a big mistake."

"Mistake?"

"Yeah, place is cursed as fuck."

"This house, you mean?" Patrick asked.

"Nah, The Gulp. Whole fucking town."

Ciara laughed nervously. "Really?"

"Yep. Place is fucked." Edgar grinned, led them over to the drinks. He opened the fridge and handed around stubbies of Little Creatures pale ale. "Good Aussie brewery, this one. Cheers!" He clinked bottle necks with each of them.

"Why stick around if the place is bad?" Patrick asked. "You guys are a successful band, I'd expect you to live in Sydney or Melbourne or something. Or even another country!"

Edgar shook his head. "Nah, this place is fucked, but it's home. Been here ages."

"You don't look over thirty! Were you born here?"

"Don't let looks deceive you, we've been around a while longer than that."

Patrick opened his mouth to ask more, but Edgar slapped his shoulder and turned away, effusively greeting another small group sitting nearby. He fell in amongst them, talking and laughing.

"There?" Simone said, pointing.

A collection of three sofas in one corner was mostly empty, except for two young women and the drummer, Shirley. The four of them wandered over.

"Can we join you?" Ciara asked.

"Of course," Shirley said. She was strikingly beautiful, Patrick thought. Her hair was so thick and straight and red it looked like crimson silk.

The other two women stood up and one said, "We're going for another drink." They smiled at Patrick and his friends and strolled off.

"Amazing gig," Torsten said, sitting down. The others followed suit.

Shirley raised a glass with a generous measure of something like bourbon in it. "Thanks. Glad you enjoyed it."

She still had her contacts in, Patrick noticed, her irises a deep red-brown. But the dark makeup around her eyes seemed to have faded a little, the branches of capillary-like lines not so evident. Rubbed off a bit, maybe. But it wasn't smudged.

"We're infamous around here for always being in character," Shirley said, as if reading his mind.

He realised he'd been staring. "Oh, sorry."

"Don't worry about it. We're either 'that cool band' or, especially among the older folks, 'those fucking weirdos'."

"I think you appear cool," Simone said.

Shirley laughed. "Thanks. I like the way you put that."

Simone blushed slightly.

Patrick was mesmerised by Shirley's languid grace. Her hair gleamed in the low light. She was not only a beautiful woman, but powerfully confident. That came, he supposed, with being hugely successful and popular. The three men in the band were equally good-looking and relaxed in their skins. "I don't mean this as an insult," he said, "but we've never heard of Blind Eye Moon before. I know we're from far away, but you guys are amazing, it's incredible we don't know you."

Shirley smiled, shrugged. "We're big on the local circuit, we tour Australia every year. But we've never really felt the need to go overseas. None of us are great with air travel. And we're more about the live moment than the studio album, you know?"

"You must have a Soundcloud or something though?" Ciara said.

"Nope. We don't like that stuff. Just old-fashioned CDs. We're not about the commercial side of music. We play gigs, sell CDs, merch, make enough money and that's it. We're about experience, not riches."

"Well, good for you," Torsten said. "That's real integrity."

"Just a shame for all the people elsewhere in the world who'll never hear your music," Patrick said.

"They'll have to come to us."

Ciara gestured around herself. "You're obviously doing well for yourselves, living in a place like this. You own it together?"

Shirley looked around the large room, blood red fingernails tapping against the cut glass of her tumbler.

"It's a fine place, hey? But nah, we don't own it. Bram owns it. He lets us live here."

"Bram?" Ciara asked.

"Edgar's... father, I guess? It's complicated, you know how family can be."

There was a moment of silence, then Shirley said, "Edgar tell you about the house?"

"1862?" Patrick said, trying to remember. "Governor Charles Gulpepper."

Shirley nodded. "He tell you what happened to Gulpepper?"

"No."

"Went mad. Had a wife." Shirley pointed to one of the portraits. The woman depicted was beautiful, and young, with long straight brown hair. She had incredibly sad eyes, Patrick thought, despite the gentle smile she wore. Next to that was another painting, the same woman with a man in a suit, looking grave. Gulpepper himself, Patrick presumed. Another painting showed Gulpepper with a tall, thin, white-haired man.

"Gulpepper married her in Sydney and brought her down here," Shirley went on. "She gave birth to four children in six years while the town grew. There's a museum in town, talks all about the early history of The Gulp. You should take a look. Anyway, he killed them all."

"What?" Simone's word was more a gasp.

"I told you, he went mad. One night, people saw him on the cliff top, where the lighthouse is now? The lighthouse wasn't finished at the time, only half-built. Anyway, a few people saw the Governor standing on the cliff edge, arms raised like he was addressing some gathered crowd, but only the ocean was there. Then he stretched up and leaped, dived right off the cliff. The people ran to see, and his body was washing back and forth against the rocks, broken and bleeding. They weren't able to retrieve him from there, and by the time they'd rowed a boat around the point, the body was nowhere to be found. So the story goes.

"Anyway, they sent a couple of people up here, to tell his wife. They found four long wooden stakes standing up in the garden, out there by the front of the house. On each stake, one of his children had been impaled, skewered from arse to mouth like little human kebabs. All of them between three and nine years old."

"Fucking hell," Patrick said. Ciara was silent and pale beside him. Torsten and Simone sat tight-lipped, both leaning forward in fascination.

"His wife was inside. She was naked. Laid out on the floor like a star, like when you make a sand angel on the beach, yeah? Except her arms and legs and her head were all chopped from her body and separated by a few feet. Sorta spread out."

"That's horrible," Ciara said.

"That's The Gulp," Shirley said.

"Why did he do it?" Patrick asked.

Shirley shrugged. "No one knows. He went mad. Why does anyone do the mad shit they do? Especially here. Kept talking about dreams, people said, but no one really understood it."

"I'd have trouble living in this place knowing that history," Torsten said.

Shirley pointed to a spot in the middle of the large room. There were no seats there, just a big rug. "Right there is where they found her. If you move the rug you can still see the blood."

"After more than a hundred and fifty years?" Ciara said, aghast. "Surely not."

"Soaked into the wood and never came out. Sanded, stained, varnished, the blood always comes through. Have a look if you want."

"I don't want!" Ciara said. "Why hasn't anyone just torn up the floorboards and replaced them?"

Shirley grinned. "Apparently they have. Three times. The blood always comes back. I need another drink." She stood and walked over to the large dresser with the bottles without another word or a backward glance.

"Fucking hell," Patrick said. "Think that's true?"

"I think maybe some is true and a lot is embellished," Torsten said.

"Embellished?" Simone asked. They spoke a moment in German, then Simone nodded. "Yes, agree. They have a..." She looked at Torsten again. "*Das Ansehen.*"

"Yes, a reputation," Torsten said. "A brand to maintain, yes? They're even still in makeup."

"Musicians," Ciara said. "Like all creatives, they're a bit weird."

"Shots!"

The room cheered as Edgar turned from the dresser with a large silver tray. It was covered in shot glasses, each filled with a pale green liquid. He moved around the room and each person took a glass, then held it, waiting. He got to Patrick and friends and they followed suit.

"Absinthe?" Patrick asked.

Edgar grinned. "Sort of. It's a Blind Eye Moon special. We call it Blind Eye Moonshine."

He put the tray down and took a glass of his own, then turned to the room. "To the mind! To the power of the intellect! To imagination!"

"To imagination!" everyone shouted back.

Patrick looked at his friends. "To imagination!"

They smiled and slammed their shots, along with everyone else. The Blind Eye Moonshine was sweet and tart at the same time, and hellaciously strong. It burned on the way down and then seemed to instantly heat Patrick from the inside out like a supernova in his gut.

"Holy shit!" Ciara said, looking at her empty glass.

Torsten blew air out and Simone said, "Phew!"

"That was quite something," Patrick muttered. His vision swam a little.

"You like it?" Edgar asked. "This is the only place in the world you can get it."

Patrick's lips felt numb, his tongue swollen. "It's

quite something," he said again, lost for any other words.

Edgar leaned over behind where Shirley had been sitting and came up with an acoustic guitar. He sat on the arm of the sofa, put the guitar on his knee, and began to play. He picked out a haunting melody that immediately insinuated its way into Patrick's blood. Then he began chords and started to sing in a strange language. It was similar to Gaelic, which Patrick spoke, but not quite the same. He listened hard, almost understood phrases, then they slipped away again.

A clean, lilting melody came over the top and Patrick saw Clarke had found a guitar too, playing along in harmony. Shirley came and stood behind a nearby armchair, using her palms to play a soft beat against its leather back. Howard, short of a bass guitar presumably, picked up the tray of shots and went around the room again. Everyone held their glasses up and Edgar paused briefly and said, "To imagination!" then continued his song.

"To imagination," the others in the room said and downed their shots once more.

The heat grew in Patrick, spreading through his body like ink dripped in water. He decided maybe he wouldn't have any more if he was offered, it seemed like more than simple alcohol, however strong. He liked it a lot, and that's what gave him pause. He liked it too much.

The night grew late, the band playing quiet and powerful acoustic songs. Howard even came up with an acoustic bass and played a hypnotic solo that seemed to stretch sound like rubber.

Despite his earlier decision, Patrick had a third shot of Blind Eye Moonshine and time stretched then as well. He and his friends talked with other partygoers, they talked with the band between songs, they drank more still, but bourbon now, and Bundaberg rum. The strange green liqueur wasn't offered again, for which

Patrick was vaguely thankful, though he missed it too.

He found himself staring out the front bay window of the large room, across a well-manicured lawn and old, established shrubs. The view dropped away after the garden and he realised he saw a faint pale smudge in the distance and a soft horizon. He was looking at the ocean, far away over the roofs of the Gulp, and dawn had begun to lighten the sky.

The room had fallen to silence and Patrick tore his gaze away from the view to see why. As he did so, Edgar began to sing. That same strange almost-Gaelic language as the first song, but no guitar now, no accompaniment. Just Edgar's voice, pure and soft, as pitch-perfect with the lilting melody as it had been belting out heavy metal anthems. This melody had something of the lullaby about it. As that thought occurred to Patrick, his eyelids became heavy. He managed to think, *He's putting me to sleep*, and a swift, icy rill of panic went through him, then his eyes closed and darkness swept in like the tide.

Patrick dreamed.

The house was dark and still, a cold breeze rippled his hair. Ice rimed every surface, glittering softly in moonlight that leaked through the windows. He took a step forward and something sucked at his shoe. He looked down. He stood in a massive pool of blood, almost black in the darkness. He tried to call out Ciara's name, but his voice was a whistling wheeze. His throat tightened. His heart began to race, breath short and shallow. He ran to the front window, wet footprints in his wake, and looked out. The moon hung full and heavy over the ocean far away. Then clouds rolled in, roiling dark black and purple. Lightning forked and the surface of the ocean heaved as rain fell. Then the sky split, deep red like a wound, and creatures fell from the clouds. All manner of shapes, long and gangly, short and squat, limbs writhing as they tumbled to the waves. Only tiny silhouettes in the distance, he had no idea what they were, people or something different. A sound forced the hairs on his neck to stand up, a howl, but not animal. Not exactly. Like a person trying to howl like a wolf.

Pounding feet on floorboards, rushing up behind him. He spun around, but no one was there. He tried to call Ciara's name again, but only croaked a cloud of condensed breath. A shadow passed the door, out in the hallway, a tall, sinewy figure loping by.

He ran to the door, looked out. No one there. More ice over everything in the hallway, the side tables, portraits, coat rack. A frozen draught came in through the open front door. He went to it, looked out over the opulent entrance, stone steps leading down to the gravel driveway. The dark roiling clouds churned above, a wind blew, cold and carrying the salt scent of the ocean, and something less pleasant. Something rotten.

A long, bony hand with blood red fingernails came down on his shoulder. He cried out, though it was barely a sound, as the hand turned him. The arm was as long and thin as the fingers, attached to a hunched body over seven feet tall, skeletal, with fish-belly pale skin. Except around the eyes, where the flesh was blackened, cobwebs of black veins spreading out over the cheekbones, up over the forehead. The eyes were glowing deep, dark red. The other hand rose in front of his face, the overlong fingers weaving hypnotising patterns in the air. Those deep red eyes stared hard into his as the creature leaned forward, face to face. Its breath was a marine stench.

He sensed it drawing something from him, sucking something out, some essence. Something important. Whatever it was taking, he needed it, couldn't spare it. He tried to scream no, but his breath was a whisper. His legs numb, face slack, darkness lay gently over him.

Patrick awoke with a pounding in his head and a mouth like the bottom of a birdcage. He groaned and rolled over, and fell off the couch onto the rug with a thump. He grunted and turned into a sitting position.

"Yeah, it's a bit like that."

He looked up to see Ciara smiling at him from an armchair, where she sat curled up, knees to her chest, eyes narrow. "You too?"

She grimaced. "Haven't had a headache like this in a while."

"We haven't drunk like that in a while."

"Truth."

Patrick looked around the room, saw most of the previous night's revellers were gone, but four or five remained. Torsten and Simone were spooned on a couch perpendicular to the one he'd just fallen from, both still sleeping. "We all just passed out last night?" he asked.

"Guess so. I don't remember."

"Can I smell bacon?"

Ciara nodded, then winced. "Coffee too."

"Gods be praised."

"Careful who you pray to in this town, hey."

They turned to see Howard, the bass player, carrying a tray piled with bread rolls and that enticing smell of bacon. He leaned down and let them take one each.

"Get these into ya," Howard said. His voice was gravelly, but kind. "They'll cure what ails ya."

"Coffee," Shirley said, putting a large metal jug on the same dresser as the booze that had caused all their problems.

Well, maybe not all of it, Patrick reflected. The green moonshine Edgar had shared around was nowhere to be seen. He hadn't seen where that came from.

The bacon roll was amazing, greasy and salty enough to start counteracting his hangover. As he chewed, he went and fetched himself and Ciara a coffee. Torsten and Simone had woken when he came back, so he turned right around and got them one each too.

When he came back, Howard offered him another

bacon roll. "Plenty to go around."

Shirley put some music on, but turned down low. Patrick recognised it but couldn't place it. Nineties grunge of some kind. The few remaining revellers drifted off over the next half hour or so, thanking the band for the hospitality. The last one to leave spoke quietly to Edgar for a moment and kept glancing back at Patrick as he did so. Edgar squeezed the guy's shoulder, said something with a reassuring face. The guy nodded and left and Edgar came to sit next to Patrick. The rest of the band joined them, all eight sat in a loose circle on two couches and three armchairs.

"Had enough to eat?" Edgar asked.

They nodded, smiled.

"You're very kind," Patrick said. "It's good of you to do this, something for your real fans after a gig, yeah?"

Edgar smiled. "Something like that. Some of these people have followed us for a while."

Patrick realised all four band members still had the dark makeup, the crimson contacts. It hadn't registered at first, and that surprised him. He nodded at Edgar's face. "You're really committed to your bit, huh?"

"It's just who we are, man."

"Must be tiring. Don't you feel like some days you just can't be bothered?"

"How do you know we don't?"

Patrick nodded. "I guess you keep it up while people are around or when you go out, but that's all?"

"Maybe."

"I feel strange," Simone said quietly.

They all turned to look at her. Torsten said something in German and the two had a quiet conversation for a moment.

"Everything okay?" Patrick asked.

"Probably the drink, that's all," Torsten said.

Edgar laughed, but good-naturedly. "Our moonshine can have a lasting effect, especially if you're not used to it."

"What is that stuff exactly?"

"Exactly, Patrick? I can't tell you. Secrets! It's just a homebrew spirit, that's all."

"If I'm honest, I feel a little weird too," Ciara said. "I'm wiped out."

"Everyone drank a lot," Clarke said. "And we were up all night. It's barely noon now. You don't have to be anywhere, do you?"

Ciara shook her head. "We were going to stay in Monkton last night and tonight. Find a motel bed instead of cramped together in the campervan. Then head on towards Sydney."

"Ended up cramped on couches and armchairs instead," Torsten said with a rueful laugh.

"Well, you're here now," Edgar said. "You want to stay with us tonight as well? We've plenty of rooms, you can have a proper bed tonight, showers, all that stuff. Better than a Monkton fucking motel, that's for sure. Have a look around The Gulp today. There's really nowhere else like it."

"Thankfully," Shirley said quietly.

The other band members chuckled softly.

Edgar stood up. "You want to? Come on, I'll show you your rooms. All your stuff is in your camper outside, right?"

They looked at each other and Ciara and Torsten nodded. Simone looked uncertain, but she also looked a little more sick and pale.

"Sure, why not," Patrick said.

Edgar gave them rooms side by side. There was even a door inside, joining the two. Each room had a large bed of dark wood, a small sink in the corner, a set of drawers and a dressing table. They were like nicely appointed rooms in an old-fashioned hotel. Across the hall was a huge bathroom with a shower cubicle and a claw-foot bath, which was theirs alone to use. The band apparently had other rooms and bathrooms, at the opposite end of the sprawling upper storey.

"People usually crash on the couches like last night," Edgar said. "But we often have people stay for a while, so we keep the guest rooms nice. Pretty good, eh? Anyway, we have to practice, so make yourselves at home. Head off into town whenever you like, and if you're back by about seven you can eat with us. Howard is whipping up one of his famous curries tonight. You'll like it, I promise." Without waiting for a response, he turned and strolled away.

"Great local hospitality," Torsten said. "This is the beauty of travelling with no agenda. Cool things happen."

"Shall we take a look around The Gulp?" Patrick said.

Simone groaned. "Shower and change first." She went through the adjoining door to the room she was sharing with her brother. Edgar had offered them each a room, but Simone had said she wanted to stay with Torsten.

"See you downstairs in half an hour?" Torsten said.

"Perfect." Patrick fancied a shower and change himself.

They walked down the hill and came to the main street leading into town, turned right towards the harbour. A park with a decent sized playground on one side, shops and a few cafes on the other. They found the museum, an old sandstone building, but it was closed up, with no opening hours displayed anywhere. A tattered poster had been pinned to the door, faded with time and rain. It asked, *Have you seen Daniel?* and featured a grainy photo of a lank-haired youth.

On the far side of the park, a road led back up to

the north side of town, more houses of varying age spreading out. Then a path ran around the harbour. The water glittered in a large half circle and on the far side was the harbour proper, with breakwater walls and a variety of boats moored up. Most were fishing boats, but a few leisure vessels bobbed among them. On the far side of the harbour was a row of buildings that ended with a large fish and chip shop.

"Back here for lunch?" Ciara said.

They walked out along the headland beyond the harbour, all the way to the lighthouse that marked the end point. It was tall, stark white against the sky. Patrick imagined it half-built, Governor Gulpepper standing on the cliff edge with his arms raised. He vaguely remembered blood red clouds and things falling but had no idea why that image was in his mind. A cold wind blew across and he shivered.

"I can't get used to it being winter in the middle of the year," Patrick said. "Nearly July and it's cold."

"Hardly cold compared to our winters," Torsten said.

"Well, no, but you know what I mean. I'm glad I have a sweater on."

"I like it," Simone said. "Clear and sun but not hot. Remember you the last trip?" she asked Torsten.

He laughed. "Yeah, that was hot! We came to Australia once before, and we started in Darwin, but it was January. So hot and humid, it was awful."

"There's a beach down there," Ciara said, pointing over the south side of the head.

They walked down that way, taking their time to enjoy the views, and found the beach was quite small, but it had a nice aspect and was low between the head and the next rise of land, so it was sheltered. Behind the gravelly black sand was another park, another set of bright plastic play equipment. Four people sat at one of the picnic tables, the only others there. They were a strange bunch, Patrick thought. A young woman, a middle aged woman and man, and an elderly man. Maybe a family group? But they didn't look alike other than they were all incredibly pale. They just sat there, staring at nothing, not talking. They gave Patrick the creeps.

A noticeboard stood at the corner of the park, weathered wood with scratched Perspex in front. It had a variety of community notices, flyers for yoga classes, local produce, Man And A Van For Hire. But one entire side was dedicated to posters about missing people. The *Have you seen Daniel?* poster was there again, along with about a dozen others. Mostly young people, but not all, with bold headings like *MISSING* and *HELP US FIND STACEY.* Ciara stood staring at them and Patrick looked over her shoulder. He opened his mouth to say something, but Torsten interrupted his thoughts.

"It's volcanic."

Patrick turned. "What is?"

"The sand. Well, the whole area, I suppose. Lots of white sand beaches and wide-open bays along the coast of Australia, but this rough black stuff has to be volcanic."

"Danke, nerd," Simone said.

"Let's go back for lunch," Ciara said. "I'm getting hungry again."

"Two bacon rolls weren't enough?" Patrick asked.

"I only had one!"

They went back to the fish and chip shop and stared at the menu board. Eventually they picked a combination of blue grenadier, chips, a seafood basket and four cans of soda. The woman behind the counter seemed entirely uninterested as she took the order, almost as though she were annoyed they were there at all. Patrick took out his credit card and she said, "Cash only," in a tired, put-upon voice.

"In this day and age?"

She pointed to a small A4 sheet of paper with CASH ONLY typed on it that had been taped to the bottom of the menu. "It's right there."

Patrick turned to the others. "We have any cash?"

Between them they came up with enough for about half the order and adjusted it accordingly.

"You must lose a lot of business this way," Patrick said as he paid.

The woman ignored him, put the cash in the till, and turned away to start preparing the food.

"Jesus, between the rudeness and the cash only thing, I'm amazed this place is still in business."

"Maybe it's a front for organised crime," Torsten said with a grin.

"Let's draw some cash out on the way back," Ciara said. "In case other places are like this."

There were tables and chairs out the front that overlooked the water, the harbour to their left, open ocean to the right. After about ten minutes, Patrick went back inside to check on the order and there were several wrapped parcels on the counter.

"Is that ours?" he asked.

The woman looked around theatrically. "You see anyone else here?"

"Were you going to call us or just leave it there to go cold?"

The woman rolled her eyes and went back into the kitchen area behind the counter. She scowled at him through the long hatch until he turned away.

He gathered up the food and, unable to help himself, turned back. "You're fucking rude, you know that? Maybe you'd be better suited to a different job."

The woman stared at him, face blank, until he shook his head and took the food back outside.

For all the terrible service, the meal wasn't too bad, but far from the best they'd had. Regardless, the extra grease seemed to chase away the last of the previous night's over-indulgence. Even Simone looked more or less back to normal as they walked back around the town, idly browsing shops.

Patrick chose not to say anything, he didn't want to seem judgemental, but there were a number of odd-looking people in The Gulp. One fellow he saw walking a dog had no nose, which he found strangely disturbing. Maybe cancer had eaten it off? Others seemed overly pale, or strangely long of limb. Still others, the majority he supposed, were entirely normal-looking folks. But there was an edge of oddness to the town he couldn't quite put his finger on. Maybe it was simply isolation.

As he stood outside a bookshop while his friends browsed the shelves, he looked out towards the north. The houses climbed the hill, lots of them in undulating geological waves, leading up to thick bush in the distance. The cliff of the northernmost head was just visible, crowded with vegetation right up to the edge. Given what they'd driven through, he assumed the south side of town was largely the same. A weird little pocket of civilisation in what Torsten had called unusually old forest. He was fascinated by the place but would be happy to drive on the next day.

It was a little after five and beginning to get dark as they trudged up the steep hill on the western edge of town, back to The Manor. The band were there, all in their makeup like before. Patrick was getting used to it but thought their commitment to it was a little bit try-hard. He'd like to see them without it, see the real people beneath the façade. He mentioned as much to Torsten as they sat with a beer in the large lounge room, night darkening the windows.

"Maybe it's like Batman," Torsten said.

"What?"

"Is Bruce Wayne the real person, and Batman his alter ego. Or is Batman real and Bruce Wayne the fake mask he wears?"

"Well, it's obviously..." Patrick didn't finish as the thought took root in his mind. "Actually, now you mention it." He laughed.

"You see. So maybe the band is real, yes?"

Edgar stuck his head in the door. "Grub up!"

They followed him to the back of the house into a big kitchen. It had a massive iron range cooker, copper pots and pans hanging from a cradle over a wide marble work surface. At the far end was an old oak table, scored and stained, but solid as the day it was made. Which must have been a long time ago, Patrick thought. It easily seated twelve given the dozen chairs around it, so the eight of them had plenty of room.

Howard put plates down and then a metal pot of steaming rice. They served themselves as Howard went back to the stove, then came back with two more oversized saucepans, one in each hand. Patrick marvelled at the man's grip strength, carrying them easily. He put them on the table and pointed.

"That one is chicken masala. That one is beef vindaloo. I hope you like it spicy."

"How spicy?" Ciara asked with a wince.

"You're not into hot food?" Howard said. "Hmm. Better stick to the chicken then."

The food was incredible. The vindaloo blisteringly hot, but so full of flavour, the masala smooth and creamy. They all had second helpings, Patrick and his friends repeatedly telling Howard how good it all was. He smiled and nodded but said nothing. Once they were full, they retired back to the lounge room. Shirley put a DVD into the player under the huge TV and John Carpenter's *The Thing*, started up.

"Oh, this is one of the best horror films ever made!" Torsten said happily.

"Oh no. Not for me," Simone said.

"You don't like horror films?" Shirley asked.

"Not really. But is okay, I am tired. I go to bed. Maybe read. I don't want more..." She glanced at Torsten. "*Der Albtraum.*"

He nodded. "Nightmares. We both had bad dreams last night."

"Nightmares, yes. Thank you for lovely dinner." Simone smiled and left the room, headed upstairs.

"I had terrible dreams last night too," Patrick said. "I'd forgotten, but she just reminded me."

"Did you dream of the fall?" Edgar asked.

"The fall?"

"When the creatures fell to the sea, off what's now Carlton Beach."

"How do you know that?"

Edgar laughed. "Everyone who sleeps in The Gulp dreams of the fall."

Patrick looked at Torsten, then Ciara. They both nodded, eyes concerned.

"How can we have all dreamed the same thing?" Patrick asked.

"Just one of the many strange things about this cursed town, my friend." Edgar turned back to the movie, slumping down in the couch. The other band members all kept their eyes on the screen.

Patrick wondered about the other part of his dream, that was only flitting around his mind in disconnected gossamer images. Something tall and thin. Some sensation of loss. He wanted to ask Torsten and Ciara about that but couldn't find the words.

He watched the film, uncomfortable. And he had even more reason to look forward to the morning and their onward journey.

Halfway through the movie, Edgar got up and offered drinks. Patrick had a bourbon, but decided it would only be the one. He didn't want to feel again what he'd felt that morning. Ciara and Torsten both accepted a second round a little later as MacReady dipped red hot wire in a petri dish on screen. Ciara threw Patrick a surprised look when he declined, but she said nothing.

When the film ended, Edgar said, "Shots!"

"Oh, not again," Torsten said.

Edgar went to the drinks dresser anyway and turned

back with several shot glasses of the pale green Blind Eye Moonshine. He walked over, offered them around.

"I don't think so," Torsten said.

"Come on, man! Just one. Especially if you're leaving tomorrow. You can't get this anywhere else in the world."

Torsten laughed and took a glass. "Just one!"

"Same for me," Ciara said, taking one.

Edgar turned to Patrick, but he shook his head.

"You sure?" Edgar asked.

"Yeah, really. Thanks though."

"Okay, it's your loss."

The band took one each and Edgar said, "Imagination!"

They all downed the shots. The band made no reaction at all, but Torsten and Ciara both shuddered and grimaced.

"It's so weird," Ciara said. "The sensation is kinda horrible, but it's also delicious." She drew in a long breath. "And there's that lovely spread of warmth. Really, what *is* this stuff."

Edgar smiled, and shook his head. "Another?"

"No, thanks," Patrick said. "Come on, let's go to bed."

Ciara shook his hand off her forearm. "It's barely after ten o'clock."

"You know, I will have another," Torsten said.

"Me too!" Ciara said, casting a defiant glance at Patrick.

"Shirley, you want to get the drinks?" Edgar said. "I feel like playing a song."

Several guitars were on their stands along one wall behind a sofa and Edgar picked one up. Patrick had a sudden and urgent desire to not hear the man sing. He didn't want to hear that strange not-quite-Gaelic language again. His gut shivered with a kind of trepidation.

"You sure you won't come to bed?" he asked Ciara.

He tried to put a little intent into his voice, tried to make something tempting of his expression like he wanted to spend some private time with his girlfriend. But his discomfort must have simply made him look weird.

Ciara frowned, then laughed, a little embarrassed. "You can crash if you like. Are you feeling okay?"

"A little off if I'm honest. Will you come with me?"

She tipped her head to one side. "You really want me to? I'd like to stay and hear Edgar play." Her eyes seemed more challenging than sympathetic.

Patrick chewed his lower lip, uncertain. Should he insist on her coming? Would she, even if he did? And why was he so uncomfortable?

"You go," Ciara said. "I promise I'll follow you up soon, okay? I'm tired too. Maybe half an hour, I'll join you."

Patrick nodded. He could hardly insist she come now when she'd made such a seemingly reasonable offer. "Okay."

Edgar grinned and perched on the arm of a couch, put the guitar on his knee. Patrick almost ran up the stairs, so desperate was he not to hear the man's song.

He waited half an hour, and Ciara didn't come. He thought about going back down, checking on her. But he'd looked like such a fool if he pulled a stunt like that. They were leaving the next day, he decided to focus on that. He got ready for bed, brushed his teeth, took a leak, then padded back across the hall to his room.

He'd been in bed only a few minutes, still no sign of Ciara, when he heard a sound. He froze, listened hard. Something was moving above the ceiling. He remembered the high, A-frame roof of The Manor, imagined there must be quite an attic up there.

The sound stopped for a moment, then resumed. Something moving, something quite large. Then definite footsteps. Was a person up there? One of the band?

He heard Simone's voice from next door. Something in German, and he caught Torsten's name. He smiled. If

Torsten was heading to bed, surely Ciara would be up any moment. He turned his ear back to the ceiling, wondering at the possibility of a person there, but was distracted again by another voice from the room next door.

"Not Torsten. It's Clarke."

Patrick sat up in bed, alarmed, then hurried to the adjoining door and put his ear to it. Clarke was so quiet and unassuming compared to the others in the band.

"Clarke? What you want?"

"Torsten is enjoying a drink and a song downstairs. You want some company?"

"Clarke. I don't know."

"I've seen the way you look at me. You like what you see, huh?"

Patrick frowned. If he was honest, Clarke was probably the best looking of the guys. They were all lean, that hard-body rock star aesthetic. The three of them all had long hair, Edgar blond and the other two black, whether natural or dyed he couldn't tell. But Clarke's hair was thick and shining, his jaw square, strong cheekbones. And he had that quiet, brooding thing going on.

"I've got a little drink for us," Clarke said. His voice had moved into the room now, Patrick imagined him at the foot of Simone's bed.

"What is it? Not the moonshine?"

Clarke laughed. "Of course the Blind Eye Moonshine. Come on, just a sip."

"I don't know."

Patrick fought an urge to swing the door wide, confront Clarke, tell the bastard to leave Simone alone. That would be the worst white knighting. She was a grown-up, she didn't need saving. Not yet anyway. If she tried to send Clarke away and he refused, then Patrick would get involved.

Simone's bed creaked. "Clarke, I don't know."

"How about I try to convince you?"

"Oh? How?"

"Here, take this. Have a drink. Just a sip. That's the way. Now lie back and spread these lovely long legs."

Simone gasped.

"Good?" Clarke asked, a little muffled.

"Oh... OH!"

Patrick shook his head and moved away from the door. It was all their business now. And if Clarke was so certain Torsten wouldn't disturb them, perhaps it was a safe bet that Ciara would stay for more drinks too. He felt at a loss, stranded on his own in a crowded house.

The noises from the next room became more urgent, more excited. Patrick got back into bed and pressed the pillow over his head. Eventually, despite all his discomforts, he fell asleep. And dreamed.

He stood on a beach surrounded by thick, verdant bush. Strangely ancient vegetation, thick trees with even thicker undergrowth. He couldn't imagine being able to fight his way through it, but where was the town? A stench of rot filled his nose, made his bile rise. He looked down to see the gravelly black sand was slick with even blacker, oily slime. Rain fell, cold and stinging against his face, stuck his hair flat to his head. The wind was cold and heavy, pendulous clouds, arcing with streaks of purple lightning, filled the lowering sky. He almost felt as though he would be able to reach up and touch them. Gaping red wounds opened in the clouds and things fell, far out near the horizon. Things that writhed and flapped and flexed as they tumbled down. Then nearer, close enough to see some details, though most was lost to silhouette through the haze of rain and darkness. Was it night or a stormy day? Some creatures had seemingly too many limbs, certainly more than four. Some had appendages that whipped like tentacles in the wind of their falling. They hit the turbulent waves and sank away.

He sensed eyes on him and turned. A tall, thin, pale figure stood just past the tree line, watching him. Its long arms hung at its sides, blood red nails pointing at the slime. Ribs and hips jutted from that too pale skeletal frame, red eyes in their black nests of cobwebbed veins never left his, never blinked. Another joined it. Then a third. Then a fourth, though this one was a little different, slightly altered in shape. Three male and a female he realised, his thoughts almost too slippery to lock down. Something roamed back and forth just behind the four, in the shadows of the trees. Something like them but taller, more bent and crooked. They raised their long-fingered hands, the four, and beckoned to him. He shivered, knowing that to go to them meant certain doom, but compelled to do just that. He tried to cry out a denial, but only managed a broken croak. He turned to run, slipping and sliding on the rotten ichor that covered the beach, washing up with the churning waves. Out there, the creatures continued to fall from rents in the heavy, lightning-struck clouds.

He ran anyway, falling, hands slapping into the ooze that stank like rotten flesh. He staggered up, ran again, fell again. Over and over he climbed to his feet, ran, and fell, but he refused to look back towards the trees, refused to even acknowledge their presence, beckoning him. Over and over again he ran and fell until, exhausted, sobbing, he lay in the fetid slime and didn't try to rise again.

Patrick woke as the grey light of dawn smudged the windows where he'd neglected to draw the curtains. He felt more exhausted than when he'd gone to bed, his dreams fresh and frightening in his memory, but tattering and fluttering away even as he tried to hold onto them.

He sat up, bereft. Ciara lay next to him, calm and relaxed in her sleep. In the low light, she seemed thinner, her cheeks hollowed by shadows. But he smiled, glad to see her there. She'd come to bed eventually, and today they could leave.

He didn't want to wake her even an hour later as

the sun streamed in through the window. Another bright, clear, blue day, but cold outside, dew glittering on the grass below. Patrick trudged downstairs, found Howard and Edgar talking quietly in the kitchen as they worked on breakfast. A huge pan of scrambled eggs sat on the stove. If nothing else, the band were feeding them well.

"Mornin', champ," Edgar said. "Sleep well?"

"Not really, no."

"That's a shame. After your early night and everything."

"I seem to have bad dreams here."

Howard laughed. "Everyone has bad dreams here."

Patrick frowned. They were still in makeup. Could he fool himself any longer? It clearly wasn't makeup. But what the hell did that mean. The two stared at him with their dark, crimson eyes. Their red nails glittered. Patrick's dreams skittered around the edges of his mind, details smudging even as he tried to hold onto them.

"You can go whenever you want," Howard said.

"What?"

"The Gulp has a habit of swallowing people," Edgar said. "But sometimes it spits one out."

"What?" Patrick said again.

"Mornin' all youse cunts."

They turned to see Clarke stroll in, grinning.

"Seen a ghost, Patrick?" he asked.

Patrick ran a hand through his hair, trying to get a grip on the morning's proceedings. Leave, that's all there was to it. They were leaving today. Concentrate on that.

Shirley came in, went to the counter. "Morning, fuckers. I'll get the toast on. Get your friends up, Pat, or the eggs will be cold."

"Fuck." At a loss, he did as he was told. He knocked on the Germans' door first, and Torsten grunted a query. "Breakfast is ready."

"Okay, be right there."

He went into his own room, sat on the edge of the bed. Ciara turned over and smiled up at him. "Morning." She looked pale, and he thought she really had lost weight. Her cheeks were hollow, not just shadowed.

"You okay?"

"Sure. Just really tired, is all."

"Sleep well?"

She grimaced. "Ugh. Nightmares, I tell you. These tall creatures with black and red eyes, chasing me."

A shiver passed through Patrick. "They catch you?"

"Every time! And they kinda suck something out of me, like they're draining me, then I wake up. Then it starts over again."

Patrick shook his head. "Fuck this place. We're leaving today, heading on towards Sydney, yeah?"

"Sure, if you want."

"I do want."

"Okay. You all right?"

She looked suddenly scared. Was she taking his lead? If he seemed scared, did she take that seriously? Perhaps, and if so, that was okay with him. "Yeah, I'm all right. I just want to get on, that's all."

They sat around the big kitchen table and tucked into the eggs. For a couple of minutes it was a companionable silence, then Edgar said, "So what's the plan for today?"

"Heading off," Patrick said quickly. "On up the coast towards Sydney."

"You don't fancy staying a bit longer? You're welcome, you know."

"Thanks, but I think—"

"I want to stay," Simone said. She glanced at Clarke and gave him a sly smile. He winked at her.

Ciara looked from Simone to Clarke and back again. "Oh! That's where you went last night?"

Clarke shrugged, grinned at his breakfast.

"We need to get on," Patrick said.

"Stick around for the week," Edgar said. "We're playing in Enden on Friday, you could head off from there."

"It's only Monday," Patrick said, and hated the edge of panic in his voice.

"Farmer's Markets today," Shirley said. "This afternoon. You should check them out, down at Carlton Beach."

"Oh, hey, get me some bugs!" Howard said. "I'll make a special dinner."

"Fucking bugs?" Patrick said.

Howard laughed. "You heard of Moreton Bay Bugs? No? Sometimes they're called slipper lobsters or flathead lobsters. Anyway, they're a kinda of lobster, obviously. There's a variety you can only get right here, around this part of the coast. Go north of Enden or south of Monkton and you don't get them any more. A few of the local fisherman always have them for sale at the markets. Get a bunch and I'll make this amazing chili pasta dish with them for dinner."

"Sounds amazing," Ciara said.

"It's to die for," Edgar said with a grin. He looked at Patrick as he said it.

"Okay," Torsten said. "Let's stick around a bit longer, yeah?"

"Sure," Ciara said.

"I want to," Simone said, and shifted her chair nearer to Clarke's. He leaned over and kissed her. The other band members laughed.

Edgar still held Patrick's gaze.

Patrick tore his eyes away. "I thought we agreed to leave today."

"Does it matter?" Torsten said. "We have no real agenda." He rubbed under his eyes and Patrick thought the German looked a little pale and drawn too. All three of his friends did.

"I want to hear the band play again," Ciara said. "You really don't mind us staying here the week?" She looked at Patrick. "It's free accommodation too!" She quickly turned back to Edgar. "We'll buy some food and booze, of course! We don't expect you to keep us."

Edgar shrugged. "I already told ya, me cassa, you cassa."

"Tell you what," Patrick said. "We'll stay if you four wash off your makeup!"

Edgar laughed, the other three grinned.

"Patrick, don't be rude!" Ciara said. She looked at him with a shocked expression.

"How is that rude?"

"Excuse him," Ciara said to the band.

"Don't excuse me!" Patrick looked around the group and they all looked back, every one of them with some kind of surprise or pity in their eyes. How was he the odd one out here? "You won't take it off? Or you can't?"

"Patrick!"

Edgar raised his palms. "We are who we are, mate."

"And who are you, exactly?"

"You want to change us?" Shirley asked. "We would never ask you to change."

"Patrick, please," Ciara said. "What's got into you?"

"Nothing! I'm not the one under their fucking spell."

"Chill out, yeah?" Ciara said, laying a hand on Patrick's forearm. "It's cool here, is it not? Hanging out with a rock band, immersing ourselves in local culture."

"I'm not really a fan of this culture, Ciara."

She smiled, shook her head. "Chill out. It'll be a nice week, then we can get a room in Enden, watch the gig, crash there, and hit the road again on Saturday. No real plans, remember? Let the trip take us where it will, isn't that what you said?"

"Yes, but–"

"But nothing. We made new friends, we're seeing new things. It's just a week, we have months more ahead of us."

Patrick ground his teeth, looked around the group.

They band smiled, patient and relaxed. Edgar seemed a little more smug than the others. Torsten and Simone wouldn't meet his eye. He turned back to Ciara, but her eyes had hardened a little, daring him to challenge her further. He knew the look.

"Fuck it, I need some fresh air."

Outside was still winter cool, but the sun warm as he walked across the grass. Patrick felt untethered, lost.

The Gulp has a habit of swallowing people. But sometimes it spits one out.

Patrick took a ragged breath, glancing back at the house. As he started to turn away, movement caught his eye. Something up above. He turned back and saw a window high on the house he hadn't noticed before. Above the second storey, in the apex under a heavy chimney, a round window with a wooden cross in it making four even quarters of glass. An attic window. Someone looked out of it. Patrick frowned. It was an old man, pale, with long white hair. A moment of recognition tickled Patrick's mind, but slipped away. He'd heard those footsteps the night before... The man snapped his head around and pinned Patrick with his gaze. Patrick gasped and took an involuntary step backwards, tripping on the edge of a flowerbed. He staggered but managed to regain his balance. When he looked back up, the round attic window was empty.

The Farmer's Markets transformed the park behind Carlton Beach into bustling activity. Dozens of stalls under Easy-Up canopies were selling pretty much everything imaginable. Fruits and vegetables of every kind, nuts, herbs, mushrooms. Some of the mushrooms on sale looked decidedly weird to Patrick, but he chose not to mention it. There were arts and crafts too. Beeswax candles, watercolours, wooden carvings, leather belts.

"Here's a seafood stand," Ciara said, dragging on his hand.

Patrick was still smarting from the earlier shutdown of his concerns, but he tried to play along for now. If nothing else, he needed Ciara to trust him, not start hating him.

They went over, Torsten and Simone with them. The seller had several polystyrene boxes filled with ice, various fish and shellfish laid out on top.

"You have any bugs?" Ciara asked.

The man behind the table was short and squat, with a wide face and eyes too far apart. *Looks like a bug himself,* Patrick thought uncharitably.

But the man smiled warmly. "Gulpepper Bugs, eh? Keen to try the local cuisine? I can tell from your accent you're not from around here."

"We're told they're really good."

"They are, but you have to know how to prepare them safely."

"Safely?" Patrick asked.

"Yeah, they have a poisonous bit, like some crabs do. You know what to do with them?"

"A friend is doing the cooking," Ciara said. "A local."

"Ah, you'll be right then. How many?"

"Eight, I guess?"

"All right." The man stepped back and slid a large plastic tub out from under his table. It sloshed with water and he popped the lid off. Dozens of large shellfish, like wide, flat, shortened lobsters hunched and jetted over each other inside.

"Oh, they're alive?" Ciara said.

The man looked up. "Yeah. You gotta cook 'em fresh. I'll box 'em for ya, though, make it easy to carry."

"Can you keep eight aside for us, so we can pick

them up later when we're ready to go back?"

"Sure, if you pay me now."

"How much?"

The fisherman eyed Ciara for a moment, then smiled. "Let's say ten bucks each, as you're new to this."

"Eighty bucks," Patrick said. "We're on a budget." Ten bucks each for something like lobster actually seemed pretty reasonable, but he didn't like the idea of eating anything so specifically local to this weird place.

"You'd pay three times that for lobster tails at the supermarket," Ciara said. "Besides, we're saving a lot staying with the band and they've been giving us loads of food and booze. This is a steal!"

Patrick kept his mouth closed, teeth clenched, as Ciara counted out the eighty dollars. She was right, after all, they'd had a free ride so far. Torsten handed her forty and she smiled at him, slipped some of her money away again.

"We'll be back in an hour or so, okay?"

"Whenever you like before six."

It was only a little after four by the time they headed back up the Manor, taking turns to carry the polystyrene box with the shellfish scratching and scuttling around inside. Howard was overjoyed to receive it.

"You remembered!"

"Of course," Ciara said.

"You beauty! We'll eat well tonight!" He took the box into the kitchen.

Simone went off with Clarke, holding hands as they went upstairs. Torsten slumped onto a couch next to Edgar and Shirley, where they were watching a movie, drinking beers. He took a bottle from the fridge, held it up asking Patrick if he'd join them.

Patrick shook his head. "Might have a nap."

He went upstairs, with no intention of sleeping. The stairway gave out onto a wide landing and immediately to the left were four doors. The two rooms they occupied, the bathroom they were using, and one other. He opened that one and saw another guest room, made up like theirs had been. The other way from the top of the stairs led down a long hallway with three doors on either side and one more at the far end. Among those would be the rooms the band members used. He glanced back down the stairs, saw no one, and ventured along.

The first doors on either side were locked. The next two were both bathrooms. The next two were locked. Maybe the band kept their rooms locked, but he wondered why. Perhaps because they had house guests so often?

The door at the end drew his eye. He opened it, surprised as he had expected that to be locked as well. A narrow staircase went up along the wall, into darkness.

Heart hammering, Patrick climbed the steep wooden stairs. They creaked softly, made him wince. When he neared the top, he looked cautiously into the attic space. It was huge, running the entire length of the massive house, with a high, vaulted ceiling under dark A-frame rafters. The floor was solid, polished floorboards. Candles burned here and there, bookcases lined the walls, jammed with hundreds, maybe thousands of books. Light leaked in at the far end from the round window he'd seen from outside. In one far corner was a curtained off area, but he caught a glimpse of a ceramic sink through a gap in the curtains. In the other far corner was a huge, mahogany four poster bed. It had a heavy, deep red velvet canopy, with side curtains all tied back to the posts. Someone lay in the bed.

As Patrick noticed them, the person moved, began to sit up. Cadaverously thin, moon pale, with long, white hair. Patrick ducked back out of sight and froze, heart hammering.

"Edgar, lad?" The voice was wheezing and thin but echoed with lost strength. Something about it chilled Patrick to his bones.

There was shuffling and soft grunts of effort as the old man moved.

"Someone else, eh? Have I got a visitor? Or did I dream it? Hard to tell these days..."

Patrick gritted his teeth in panic, looked down the steep staircase to the rectangle of inviting light below. He didn't dare move, give himself away. He looked up again, into the gloom of the attic. Another grunt and the definite sound of a footstep. The old man groaned softly, then made the universal noise of someone stretching, though it was a dusty, weak sound.

"Let's have a look at you!" The old white head surged into view right above him and Patrick yelped in surprise. How had he covered that distance so fast? Without thinking, Patrick half ran, half fell down the thin wooden stairs, clattering as he went, and stumbled out onto the landing. He slammed the door behind him, shutting out a peal of harsh laughter that was anything but frail.

Swallowing hard against powerful adrenaline, he went directly to his room and closed the door.

The meal Howard made was indeed amazing. Even Patrick had to admit it. The bugs had been cleaned, the tender tail meat cooked up into a spicy tomato sauce and served over linguini. Howard had even baked fresh bread and then toasted it with generous slatherings of garlic butter.

"You lucky to have Howard as chef," Simone said to the others.

"You do all the cooking?" Torsten asked him.

Howard nodded. "Usually. I enjoy it, it's like a hobby. These fools have a go sometimes when I can't be bothered."

"The famous Edgar spag bol!" Shirley said with a laugh.

"Hey, fuck yas!" Edgar said. He turned to Patrick and his friends. "I'll make my spag bol tomorrow night, see what you think."

"Ah, what have I done?" Shirley said, slapping the back of her hand to her forehead.

Three bottles of crisp white wine were on the table and Clarke kept everyone's glass full. Patrick took full advantage, shaken by recent events, thinking maybe a few wines would help. There was no way he would be drinking the Blind Eye Moonshine again though.

The wine did indeed relax him, especially his tongue. After they sat back, sated, and Howard had collected up the plates, Patrick said, "So who's the old guy in the attic?"

Ciara, Simone and Torsten flashed confused glances his way. Howard, Clarke and Shirley seemed to still, attentive.

Edgar remained relaxed, smiling. "You met Bram?"

Patrick hadn't expected such a casual response. "Well, not met him exactly."

"You just had a quick spy on the old fella, is that it?"

"I was exploring the house, is all."

Edgar nodded. "That right? He's my... father, I suppose. I told you the house was his."

"I didn't know he was in the attic!"

"He lives up there, rarely goes out. He's *very* old."

The other band members snickered.

Patrick had a sudden pulse of realisation. The moment of recognition from the garden earlier, confirmed with his close encounter upstairs. He'd been too shocked to make the connection before, but the old man in the attic, Bram, and the white-haired man in the portrait with Governor Gulpepper... He shook his head. Surely not. Not *that* old. But they were the same person, he was sure.

"Wait," Ciara said. "There's an old man in the attic?"

Edgar laughed. "Don't sound so shocked. He's got an entire apartment up there. It's not like we keep him in a fucking box or something."

"Your father?" Simone asked.

Edgar paused a moment. "Sort of. The man who made me, shall we say." He smiled at his band mates. "I guess he's responsible for all of us in a way."

"We look after him," Shirley said. "And he lets us have the house."

"It works for everyone," Clarke said.

"Sounds like a good arrangement," Ciara said. "But we've made a lot of noise here and there. We should be more mindful."

"Don't worry about it," Howard said. "The attic is a long way from downstairs. It's a big house. He doesn't care anyway."

Patrick was disarmed. He'd thought to drop a bomb with his revelation but had barely made a ripple. He jumped at a sudden rapping at the front door.

Edgar hopped up. "Company!"

"Expecting guests?" Torsten asked.

"Yeah, few mates coming over. Bit of a party!"

"On a Monday?" Patrick asked and immediately felt stupid.

Everyone laughed, throwing him pitying looks.

"It's always the weekend in rock'n'roll land!" Edgar said, and went to answer the door.

Patrick shook his head, frowning at the laughter of the band and his friends alike. His stomach churned, like the strange bugs he'd eaten had reanimated and were squirming around inside him.

The others all left the kitchen and headed towards the large living room as voices swelled. Several people must have arrived at once. Only Patrick and Ciara remained sitting at the table.

"What's up with you?" she asked.

He stared, lips pressed together. "You really can't see it?"

"See what?"

"This!" He gestured vaguely around himself. "All this. It's fucked up. It's wrong."

"Patrick, you're the one being weird. Like going to bed early, on your own. You used to love a party, I'd have to drag you home."

"These people are messed up, Ciara. They're not good for you."

She frowned, shook her head. It was almost like she pitied him.

"Have you seen yourself?" he asked. "You're so thin, so pale. All three of you are. You all look bad. Unhealthy. They're doing it to you. The band."

"Are you jealous, Pat?"

"What? No! I'm fucking scared, Ciara. This is not right!"

"Youse coming or what?"

They turned to see Edgar hanging off the kitchen doorframe, grinning.

"Yes, coming," Ciara said, standing.

Edgar held Patrick's eye for a moment, then winked, slow and condescending. He turned and left, Ciara close behind. She didn't look back. Patrick sat alone at the table, feeling hollow inside.

The sounds of partying grew as he sat there, seriously considering slipping away. If it wasn't for Ciara, if it was just Torsten and Simone, he would get in the campervan right now and drive away. The urge to do just that was strong. But he couldn't abandon Ciara. He loved her. He wanted to marry her. Somehow, he needed to convince her to see what he saw.

The noise of the party increased. Eventually, Patrick got up and walked around the big house to the front room. He looked in and saw more than twenty people sitting and standing around. The booze was in full flow, people laughed, the music pounded out. "Jesus Saves" he realised, from Slayer's "Reign In Blood" album. Seminal bloody classic.

Simone sat on Clarke's lap, their faces close together. Ciara was standing with a group of three strangers, all laughing at something one of them had said. She held a frosty beer bottle. Edgar caught Patrick's eye and smiled. He gestured, crooking one index finger to invite Patrick in. Patrick scowled, shook his head.

"Let's start early tonight!" Edgar said loudly. "Shots!"

A cheer went up and the lead singer went over to the drinks cabinet. He glanced back, flicked another wink at Patrick. Patrick wanted to beat the fucker within an inch of his life. He wanted to pound on those weirdly blackened eyes, that he was convinced now weren't makeup. Why couldn't the others see it? And he could beat Edgar too, he'd easily smash the skinny musician to a pulp. But it wasn't just the one man. Patrick couldn't fight everyone. He turned and trudged upstairs to hide out in his room again. He planned to stay awake until Ciara came up, whenever that might be, and convince her to leave with him.

Despite his determination, sometime after midnight, the muffled thumps and laughter of the party still in full swing below, he fell asleep.

He stood on that slick, blackened beach and stared out over a turgid sea. Something huge and bright and red boomed in the sky and thick clouds blossomed down, arcing with purple lightning. The creatures began to fall. He turned a circle, saw the beach was entirely surrounded by thick bush. Another sudden split in the sky, out there over the land, bright red like an explosion, and another rain of creatures. Some looked dead already, falling limp and unmoving. Others writhed, some vigorously, some weakly. Surely the fall would kill them? The ones over the ocean might survive if they didn't drown, but these, slamming down into the bush from thousands of feet up, would be smashed to pulp. He squinted into the sudden and drenching icy rain, tried to see what they were, but even in the stark flashes of lightning, they were featureless. Twisted bodies, often too many limbs, tumbling and turning.

He heard scraping sounds behind and spun around, saw those horrible flat, wide lobsters crawling from the surf onto the slimed black sand. Only these were huge, the size of small cars, and their bodies swarmed with hundreds of the small ones, skittering all over their hard carapaces. *Babies*, he thought. *We ate their babies.*

He turned again, nervous of the tall, pale creatures wanting him, but they were nowhere to be seen. Some dream fugue part of his mind suggested they wouldn't come, not yet. Because they weren't asleep yet, they still partied downstairs. But they would come, soon enough. He wanted to run away and started along the beach, looking for a way out. But the bush was thick and unbroken. He reached one end of the beach and the rocks were rough and climbable, but only to a certain point before they became treacherous and led only to another small cove, this one all rock, the ocean crashing against the stone. He stood on a jutting point and bellowed his rage.

No one heard.

In the early hours of Tuesday morning, dawn smudging the sky outside, he was woken by movement. Ciara crawled into bed beside him.

"We need to talk," he said. "Please."

"Later, Pat." Her voice was thick with sleep and booze. She stank of alcohol. And something he couldn't place in his half-awake state.

"Please," he said. "Ciara, it's too important."

She turned onto her side, but reached one hand back, patted his chest. "Okay, but in the morning. I'm so tired."

He sat up, stared at her as her breathing sank instantly into the long, deep cadence of sleep. Maybe he should pick her up while she was passed out, carry her to the campervan and just drive away. Leave everything behind and get out while he still could.

His heart raced at the thought, it was so simple and so perfect.

Soft voices came from the hallway outside. Patrick hopped up, went to the door and opened it a crack to peer out. The four band members came through the door at the far end of the hall. The one that led to the attic where the old man lived. The four of them looked fresh, invigorated even. Did they draw power from the old man somehow? *The man who made me, shall we say*, Edgar had said.

"Let's feed," Edgar said quietly. "See you all in the morning."

Shirley laughed. "Sweet dreams, my brothers."

They each slipped into their own rooms using keys from their pockets. At the last moment, Edgar paused and turned to stare right at Patrick. Patrick gasped, jumped, but Edgar only smiled. He winked again, slowly, then went into his room.

"That's it," Patrick said, closing his door. "That's fucking *it*!"

He dressed and looked at their few belongings. They were backpacking, so travelling light. Mostly clothes and toiletries. He could easily just leave all that behind. He put his phone and wallet into a bumbag he always wore when they travelled across borders. His passport and other important documents were in there. If they lost everything else, this small and ridiculous bag on a belt was all he really needed. Ciara had one too. He searched her side of the bed.

As he looked for her stuff, she moaned and rolled over. Her back arched gently off the mattress and her lips fluttered, almost as though she dreamed of being kissed. Her breath stuttered softly out. Her cheeks seemed to tighten against her skull.

"Fuck it!" Patrick muttered.

Let's feed...

He found Ciara's small leather bumbag half under the bed and quickly checked it. Passport, wallet, phone. All the essentials. He strapped that to himself too, his in front, hers behind. Then he turned to the bed, carefully moved back the covers. She wore only an oversized t-shirt and shorts, but that would have to do. He couldn't hope to dress her.

He slipped his arms underneath and lifted her off the bed, then remembered the closed bedroom door.

"Fuck it!"

He put her down, hurried over and opened the door. Then he remembered the front door downstairs. And the door to the campervan. It had a sliding side door, he could put her in that way, but how would he carry her and open it up. And what about the keys.

A slight sob escaped him. "Think, Patrick!" he told himself. He checked the bumbag and the keys were there. But should he open up all the doors first and then grab Ciara and run?

"What are you doing?"

He gasped, turned back to the bed. Ciara stared at him, frowning. Her eyes were dark as night even though dawn was slowly brightening the room. He was so tired, so confused.

"Ciara, I want to go. I want to go right now."

She furrowed her brow, like she was seeing him for the first time. "Patrick?"

"I'm serious, Ciara. Please. I can't explain, and I'm sure you'll understand more once we get some distance between us and this place. I want to go. We *have* to go."

"Patrick, I'm tired. Too tired."

"Ciara!"

"But okay. Just not right now. It's the middle of the

night."

"It's dawn."

"You know what I mean. And what about Torsten and Simone?"

"I... I don't know."

She patted the bed beside herself. "Rest, yeah? For now. In the morning, the four of us, we'll talk about it."

"I just want to go!"

"All right. But in the morning. We'll tell Torsten and Simone."

"If they won't come, we leave anyway, yeah? Ciara? Please?"

She gave him a crooked half-smile, but her eyes were sad. "Okay, Pat. Okay."

He drew in a ragged breath and came back to the bed. As Ciara lay down again, he unclipped the two bumbags and tucked both safely just under his side of the bed. He didn't think he'd sleep any more, but he was so very tired. He drifted in and out of fitful, restless dozing.

The winter sun was bright through the room when he woke. He jerked up, turned to see Ciara, but her side of the bed was empty. Looking at his watch, it was past noon. How had he slept so long? He got up, headed for the door, then paused. He fetched the two bumbags, put them both on as he had the night before, then zipped up his baggy black hoodie. It covered both well enough.

Downstairs a few stragglers from the previous night's party loitered around on the couches and armchairs. No sign of the band or his friends. He went back upstairs and checked the siblings' room, but it was empty, the bed neatly made. Or not even slept in.

Back downstairs he searched the kitchen and other parts of the house. Nothing. Back in the lounge room he approached the nearest reveller, a small blonde woman with goth makeup wearing a tight, short-skirted dress and Doc Martens.

"Have you seen my friends?"

"I dunno. Who are your friends?"

"What about Edgar? The rest of the band."

"They went out. With that German pair and the hot Irish chick."

"Went out where?"

"I don't fucken know, mate. I'm not a cop."

"What?"

The woman hauled herself up out of the chair and staggered off towards the front door. She let herself out. Patrick turned back to the others in the room and they were all getting up, some casting suspicious glances his way.

"Do any of you know where the band went?" Patrick asked. "Or my friends? Ciara, Torsten and Simone?"

"What are you, their fucken dad?" one tall, long-haired young dude asked. He laughed and left the house.

The others followed and in moments Patrick stood alone in the lounge room, surrounded by the litter of the night before. Bottles and glasses, ashtrays with spliff butts, someone's shoes. Who had left without their shoes?

Patrick turned a slow circle. Alone in the house. His gaze drifted upwards. Well, not entirely alone...

The man who made me, shall we say.

Patrick began to tremble as thoughts that had been orbiting his mind at a distance began to coalesce. He remembered one of his favourite films, *The Lost Boys*. Grandpa, right at the end, casually taking a drink from the refrigerator. *One thing about living in Santa Carla I never could stomach: all the damn vampires.*

Blind Eye Moon weren't vampires, not exactly, but they were something similar, weren't they? A week ago, Patrick would have scoffed at the idea, but the things he'd seen the last few days, the realisations he'd made. And they protected that old man upstairs.

The man who made me, shall we say.

Patrick could end all this, if that old man did hold the key to the power the band wielded. Ciara had said she'd talk in the morning with Torsten and Simone and they would leave. So where was she? She'd gone out with the band instead. Didn't even wake him to invite him along. She'd said they would talk. She didn't mean it, or didn't remember. Either way, Edgar and his friends had a hold over her.

Patrick realised he was already heading towards the stairs. He stopped and went to the kitchen instead. He took the biggest carving knife from the wooden block by the stove and returned to the stairs, went up and headed along the hallway. His hand shook as it fell on the door handle but he clenched his teeth and pushed on. It was insane, but he had made a decision. Everything about this was insane. Even the fact that a band as good as Blind Eye Moon would play shitbox gigs like Monkton. From the moment they had struck those first chords, they had been putting spells on Patrick and his friends. But he saw through them. And he had a way out.

He mounted the narrow staircase leading up to the attic, breathing hard through his nose. Though his hands shook, his grip on the knife was unbreakable. The attic was lit from the large window at the end, the old man a collection of sticks under the covers of his bed. Bram, Patrick remembered. Edgar had called him Bram. Patrick braced himself, crept forward. He didn't know what kind of strength to expect, but thought if he moved fast enough, it wouldn't be an issue.

He was halfway across the large space when the old man stirred, turned to sit up. "Edgar? That you, boy?"

Bram was skeletally thin, long white hair in greasy tails around his skull-like head. His eyes were dark pools, those same black filament capillaries lost in the wrinkles of his cadaver-pale skin. His eyes were bloodshot, the pupils clouded over, but red like the band. In his shock before, Patrick hadn't taken much in, beyond that flash of recognition. Now he saw it was indeed the man from the portrait, but so much older. He'd seemed elderly in the painting, now he was ancient.

Bram squinted as the covers fell from his bony shoulders. He wore stripy pyjamas. As Patrick got within a few metres, Bram said, "You again?"

The old man's eyes widened and he hissed, opening his mouth wide to reveal half a dozen blackened teeth in red and bleeding gums. He lifted clawed hands up like he was about to cast a spell even as he surged from the bed with unnatural speed and agility. Patrick felt a harsh dragging on his chest. He remembered the dream when the creature had seemed to draw something out of him. He imagined the band drawing from his friends like that every night.

Let's feed.

His breath left him and his vision blurred at the edges, like he was about to pass out. Bram continued to hiss, striding towards him, eyes flickering with red light like a fire burned in them.

Patrick hauled the knife up and it *thunked* into the old man's toast rack chest as the distance between them closed. Bram coughed and wailed a high, thin sound. The sensation of drag eased so suddenly that Patrick nearly fell. He drove forward, pushed the old man back onto the bed. He pulled the knife out and slammed it down again. And again. Something warm spattered his face and the bed clothes blossomed with red stains. Bram's pyjama top was soaked, the blood dark crimson, and he collapsed back.

The thin, keening wail faded and the old man lay still, head tipped back, red eyes staring sightlessly at the headboard. His mouth remained open in a silent scream.

Patrick staggered back, leaving the knife sticking up from Bram's chest. He looked at his hands, saw them soaked in blood. "I did it!" he laughed, a thrill rushing through him. "I fucking did it!"

He staggered through the curtain into the old man's bathroom and turned the taps on, washed his hands in the sink. A small mirror hung from the sloping roof above and he saw a scarlet spray of freckles across his face, even over his lips. He gagged and washed his face, again and again. Eventually he felt clean and thought for a moment he might vomit but swallowed it down.

Had Edgar and his friends just crumbled to dust out there in The Gulp, wherever they'd gone? Or had they lost their powers and aged in an instant. Were they older than they looked or not? Edgar had said something about them being around a long time. Patrick grinned. What did it matter? He had destroyed the man who made them. He needed to find his friends. They'd listen now, and they could leave.

He went back into his room thinking about how much other stuff he could take and decided to let his friends decide. They could pack if they wanted, or simply go. He had the most important stuff for himself and Ciara.

He went downstairs, headed for the kitchen and fixed himself a feed. An hour later he began to wonder if he should go out and look for Ciara, but The Gulp was a fairly big town. He could easily miss her. She would have to come back to the Manor at some point. If Edgar and the others had come to some horrible grief when old Bram had died, perhaps Ciara, Torsten and Simone had run into problems. If only their damn phones worked in this gods forsaken corner of Australia. Then again, Ciara's phone was in the bag at his waist.

What if he was too late? What if Edgar had taken his friends somewhere and done away with them?

The days were short and it began to get dark a little after five. Patrick was beside himself with nerves, alone in the big house for hours, mind churning with possibilities. Just before six he heard voices outside. He jumped up and ran into the hall as the front door opened. The first person he saw was Edgar, looking hale and hearty. Behind him were his bandmates, and Ciara, and Torsten and Simone. His girlfriend and the Germans all looked thinner and paler than ever. He was reminded of his uncle, who had died from cancer in his fifties. The poor bastard had looked like Ciara looked now only days before his death. Patrick suddenly wished he still had the knife.

"We have to leave, right now!" he said.

Ciara frowned at him, again with the pitying look. Edgar half-smiled. "What have you done, Patrick?"

Patrick stood trembling as the group came into the hallway and Howard closed the front door.

"Where have you all been?" Patrick managed at last.

"Just into town, showing these guys around," Shirley said.

"We saw the museum," Ciara said. "Patrick, what is wrong with you?"

Edgar began to chuckle, shaking his head. He turned slightly, looked up the stairs, then back at Patrick. "You fucken killed him?"

Shirley, Howard and Clarke all seemed to still a moment, eyes turning up, then they looked back at Patrick too, all smiling. They were all healthy, all completely unbothered.

"Killed?" Ciara said, looking from Patrick to Edgar and back again. "Killed who?"

"You killed Bram?" Edgar said with a laugh. "Wow, fuck me dead, you mad bastard!"

"Fuck you!" Patrick shouted. "Ciara, we have to go!"

"The fuck is wrong with you, dude?" Edgar said, still laughing. "You murdered an old man!"

Patrick shook his head, felt tears sting his eyes.

"He was so old," Shirley said. "Too old to even feed any more. Couldn't hold himself together in the dreams, but he was happy up there."

"He liked his books," Clarke said. "You fucking dickhead. What did you think that would achieve?"

"Patrick, did you really?" Ciara asked. Her face showed her dismay, despite her obvious weakness.

How was Patrick the bad guy in all this? He didn't understand. What should he do? "Ciara, please, leave with me now! Torsten, Simone, you too, yeah?"

"Your friends are feeding us well, every night," Edgar said. "There's a bit left in them still. A few more nightmares."

"You see!" Patrick said, triumph in his tone. But Ciara didn't react, like she hadn't even heard what Edgar had said.

"Hey, we can finally convert the attic in to a practice space," Howard said. "No more rehearsals in the cold garage."

Edgar laughed. "Good point."

Patrick snapped. He ran over, grabbed Ciara's arm and tried to drag her back to the front door. He had the bumbags, all they needed.

She cried out, managed to shake him off, though she staggered with the effort. "Get off me, Pat! What is wrong with you?"

"Ciara, please, I love you. It's not safe here!"

She shook her head, those pitying eyes again. "You're so weak. Why did you have to be weak about this?"

"What?"

"What they give us, Patrick. You could have it too."

He was incredulous. "They're not giving you *anything*. They're taking *everything* from you. Didn't you hear him? There's a bit left in them still, he just said. A few more nightmares. They're going to kill you soon."

"Oh, Pat. I really wish you'd been stronger about this." She stepped back from him, reached out and Howard took her hand. "I'm staying. For the same reason as Simone."

"What?" He felt numb, and stupid, saying the same word over and over.

"I'm fucking Howard, Patrick. He's *good*! You go to bed early like a child every night and Howard is still here. And Torsten is with Shirley. It's worked out really well. For us anyway. We're staying, Pat."

"Ciara!" His stomach roared, bile rose in his throat. "I want to marry you! I was going to ask you, after... When we got back home."

She laughed and leaned into Howard. "It's too late, Pat."

"Too late for them," Edgar said. "But remember what I told you? Sometimes The Gulp spits one out, mate."

"You're going to die!" Patrick shouted, staring hard at Ciara, trying to make her understand. "And you two are as well!" he said to Torsten and Simone. "Any day now, you'll be dead and these fucking freaks, these monsters, they'll probably bring other people home from their next gig. Fuck them and feed on them too."

Edgar grinned, nodded enthusiastically. Ciara, Torsten and Simone seemed oblivious, just stared blankly back at him like he was speaking a language they couldn't understand.

Patrick choked back a sob. He took off Ciara's bag and threw it at her, and then he ran. He pushed out the front door, scrabbling in the bag still at his waist as he went for the campervan keys. He climbed in and it started on the first try. The tyres skidded on the gravel, then he was driving hard down the hill, away from the Manor. He turned left, past the bright white and green Woolworths supermarket, and onto the dark and straight Gulpepper Road.

What the hell would he tell people? That he and Ciara had a fight? They broke up? He last saw her in Monkton with their German friends after a gig? He knew damn well there was no point in trying to tell anything like the truth. No point in trying to send authorities into Gulpepper.

His vision blurred with tears as he drove. He reached the T-junction and turned right towards Enden. He sobbed, gripped the wheel hard, and didn't dare look in the mirror again, planning to drive all night.

48 To Go

48 To Go

Blind Eye Moon pounded from a JBL Bluetooth speaker as Dace Claringbold guided the small boat through darkness close to shore. He threw a grin at Sasha in the passenger chair beside him, feeling good. She smiled back, long brown hair streaming in the wind, nodding subtly with the music.

"Hey, wanna stop for a spliff?" Dace said, loud enough to be heard over the music and the wind.

"Stop?"

"Sure. It's relaxing out here, especially at night. No one around. We're about halfway to Enden, the whole trip takes less than forty minutes. Got plenty of time."

She shrugged. "Sure, why not? Didn't know you had any weed."

"I've always got weed."

He hoped that was cool in Sasha's eyes, not lame. Her smile stayed put, so he figured she was into it. He throttled off until they were drifting, then killed the engine. The large outboard dropped into silence and Blind Eye Moon was suddenly beltingly loud as they bobbed gently in the night. He grabbed his phone from beside the wheel and tapped it down a few notches. Still loud, but not so much they'd have to shout over it. BEM needed to be loud, after all. He couldn't wait for the gig later that night. The spring evening was mild and clear, not yet the close heat of summer, but warm enough so they were comfortable in t-shirts.

He swivelled in the driver's seat to better face her and pulled out the leather pouch he kept his tobacco, papers, and weed in, and began to roll one up.

"I can't believe you have this sweet boat," Sasha said.

I can't believe you finally agreed to go out with me, after I told you this was mine, Dace thought, but didn't say it. It wasn't his, after all. But he would get laid before admitting that. He had the use of it whenever he needed, one of the perks of the job, so it amounted to pretty much the same thing.

"Almost brand new Quintrex 530 Cruiseabout," he said instead. "Got an upgraded 115 horse power Evinrude Etec on the back there. Not too shabby." He grinned and licked the oversized cigarette paper, stuck it down. He turned the joint and lit it, took a big draw and held it in.

"You have to deliver something before the gig, you said?"

Dace blew out a plume of smoke towards the stars and nodded. He took another draw, then handed Sasha the joint. This was fine weed. He blew out again, then said, "We'll be met at the wharf in Enden. Once we've given over the box we can head into town. Easy as. Get a couple of drinks in before the gig, yeah?"

"Sounds good." She coughed slightly, grinned sheepishly, but took another toke. "What's in the box?"

Dace waved a hand. "It's just work stuff."

"On a Friday night?"

"Yep."

He wasn't about to tell her any more than that and she seemed happy to let it go. Preferable all around, really. At least until he knew her better. He thought about leaning in for a kiss but didn't want to push things too fast. The boat moved slightly with the current and they were turned to face the cliffs. Tumbled sandstone, striped like cake, led up to thick bush on top. As the weed kicked in, they both leaned back in their seats, mellowed with it. The myriad stars above the silhouetted gum trees made for a stunning outlook, the wide sweep of the Milky Way a river of distant diamonds.

Dace took the joint back from Sasha. Something in the bush high above them moved. He paused, halfway through inhaling, and watched as a dark shadow rose briefly higher than the treetops. It was curved, lumpy. It reminded him of a whale breaching the surface of the ocean, that slick curve of massive beast briefly rising then sinking away. Except this was on a cliff top. And the trees had to be at least ten metres high up there, maybe more.

"You see that?"

Sasha looked at him. "See what?"

He pointed with the spliff. "Watch, up there. Dead ahead of us. Something huge moved in the bush."

Sasha frowned. "You're stoned, man."

"Yeah, that's true. But I definitely saw something."

They both stared at the high vegetation, passing the joint back and forth. But saw nothing more.

"I definitely saw something," Dace said at last, annoyed.

Sasha laughed softly. "I believe it. There is weird shit in the bush around here. Wouldn't get me in there for quids. I stay on the road every time, and never stop the car."

"I hear that."

"Better yet, we do this. Going by boat to Enden is way smarter."

"No chance of some kingshit cop in town trying to RBT you either."

"You heard the McFarland story?" Sasha asked.

Dace laughed. "Everyone knows the McFarlands. Weird fuckers."

"Weird even by Gulp standards, yeah. But you know the story about their land?"

"I guess not. What about it?"

"They have over a hundred acres out on the Gulp Road, yeah? South side. Theirs is the last property before it's thick bush all the way to the Enden-Monkton Road."

Dace took the joint. It was getting short, hot. "Yeah."

"One of the earliest farms, cleared and settled by John McFarland's great-great-grandad. It's been there over a hundred years, ticking along. So back before the McFarland kids were born, John McFarland inherited the farm from his dad. He'd always said they should expand, but his dad said no way. My dad and John McFarland are mates, right, which is how I know all this. Now apparently, McFarland wanted to clear more land, but *his* dad always said they should never disturb what was out there, beyond the creek." Sasha smacked her lips. "My mouth is dry as Gandhi's sandal. Got a drink?"

Dace handed her a plastic water bottle he had in a cup holder by the steering wheel. He always came prepared. He was enjoying her stoned rambling. "What's out beyond the creek?" he asked.

Sasha gulped some water down. "That's better. I'm getting to that. Now, John McFarland would have been about twenty-five or so, his dad died young and he inherited the farm young. Gung ho, is what my dad called him. He decided fuck what the old man said, he was going to strip out a few more acres past the creek.

"So this creek runs right along the far side of the McFarland back paddock, marking the boundary of their land on that side. John McFarland decided to take down the fencing on his side of the creek, drop a couple of cement culverts in to make bridges, and then start clearing bush the other side.

"He had some help with him, a local teenage pair, brothers from one of the families in town. They were fifteen or sixteen, something like that, earning pittance bucks for back-breaking work on the farm. He still does that to this day, hires teenagers, pays them next to fuck all. Anyway, they get out there and start stripping down the fencing and one of these teenagers goes over to the creek and says, 'The water is black.'"

"The water is black?" Dace echoed.

"That's what he said. 'What do you mean, black?' John McFarland asked him, and the kid says, 'The water is black, like oil.' All this my dad told me. Apparently,

McFarland got drunk one night at Clooney's and told him the story.

"So this kid puts his hands in the creek and cups them together to get some water. Sure enough, it's black. Not like oil, McFarland said, but dark like a glass of stout. 'Probably just peat or coal or something in the ground hereabouts,' McFarland says to the boy. 'Stop fucking about, there's work to do.' Apparently the kid shrugged and said, 'Well, I'm thirsty,' and drank what was cupped in his hands."

"So this won't end well," Dace said with a grin.

"Does anything in this fucked up town? The kid screamed in agony and collapsed to the ground. Began gibbering and rolling his eyes. They all freaked out, and McFarland rushed him home. He settled down a bit on the way, but the kid has never been the same. All his teeth fell out and his skin went white, like fucking chalk. You'll have seen him around town, right? Everything about him is long and weird and floppy, he always wears overalls with that massive baggy jumper underneath, even in the height of summer."

Dace frowned, nodded. "Yeah, I know who you mean. That's how he got that way?"

"Fucked up his mind too, he's not all there, so they say. I wouldn't know, I won't go near the freak."

"This is a wind up, right?" Dace said, grinning.

Sasha shook her head. "Nah. Unless my dad was winding *me* up. He told me it was all true, John McFarland got drunk that night and spilled it. Says he still feels guilty for how that kid got fucked up. I mean, he's a grown man now, must be around forty or something, but he *is* fucked up."

"Did he ever extend the land?"

Sasha laughed. "Nope. Said he went back the next day and put all the fence back up. Said no way he wanted that creek on his land, it could stay in the bush. And that's not even counting for whatever his dad said was out there *beyond* the creek."

They nodded along to Blind Eye Moon for a moment. Dace thought maybe he didn't want to consider too deeply what lay beyond the McFarland's creek. Or what he might have seen up on the cliff top.

"No sudden moves, you two!" snapped a gruff voice somewhere behind them.

Dace spun his chair around to see another boat not five metres from theirs. Two men were in it, one at the wheel, the other standing on the prow pointing a shotgun at him. Both wore balaclavas concealing their whole face except the eyes. They must have cut their engine and coasted in under cover of the music.

"What the fuck?" Dace said.

"Who are they?" Sasha asked, eyes wide.

"Turn that shit off," said the man with the gun. "Slow and easy as, yeah?"

Dace nodded, reaching cautiously for his phone. Blind Eye Moon stopped mid-riff and the night was heavy with silence but for the slap of low waves against the hulls of the boats.

"Give it to us then," the man with the gun said.

Dace swallowed, stomach cold, legs shaking. He was glad he was sitting down. He felt as though his bladder would let go any moment. This was bad. Really bad. "What do you mean?"

"Don't fuck with me, son!" the gunman said.

Son? Dace was thirty-four next year and the guy pointing a shotgun at him didn't look old. What did that matter? His mind was rambling.

"Give us the fucken shipment!" the man yelled.

"Jesus, Dace, whatever it is, just give it to them!" Sasha said.

"Whatever it is?" the other boat driver said, his voice strangely high. Then he laughed. "You don't know what your boyfriend here is doing?"

"He's not my–"

"Just give us Carter's weed, you fucking loser," the gunman said.

Sasha turned a shocked expression to Dace. "*Carter's* fucking weed?" she exclaimed. "You idiot, why do you have anything to do with that guy?"

The gunman laughed, loud and deep. "S'a good fucken question, dickhead! But don't answer it now. The stuff, quickly."

"Fuck fuck fuck," Dace muttered, trying desperately to think of a way out.

The shotgun boomed into the air and he flinched. Sasha screamed and dropped to the floor behind the dash and low windscreen, curled up tight.

"All right, all right!" Dace shouted. He moved to the back and pulled out a 30-litre plastic storage tub with a clip-on lid. It was lined with newspaper, concealing the contents. But Dace knew it held around seven and half kilos of high-quality bud, grown on Carter's farm above the south side of The Gulp.

"Just put it on the front," the gunman said, gesturing.

Dace hefted the tub over the windscreen, shoved it forward. The driver of the other boat started his motor and nudged in. The one with the shotgun hopped over and grabbed the tub, the shotgun held one-handed, but trained on them the whole time. If he fired it like that, Dace thought, he was liable to lose it from the recoil. But he'd still have fired it and no way would a shotgun miss at this range.

"Can't believe you made it so easy for us," the gunman said. "We were going to run you down before you got to Enden, then here you are floating about like a pair of complete fuckwits." He dropped the tub into his boat and jumped down behind it, the shotgun still aimed right at Dace.

The driver lifted a hand in a wave as he gunned the motor. "Don't you fucken follow us," he said. "You let this end here and no one gets hurt."

No way does this end here, Dace thought. He had to go back and tell Carter he'd lost the shipment. Carter would kill him. He needed something, some clue to give over so they might make this right.

But before he could say or do more, the other driver carved a tight turn, spraying Dace as he roared away, back towards The Gulp. There wasn't a single identifying mark on the boat, the whole thing plain white with a Yamaha outboard like a hundred others. He might recognise it again, but it was entirely likely he wouldn't.

They bobbed in the wake of the thieves and Dace stared, dumbfounded. Then he tipped his head back and yelled, "FUCK!" at the indifferent stars.

Sasha got up from the floor of the boat, looking daggers at him. "You can take me the fuck home right now."

Dace nodded and sat down on the driver's seat, started the engine. He had to go right back to Carter anyway. No way he could put off telling the man. He pointed the boat back towards The Gulp wondering what the hell he was going to say when he got there.

Twenty minutes later he tied up at Carter's point on the harbour. Sasha hopped straight off the boat, glared down at him.

"I was looking forward to the gig tonight," she said. "Thought you'd be fun to hang out with."

"I would be. Still can if Carter doesn't kill me." The dick wants what the dick wants, he thought to himself.

Sasha shook her head. "No way, man. I'm having nothing to do with anyone connected to Carter. You're fucking mental to think it's worth dealing with that psycho."

"You were happy to come out with me in his boat."

"I thought it was your boat, you fucking moron."

Dace stopped, stood up to yell at her. "Yeah, so you only looked twice at me when you thought I had money, that it?"

Her mouth fell open. "I thought maybe you wouldn't be after *my* money, you cunt. Half the blokes 'round here see a girl with a job and expect to mooch off her. I thought maybe you wouldn't be like that."

"Well, I'm not. I've got my own money."

She laughed and shook her head. "Nah, you take Carter's money. That's entirely different. Anyway, best of luck. I'll keep my eye open for the 'Have You Seen Dace' posters to start going up."

She turned away and stalked off before he could reply. He hoped to hell she wasn't right. He needed to get in the car and up to Carter's place right away. Come clean and figure out a way to make it right. He wouldn't say the bit about stopping for a joint and getting snuck up on. Those arseholes had said they intended to run him down. And they had a shotgun. That's the story he'd tell Carter.

Once he was sure the boat was secure, he walked across the small car park to his battered old Mitsubishi and climbed in. It started first time, something it never usually did. Dace decided to look on that as a good omen.

He drove south out of town, up the hill where the houses got a little bigger and spaced further apart. He passed the industrial area where big aluminium sheds housed mechanics, a metal machine shop, half a dozen other blue-collar industries, then he turned onto a narrow road with a *No Through Road* sign at the start. A couple of larger properties had their drives left and right, then the road climbed even steeper, switching back on itself, and became a dirt track. Carter's battered post box stood on a weathered wooden post beside a cattle grid, his name stencilled on the side. Dace's hands shook as he gripped the wheel and pointed the car up the track. It doubled back on itself a couple times as it rose through thin bush, The Gulp falling away behind. Then it levelled off onto a natural geological shelf that housed the Carter property. Some two hundred acres, if he recalled correctly, cleared and farmed right when The Gulp was first settled, before it even had its name. Ostensibly a cattle farm, Carter kept cows and horses, but made his money in variety of other ways.

As Dace drove through the night towards the house, his mouth became dry. He'd left the water bottle on the boat and lamented that oversight. Then he shook his head. He'd worked for Carter for more than ten years, they knew each other well. As well as anyone could know Carter anyway. He would explain, the man would give him a glass of water, they'd figure it out.

He parked behind Carter's Toyota Hilux and sat in the quiet car for a moment, gathering himself. Then he took a deep breath and climbed out. Carter stood on the veranda, hands on his hips.

"Trouble tonight, hey?"

Dace jumped, not expecting the man to be there. How did he always seem to know stuff? "Yeah. I'm sorry, Mr Carter, it's not good."

"In you come, son."

Dace followed Carter inside and into the large kitchen. Chrissy sat at the kitchen bench, sipping a drink. It looked like a gin and tonic. She smiled and nodded at Dace.

"Hey, how are you?" he said.

"I'm good. You wanna talk privately, Daddy?"

Carter kissed her soft and long on the lips, then nodded. "You don't need to worry about this."

She stood and strolled off towards the lounge. Dace heard the TV click on.

"You want a drink, Dace?"

He turned to Carter, determined to be chill. "Sure, got a beer?"

Carter pulled a couple of bottles from the fridge, opened both and handed one to Dace. "So what happened? You should be in Enden by now, and I should have had a call about a successful transfer of merchandise."

Of course, that's how he knew stuff. Dace turning

up here, no call from the contact. "I was robbed, Mr Carter."

"Fucken robbed?"

"Yes, sir. They must have known and followed me. About halfway to Enden they ran around me in their boat and held me up. With a fucking shotgun! Two of 'em and one yelled, 'Give me the fucken shipment!' They knew what I had."

"So you gave it to them?"

"Yeah, they were gonna shoot me, Mr Carter. They both wore balaclavas, but they were white, I saw their hands and eyes. Both men, I guess about middle-age, the guy with the gun had a beer gut, the boat driver was kinda skinny. It was a plain white boat, no name or numbers, with a Yamaha outboard."

Carter drew a long breath in through his nose, lips pursed. He wore jeans and a collared shirt, his black hair slicked back like always. His cold blue eyes were hard, unblinking. He sipped beer. "You gave it to them," he said again.

"Y-yes."

"You really think they'd have shot you?"

Dace hadn't considered this angle. "I do, yeah. I mean, out there, middle of nowhere. They could have killed me, sunk your boat, nothing would ever be found, right?"

"You've been thinking about this, have you?"

"Thought about nothing else all the way here. I'm really sorry, Mr Carter, I don't know what to say. What to do. I want to make this right."

"Who was with you?"

Dace paused, licked his lips. He took a sip of beer to buy himself another moment. Carter would know if he lied. Carter always knew. "Sasha. Just this chick I was planning to... you know. I invited her to a gig in Enden tonight. Once the delivery was made, we were going to see Blind Eye Moon, head back home afterwards."

"You made it easy for them."

Dace's heart raced. "What?"

"Distracted by a fucking woman!" Carter yelled, and Dace flinched back.

"I wasn't distracted! I–"

"They snuck up on you, don't lie to me, shitcunt. If you'd been on your own, actually motoring towards Enden, and they tried to run you down, you could have run. You could have *tried* to not get caught. But they sailed right up and caught you without even fucking trying!"

How did he *know* this stuff? "Mr Carter, I–"

Carter held up one forefinger and it silenced Dace immediately. "What's done is done, Dace. You're a fucking idiot, but what's done is done."

Dace took a long breath, nodded, lips pressed together. He knew when to hold his tongue.

"A long time you've been with me, eh?"

"Yes, Mr Carter."

"So I'm going to be generous."

Relief began to seep through Dace. He nodded. "Thank you."

"That shipment was worth, give or take, about eighty grand on the street. My contact paid me a flat sixty for it. So here's my generous offer. You have forty-eight hours to pay me back the sixty grand I will have to return to my buyer."

Dace's stomach turned to ice. "Sixty grand?"

"I will also have to smooth things over with the buyer, all that extra hassle. But like I said, we go back, you and I. So I'm generously only holding you accountable for the actual monetary loss."

"Mr Carter, I don't have sixty grand!"

Carter's eyes didn't soften at all. He sipped beer again. "Isn't that unfortunate. You were going to earn five hundred bucks for tonight's delivery, so let's say you owe me fifty-nine thousand five hundred."

"I don't have it! I have, like, eight hundred bucks in the bank. My rent is due on Monday."

Carter smiled, lifted his shoulders. "How is any of that my concern?" He walked past Dace and took the half-finished beer from his hand, stood both bottles on the counter where Chrissy had been sitting. Then he carried on, towards the front door.

"Mr Carter, please. I just don't have that kind of money."

Carter opened the front door, then looked at his watch. It was gold, with diamonds around the face that glittered in the soft light of the hallway. Dace thought that watch alone was probably worth sixty grand.

"It's just before nine," Carter said. "You have until 9pm Sunday night to bring me my money."

Dace stared. Carter smiled, like he didn't have a care in the world. Dace wanted to ask what would happen if he didn't make the deadline, but he knew already. People often went missing around The Gulp, and often the gossip led back to Carter. Maybe he could just run away.

"I would remind you," Carter said amiably, "that I know your parents well, and where they live on the north side of town. And your sister visits often, even though she lives in Sydney now. Something to keep in mind."

If you run, I'll kill your family. The message was clear. Dace nodded. Carter gestured out the door. Dace left. The door clicked shut behind him and Dace's body was wracked with tremors. Holding back tears of panic, he went to his car and drove slowly away. Sixty grand in forty-eight hours? How the hell was he supposed to manage that?

As he drove, he went through a mental check list of everyone he knew and how much money they had. His parents were okay, but retired now. They had a pension, but nothing much in savings. His sister worked for a media company in Sydney, and no doubt had money put away, but probably not much. And there was no way she'd give it to him anyway. They were civil these days, but after a falling out in their early twenties, they were distant. Maybe if it really came down to the wire, he could ask, but he doubted she had anything like sixty grand in savings. Every other friend he could think of was like him. Scraping by or on some kind of benefits. After all, sixty grand was the kind of money that could get a person out of The Gulp, so why would anyone still here have that kind of cash?

His mind switched gears. Where could he steal that sort of money? Hold up the drive-through bottle shop around the back of Clooney's? Well, no, that would be mental. For one, they probably had nothing like that much to hand. For two, it was part of Clooney's and the pub belonged to Chrissy, which meant it was really Carter's. That whole daughter-lover thing they had going on was creepy as fuck, but everyone ignored it or gossiped about it privately. Either way, it meant he'd be stealing from Carter.

He drove back into town, heading towards the harbour. Nine o'clock on Friday night. Being part of Carter's retinue meant he usually drank at Clooney's, but he knew a couple of mates were planning to go to The Vic this weekend. Maybe he should drop into The Gulp's other pub and talk to them. His head was spinning and he needed help. Just someone to talk it out with.

He parked by the Victorian Hotel, sat in the car gathering himself for a moment, then headed in. It was heaving, music on the jukebox blaring, people talking and laughing. He saw Justin and Ahmed right away, beers in hand chatting to each other. He got himself a cold one and went over to them.

"I thought you were going to a gig in Enden," Ahmed said as all three clinked glasses in greeting.

"Yeah, kinda fell through."

They made small talk for a while, Dace's mind spinning with disconnected thoughts. If he could raise sixty grand in two days, he'd have done it before, that much was obvious. So the only way to do it was to take risks he would never have entertained before. But what risks?

"Hey guys, answer me a riddle," he said when their conversation lulled. "Say you need a lot of money in a very short time. How would get it?"

Justin and Ahmed both narrowed their eyes.

"In trouble with the boss?" Justin asked.

They both knew he worked for Carter. They both knew Carter's reputation. Everyone in The Gulp did. They also stayed well clear of the man. Justin worked in his dad's accountants office and Ahmed was a mechanic. "Nah, just a hypothetical," Dace said.

"Take out a loan," Justin said.

"What if there was no time for that, like it was a weekend and you needed money fast. And couldn't afford a loan anyway. I'm talking about a real chunk of change. Say fifty grand."

Ahmed whistled. "If I could raise fifty grand I'd be long gone."

The echo of his own thoughts made Dace nervous all over again. "Me too. But for the sake of argument..."

Justin laughed, shook his head. "There's no legitimate way to make fifty grand fast short of luck. Like a lottery ticket or something."

"Right."

Justin frowned. "So you'd have to fucking steal it or something, dickhead."

"Or you could, you know," Ahmed said, nodding past Dace.

He turned to see the Stinson brothers walk in and head out into the enclosed courtyard, where they always spent their evenings. Craig, the younger sibling, was stocky, shorter than his brother, William by a few inches. Both well-muscled, lean and mean-looking. Both with straight brown hair cut short and sharp chins. They ran all kinds of rackets around The Gulp, hardcore bastards according to some, petty criminals according to

Carter. But the rivalry between the Stinsons and Carter was well-known.

"What do you mean?" Dace asked.

Ahmed raised an eyebrow. "Use your noggin, mate. They fucking hate Carter. If you owe Carter fifty grand – and that is a deep well of shit, by the way – maybe you can offer them something. Tell them something for the money, maybe, or give them shit to use against Carter."

Dace shook his head, waved one finger. "For one thing, I didn't say I owe Carter fifty grand. For another, it would be suicide to deal with those two! What do you think I would have to give them for that kind of money, and how would that ever help me?"

"Guess you're fucked then," Ahmed said. "You'll have to think of somewhere that holds that sort of cash and rob them. You any good at bank heists? The banks are open Saturday mornings."

"Jesus fuck, you're worse than useless."

Ahmed shrugged, Justin laughed. Dace's stomach curdled.

"What about the Nikolovs?" Justin said after a while.

"The who?"

"Nah, that's a band. The Nikolovs."

Dace sighed. "Mate, you're going to have to be more forthcoming."

Ahmed nodded. "Yeah, what the fuck are you on about?"

Justin took a swig of beer, then said, "Okay, this must be one of The Gulp legends that's slipped by both of you. Honestly, I'm a little disappointed. Anyway, the Nikolovs are this weird ass old Macedonian couple here in town. Proper eccentric nutters. But rich eccentric nutters. Rumour has it they don't trust banks and sit on a fortune in cash they keep at home. Thousands under the mattress kinda thing."

Dace grimaced. "Yeah, but this town is full of bullshit rumours."

"I reckon this one's true though."

"Why?"

"Lots of little things, but here's an example. When I was going out with Tracy Briggs, her dad's a plumber, yeah. She told me about how he had to install a new hot water heater outside their place. While he was at it, he had to replace a bunch of pipes in the back yard to cope with their roof runoff or something. Anyway, the bill ended up being nearly three grand. Old man Nikolov asks Briggs how much, and Briggs writes up the invoice, expecting a bank transfer or something in a few days like normal. Except Nikolov looks at the bill, tells him to wait and goes inside. He comes back a few minutes later with the full amount in cash."

"That is a bit strange," Dace said quietly.

"We hear stuff at the accountancy office too," Justin went on. "I don't give much of a fuck, but Dad keeps an ear to the ground. He said they've never used a bank in town, never used any of the local area accountants for their taxes or anything like that. Dad's convinced they're loaded and hoarding cash."

"Why are they so eccentric anyway?" Ahmed asked. "I mean, not using banks doesn't make someone a complete weirdo."

Justin laughed. "That's barely the surface of it. You know that house halfway up Tanning Street with all the guinea pigs in cages all around the front yard."

Ahmed frowned and shook his head, but Dace said, "Yeah, I've seen that place. That is fucking strange."

Justin smiled and nodded. "That's them. Old man Nikolov is sometimes in Woollies, but all he ever buys is milk, white bread, and tinned sardines. He apparently has a deal with one of the farmers out on the Gulp Road for bales of hay once a month or so. To feed all the fucking guinea pigs, I expect."

Dace's mind began to race. He knew the house Justin was talking about. An old couple sitting on a pile of cash. It might not be sixty grand, but it might be a good start towards it. Maybe enough to show good will and buy more time with Carter. And he could go tonight, just an hour or two to plan. But he needed to change the subject. No one would have overheard them in the busy pub, but even his two mates thinking too hard on it was risky.

"Robbing a weird old Macedonian couple," he said, shaking his head. "I'm glad you two aren't in any crime syndicate. Honestly. Another beer?"

They grinned and raised almost empty glasses, and Dace went for another round. After taking his time with that one, he said, "Well, the gig tonight was a blow out, and much as I love your company, gents, I think I might take an early night."

"On a Friday?" Ahmed asked.

"It's been a long week. And I can't really afford to get drunk, so no point staying here."

Justin looked at his phone. "It's only ten."

Forty-seven to go, Dace thought, but kept his expression as neutral as he could. "I'll see you guys later."

Outside, the spring night was warm and fragrant. The salt of the ocean and sweet, cloying night pollens filled the air. Several people were about, a short queue at the noodle shop a few doors down grabbing a last-minute feed. The place stayed open until ten on Fridays and Saturdays. Times like this The Gulp seemed almost normal, not such a bad place to live. Usually. Right now, Dace felt as though he stood on a precipice, his toes over the edge and the rock beneath his heels beginning to crack and crumble.

"Fuck," he spat softly, and got in his car to drive home and prepare.

Forty-five minutes later he was beginning to buzz with a combination of stress and adrenaline. Underlying it all was a building fatigue. It wasn't yet eleven pm, but he felt as though it were the early hours of the morning and he'd been out all night. He stood in the lounge of his small one-bedroom flat on Kurrajong Street and stared at the stuff laid out on the sofa. Leather gloves, thin for driving, which had been a gift from his grandmother years before and were still tagged together as they had been in whatever shop she bought them from. He'd never imagined using them, but also never thrown them out. He was thankful for that now. Next to them lay a rubber Freddy Kruger mask that went right over his head and neck with a skirt of rubber to tuck into a shirt or jumper. It was part of a Halloween costume from a couple of years before. He had no balaclava like the arseholes who'd robbed him, so this was the best anonymity he could manage. Once he'd decided on that, he felt like keeping the theme, so next to the mask was a baggy red and green striped jumper. The Freddy mask had come with an oversized glove with plastic finger blades, so he'd asked his mother to knit the jumper for him. He'd shown her stills from the movie and she had been thoroughly horrified, but like any good mother, she'd indulged him. The jumper was exactly like the one in the film, right down to the ragged neck and cuffs. The combination of mask, glove and sweater with a pair of dark brown cargo pants with big pockets and black work boots was perfect for Halloween. The pants and boots sat on the sofa too, but the Freddie blades would stay home in favour of the driving gloves.

"One, two, Freddie's coming for you," Dace muttered, and a slightly deranged giggle escaped. "Three, four, hope you haven't locked your door."

He had no idea how to break into houses. If they'd left the back door unlocked and he could sneak in while they slept, he would be happy.

Beside his outfit – disguise? – was a large carving knife from his kitchen. It terrified him to look at it. He'd done some less than savoury things for Carter over the years, but nothing explicitly violent. Carter preferred a personal hands-on approach to any violence that needed doling out, thankfully. Dace had once joined in with a beating, but even then he'd only thrown in a couple of half-arsed punches while Carter and Stephen did the large proportion of the work. But if the Nikolovs weren't asleep, or if he woke them, he would need something to enforce his authority. And he might need to wake them and force them to tell him where the money was, but he hoped not. With any luck, waving the knife around would be as violent as he needed to get.

He also had a small Maglight torch, one of the six-inch models, and he'd put fresh batteries in it. Perfect for snooping around quietly in a house at night. The last item was a plain black backpack. He hoped to fill it with the cash the Nikolovs apparently had stashed away, but he could also take other stuff if there wasn't enough money. If they had laptops or something, maybe he could sell them at the pub on Saturday night. He'd be hard pressed to raise sixty grand with stolen household items, but desperation drove his thinking.

"They've got the money," he said to himself, willing it to be true. "They've got more than I need stashed somewhere, and I'll sneak in while they're asleep, I'll find it without waking them, and I'll sneak out again. Easy as."

He swallowed down a rill of panic, nodded to himself. Let that be true. He changed into the Freddie outfit, cut the tag from the driver's gloves and slipped them on. They were good quality, thin leather like a second skin, and fitted well. He put the mask, torch and kitchen knife into the backpack and sat on the sofa. His phone said 11.15pm. How long should he wait? An old eccentric couple were likely to be early to bed, early to rise sort of people, right? 1am, he decided. He'd leave at 1am and be back by 2 with all his problems solved.

He turned on the TV, poured a generous shot of Wild Turkey to steady his nerves, and stared at Friday night bullshit programming while he waited.

At 12.20 nervous energy drove him up from the couch. He didn't dare drink any more, and he could wait no longer. It was only about a five-minute walk to the end of Kurrajong Street where it met Tanning at a T-junction. About another five minutes south along Tanning would take him to the house with the guinea pigs in the yard. The spring night was cooling but he didn't need the sweater. It also occurred to him that he would look obvious in it if anyone drove by and saw him. He pulled it off and stuffed it into the backpack, then peeled off the gloves and put them in his hip pocket. He'd put it all back on, and the mask, when he got to the house.

What the hell was he doing? For a moment, he nearly bolted back inside. Then Carter's voice echoed through his thoughts again. *I know your parents well, and where they live on the north side of town. And your sister visits often, even though she lives in Sydney now. Something to keep in mind.*

He couldn't be responsible for the death of his whole family. The idea had floated through a couple of times in the hours since Carter's ultimatum. Once or twice he'd thought maybe he could live with it. His parents were in their late 60s, retired. Not old by any means, but not young. His sister was a pain in the arse most of the time. But then he would quickly shake off the thought. He loved them, even his fucking sister if he was honest. He couldn't let them die, much less be responsible for their deaths. He had to at least try to save them.

With the bag slung over one shoulder, he set off along Kurrajong, downhill towards the junction. He crossed the road before he passed The Vic at the end, kept his head down and hurried right onto Tanning and walked quickly up hill, past the medical centre, past Carlton Beach on the other side of the road. A group of four people stood in the park behind Carlton Beach, not far from the play area. An old man, a middle-aged man and woman, and a young girl he recognised from Woollies. Strange bunch to be there so late at night, he thought. They all looked pale in the light of the moon, standing still, staring out at the ocean. But Dace was too distracted to think much on it and kept walking.

He crossed onto the east side of Tanning Street as he passed St Augustine's Primary. He didn't remember exactly where the guinea pig house was, only that it was somewhere between the school and the Ocean Blue Motel.

Most of the houses were single storey, 60s and 70s homes like his parents' house on the north side of town. Some weatherboard, some brick, most with metal roofs. He glanced into each low-walled front yard, looking for the stacks of chicken wire cages. He heard the whiffling and caught a scent of hay right before he came to the place. Cages three deep along both wooden side fences and up against the brick house. A single storey row sat along the front garden wall, brick only a metre or so high that had been plastered over, but the whitewashed plaster was crumbling away in places. The house was run down, certainly not the sort of place a rich person would inhabit. But it did look like the sort of place that might belong to people who hoarded their money. The window frames were painted pale yellow, but the paint was peeling. The corrugated steel roof had more patches of rust than clear metal. Half a hay bale sat on the scrubby grass in the centre of the small front yard. Guinea pigs by the dozen scratched and whistled plaintively in the cages.

Dace ducked back and saw that the house next door, entirely clean and well-maintained, had a large frangipani tree in their front yard, casting a pool of shadow. He hopped over their wall and scurried into that darkness and crouched down, heart beating hard. For a couple of minutes, he watched the footpath and the street, kept glancing back at the house behind him. Nothing. No one about, not even cars passing.

He took a deep, shuddering breath, then blew it out slowly, his cheeks filling. "All right, Dace. You got this. Let's go."

He pulled out the Freddie sweater and put it on, then the thin leather gloves. He slipped the kitchen knife into the large thigh pocket of his cargoes, careful to wedge the point into one corner so it didn't stick his leg, and put the torch into his hip pocket. Then he put the backpack on properly over both shoulders and took another deep breath as he held the rubber mask in both hands.

"You got this," he said again, and pulled the mask over his head. It was well-detailed with all Freddie's burn scars. He tucked the skirt of it into the ragged neck of the sweater. It smelled of rubber and old sweat, rough and a little tacky on the inside. The fit was fairly good, lining up well with his eyes, but he still lost at least fifty per cent of his peripheral vision. His breath was suddenly hot and close, despite the small mouth hole.

He checked the road out front again, making sure there were no cars or pedestrians, then hopped over the wall to the footpath and immediately ran along two metres and jumped back over Nikolov's wall. There was a path down the side of the house, deep in shadow, and he hurried into it. As soon as the darkness covered him, he slowed to a creep, heart racing. Committed to the course of action now, he tried not to think. When he got to their back yard, four times the size of the small patch out front, he paused in surprise.

There were more cages here, dozens of them, row upon row like supermarket shelves, cages stacked four deep. They were all weathered wood and half-rusted wire, had obviously been here for years. They were as packed with guinea pigs as the ones out front, there had to be hundreds of the small rodents, all kinds of size and colour. Most were still or sleeping, but some scuffled and nosed around. Another hay bale sat in one corner of the yard, and a large wooden shed filled the far back corner, its door slightly ajar.

Dace looked long and hard at the shed and wondered if maybe the Nikolovs would keep their money hidden in there. It would make things so much easier. He stayed in the shadows of the rows of cages and crept up to the shed. The last third or so of the garden, it turned out, was given over to vegie beds. He saw carrots and parsley and tomatoes and a variety of other things growing there. He slipped into the shed and stood in darkness, holding his breath, listening. Nothing except the scratching and whistling of the guinea pigs outside.

He took the Maglight from his pocket and twisted it on. The shed was crammed with tools for gardening, sacks and barrels of food. Some had vegetables no doubt harvested from the garden outside. A couple had pale brown cylindrical pellets, presumably a kind of feed for the animals. He dug an arm into each, carefully feeling around in case anything had been concealed under the food. Nothing. The shed smelled earthy and rich, paradoxically both enticing and slightly sickening. It only took a few minutes of searching to learn there was nothing for him there. He sighed, twisted off the Maglight, and moved cautiously back outside.

In moments he was standing on a cement step by the Nikolovs' back door. Before he could second guess himself, he reached out and turned the doorknob. The door popped open with a soft scrape.

Dace jumped, hands up front of his chest as the door stood three inches open. He froze there, amazed it had been unlocked after all. Old school, he thought. Again, no sound but the animals behind him, so he pushed the door open a little wider. Just enough to slip through, then he closed it silently, twisted on his torch again.

He stood in a kitchen. Black and white vinyl flooring. Ancient Formica counters and table, the latter surrounded by three rickety wooden chairs. An electric cooker, shelves of crockery, drawers and cupboards under the counters. A bread bin and several storage jars stood against the wall on the counter beside the cooker, and an old Crosley Shelvador refrigerator filled one corner, all rounded edges and large chromed handle. The chrome had gone matt and grey. It whirred noisily.

But all that paled as his torchlight lit up a wooden rack against the far wall. The rack had dozens of little bodies hung on it. Guinea pigs, skinned and clearly roasted, all four limbs stretched out into a star on small metal braces presumably crafted for the purpose. Dace held his breath in disgust. There was a tub of thick metal wire pieces, a pair of pliers with orange rubber grips, a couple of half-finished frames, the metal twisted expertly together.

On the counter beside the rack was a plastic tub full of guinea pig corpses, pink and raw where they'd been skinned but not yet cooked. Piled beside the tub were twenty or so more dead animals, these still with their fur, half of them looking like they were simply sleeping there. A large plastic bin stood on the other side of the rack, a plastic liner in it and a rank smell rising up as Dace approached. He leaned over and gagged as the sight of animal guts half filling the bin.

"What the fuck?" he whispered. They bred the things to cook and then dry them out? Did they live on nothing but guinea pig meat and jerky? Maybe a few of the vegies they didn't feed to the animals first? If the number they kept in their garden didn't seal the eccentric label, this sight certainly did. He thought they had a crazy passion for pets, but this? Dace swallowed, desperate to be out of the place as quickly as possible.

"Okay," he said under his breath, barely louder than an exhalation. He got right to work, checked every cupboard, drawer and vessel he could find, even looked in the oven and fridge. In the fridge he found some butter and milk, but more disturbing were dozens of small bottles of dark, purplish liquid. Each only about

50ml, every one had a label with a number, dates from the next day onwards. Future doses of something? Did one or other of the old couple need this medicine? There had to be fifty doses crammed onto the top shelf, maybe more.

On the lower shelves were plastic tubs, some containing young octopuses of a strange colour, with purple and yellow markings. He'd never seen any quite like them before. Other tubs contained muddy-coloured, feathery fronds. They appeared fleshy. Dace stared, trying to remember where he'd seen such things before. Then it came to him. The bit of the local Gulpepper Bug people said was poisonous. You had to make sure to remove them before cooking the Bug, but Dace would never know. He'd never eat one. The thought of them always gave him the creeps, but some locals loved them. He shook his head and closed the fridge. It wasn't money, so it didn't matter.

He was tempted to fish around under the rodent guts in the bin, but surely that wasn't necessary. It took a good ten minutes, but he exhausted every possibility and hadn't found a cent. Not really a surprise, he supposed. Time to move on.

One door led from the kitchen and he approached it cautiously, shining his Maglight ahead. The beam illuminated a room with polished wooden floorboards, a threadbare rug under a coffee table, a TV on a wooden cabinet beside a bookshelf crammed with paperbacks. A window with the curtains closed, a kind of roll-top dresser beside it. That was promising, the kind of place people might stash their money. A long, tatty sofa, black plastic faux-leather back and arms with rough textured orange seat cushions. Dace stepped into the room and shone his light around further. An armchair that matched the sofa, a plate on the wide plastic arm, piled with tiny bones, sucked clean. An old woman sat in the armchair in the dark, staring at him, the whites of her eyes huge in fear.

Dace sucked in a shocked breath as the woman's mouth fell open, a toothless, wet O in the saggy, wrinkled skin of her emaciated face. Even covered by a blanket, feet raised on a leather ottoman, she was clearly skeletally thin, grey hair in wispy tufts on her pale, patchy head.

For a moment Dace stood frozen, then the woman screamed. Splittingly loud, an ululating wail like an air-raid siren. Dace tensed, danced foot to foot in panic. "No, stop! Quiet! Please, I won't hurt you!" He realised his face, his mask, would be terrifying to her, the burn-scarred Freddie Kruger visage.

The scream seemed endless. A man's voice, thick with sleep, from down the hall. "Elena? Dreams again?" He had a heavy accent.

"Stop, please!" Dace said, approaching the woman, one hand palm out, the other causing torchlight to dance hectically over her wailing face.

And the scream went on. She didn't pause for breath, how could she scream continuously, so loud?

"Elena, enough. I'm coming, I'm coming!"

"Please!" Dace said, almost crying with the horror of it. "Stop it! Stop that noise!"

It got, impossibly, louder.

"No!" Dace shouted and struck out with his free hand to slap her cheek, desperate to stop that scream from drilling into his brain.

The woman's face whipped to one side and a loud *snap* stopped the scream dead. She stilled, her head on her shoulder at an angle that made Dace's stomach clench. No neck should allow that. No unbroken neck. Her wide, white eyes with pale grey irises stared ahead, seeing nothing.

"No no no!" Dace said breathlessly, looking around himself. He'd hardly touched her, it wasn't a hard slap at all. Barely a tap.

Footsteps behind him. He grabbed the knife from his thigh pocket and spun around. An old man, tall and thin, iron grey hair in disarray, stood there. He wore blue and white striped pyjamas, his face hard, eyes narrowed.

"You hurt her," he said. Not a question, an accusation.

"I didn't mean to!"

Dace took a step back, the knife held in front of his chest, pointing at the old man, but he made space. Nikolov approached his wife, crouched before the armchair. Tears rolled over his high cheekbones, into his hollow cheeks.

"Elena," he said plaintively. "Elena." He turned, looked up at Dace with haunted eyes. "Why?"

"I'm so sorry! It was an accident!" Dace's mind raced. He couldn't be responsible, it would be even more trouble. "A heart attack," he said, voice desperate. "I surprised her? It must have been a shock!"

Nikolov stared, mouth half open, lips as wet as his cheeks. He shook his head. "I saw you hit her."

Dace's heart rushed, hammered in his ears. "Fuck fuck fuck." He brandished the knife. "Okay, sorry about this, but get up. Get away from her."

"You want to rob us, yes?" Nikolov said. He rose slowly, grimacing, one hand to his lower back.

These two were ancient, they had to be in their nineties at least. Dace licked his lips, dry-mouthed despite the sweaty confines of the rubber. His breath was hotter than ever. "Over there." He pointed at the sofa with the knife. "Over there, come on. Sit down."

Nikolov complied, without taking his eyes from Dace. He sat on the centre cushion of the three, back straight, hands on his knees. Dace moved to the door and turned on the light, put away his torch, then stood staring at the old man. His hand shook holding the knife, his knees knocked. What the fuck was he supposed to do now? Think. Think!

The woman was dead, that was done. Couldn't be changed. He needed Carter's money, that was still his priority. Old man Nikolov had no idea who Dace was. Get the money, leave the old man to call the police. They never came to The Gulp quickly, if they ever came at all. He'd be away and gone, he'd burn the Freddie costume, or maybe put it in the bag with a load of rocks and take it out in Carter's boat, drop it far out to sea where it would never be found. Just get the money and get out. Easy as.

Fuck.

"Yes," he said, trying to make his voice strong. "I want to rob you."

"Good luck. We have nothing."

"Bullshit!" Dace shouted. "Everyone knows you have money. This... this fucking guinea pig bullshit circus, the fuck are you even doing here?" He was ranting, rambling. Panicking. He killed that old woman. Was that murder? It was an accident. But no, he'd hit her. "You've got money!" he said again. "Where is it? Give me the money and I'll be gone. Simple."

"No money." Nikolov's face was hard, expressionless. But his eyes burned. The lower lids were loose, wet and red, but his gaze was iron.

Dace stepped closer, waved the knife under the old man's wattled chin. "The fucking money!"

Nikolov lifted his chin, exposed his throat, like a dare.

"Don't fucking move!" Dace said.

He searched the room, starting with the roll-top desk. Every few seconds he glanced back at Nikolov, but the old man sat stock still. Dace rummaged everywhere, found nothing. He saw a jacket hanging on a hook on the door and went to it, found the old man's wallet. Inside was $240 in fifties and twenties. He pocketed it with a sob of disappointment. Next to nothing compared to the sixty K he needed.

"Where is it?" he yelled, rounding on Nikolov.

The old man sat still, staring.

He would have to tie the bastard up and search the

rest of the house. Or could he convince the man to tell him? He might search for hours and find nothing. He might miss it. But this fucker knew where his money was. Dace's mind flicked back to the kitchen. The guinea pigs on their little metal stretchers. The pile of wire pieces. He was all in now, the old woman's corpse was proof of that.

"Don't move!"

He ducked around the door, grabbed the pliers. Nikolov's eyes widened slightly at the sight of his tool in Dace's hand.

"We have nothing," Nikolov said. His voice was steady, but was there a trace of fear under it now? "You should go. Just go now."

"Can't do that. I'm in a world of grief and your money is my only way out."

"No money."

"Bullshit."

Dace grimaced. These people were virtually cadavers already, eating roast fucking guinea pigs, living in a house where no single item of décor was less than thirty years old. Maybe the old man was scared because he was telling the truth. Maybe they really had nothing. But he had to be sure. Because he had no other ideas if this one didn't work.

He sucked in a deep breath, blinked, his eyes gritty with tiredness. Then he moved towards Nikolov. The old man shifted back in alarm. Dace crouched, put the knife on the ground beside him and grabbed one scrawny ankle. The man's bare foot was long and thin, the bones standing up in ridges to his knobbly toes, the nails thick and yellowed.

"No!" Nikolov said.

"Where's the money?"

"No money."

"Bullshit!"

Dace opened the pliers and put the toothed metal grips over and under Nikolov's pinkie toe. The man struggled, stronger than Dace had expected, but no match for him. Dace squeezed, enough to whiten the skin, and Nikolov stilled. "Where's the money?"

"No money!"

Dace blew out an exasperated breath. Fuck it. He gripped the plier handles hard. Nikolov howled as his toe burst, the bone crunched, blood spurted from under the nail, then the nail skidded sideways and came away. The pliers slipped off and Nikolov stamped his free foot up and down, gasping and sobbing with pain. Blood sprayed, Dace heard some spatter against the rubber face of his mask. His breath was short and shallow, furnace hot in the confines. It felt tight against the back of his head, thick and heavy around his neck and over his shoulders.

Nikolov stilled, his chest heaving, a *huh huh huh* of pain and shock punctuating his breath.

Dace sat back on his heels, looked at the old man. Nikolov stared back.

"Just tell me where your money is," Dace said. "I'll take it and be gone, and all this will be over."

"Nema da zemeš ništo od mene," Nikolov said through clenched teeth.

"What? What the fuck did you say?"

"Kopile!"

Dace frowned. He thought maybe he understood that from the delivery alone. "Speak English, old man. And in English, tell me where the fucking money is! I don't want to do this." He swallowed bile, refusing to look at the stark white bone sticking sideways from Nikolov's rent flesh.

"Then don't! Just go!"

"I need the money, man! You can't understand how badly I need the money. My whole family!"

Nikolov stuck out one bony arm, one long finger trembling as it pointed at Elena. "And what about my family?" The strength of his anger was surprising.

"I'm sorry, that wasn't supposed to happen." Dace

gestured at Nikolov's foot. "This wasn't supposed to happen. Any of this. But here we are."

A surprising amount of blood still pulsed from Nikolov's little toe. Dace didn't want to do it again, but he would. He was committed now. If the man truly believed Dace wouldn't stop until he had the money, Nikolov would tell him where it was. But he couldn't bear to look at that mangled toe. He grabbed the other foot.

"Ne Ne Ne!" Nikolov said, thrashing harder this time. He leaned forward and rained blows with his bony fists and forearms onto Dace's head. They were incredibly strong strikes, the mask slipped and shifted on his sweat, the eyeholes moving down, blinding him. Nikolov kicked his leg, hammered at Dace, even kicked at him with his other foot, heedless of his ruined toe.

Dace didn't let go of the skinny ankle, thrashed blindly above his head with his other hand, still gripping the heavy metal pliers. He struck into something, maybe a hand, and Nikolov yelped. Dace rose onto his knees and swung his arm forward, felt a sudden and jarring impact, a crunch, a grunt from Nikolov, then the old man stopped fighting.

Dace shifted the mask back into place, looked up to see Nikolov sat back on the sofa, eyes swimming a little, blood flooding from his crushed nose. It sluiced over his mouth, stained blackly into his pyjama jacket.

Nikolov blinked, brought his attention back to Dace. Dace gripped the old man's uninjured pinkie toe in the pliers. "Where's the money!"

"No... fucking... money..." Nikolov panted. Hate emanated from his gaze like steam.

Dace gripped hard, the toe crunched, blood sprayed.

Nikolov yelled, a formless roar of pain and anger as he sat bolt upright. Dace hoped desperately none of this was loud enough to alert any neighbours. Nikolov leaned forward, gasped quick, short breaths. His eyes widened, he clamped a hand against his chest. His already pale face went grey, his lips blue. He shuddered. His breath hitched, like he had something stuck in his throat. Dace stared. What the fuck?

Nikolov tipped forward and sideways and thumped onto the floor.

Dace jumped up, dropped the pliers and stumbled back. "Oh, fuck, no!"

Nikolov lay on his side, eyes as wide and staring as his wife's. And equally devoid of life.

Dace turned a slow circle. "Fuck fuck fuck fuck fuck!" He staggered back further and sat against the roll-top desk, leaned forward, hands on his knees. He gasped for breath, dizzy, like he might pass out at any moment. He'd killed them both. He forced himself to suck in long, deep breaths. His face was slick with sweat, so hot in the damned mask. But they were dead! He grabbed it by the top and pulled it off. It slid away and cool air flooded over his skin. His vision widened to take in all the murder he'd done, but his head cooled and his breath came easier.

"Okay, this is fucked, but it is what it is." What did that even mean? It meant he had to search the rest of the house, that's what. Simple.

The house was long and narrow. He saw the front door dead ahead, the frosted glass in it glowing orange from a street lamp outside. A short hallway led from the front door to the lounge where he stood, and that led back to the kitchen. Either side of the hallway were four doors, two on each side. Three bedrooms and a bathroom, he presumed. The first stood open, from where the old man had emerged.

Dace walked to it and looked in. He couldn't see much. He felt around the walls until he found the light switch. The room was simply furnished. A wooden double bed, a dresser with a variety of creams and brushes, a tallboy with six drawers, and an old-fashioned freestanding wardrobe with arched doors, mirrors on each. He went to the dresser and searched it, and the two drawers underneath. No money. He pulled every drawer from the tallboy and upended each one. Nikolov's clothes fell out, but no money.

The wardrobe was crammed with dresses and coats, he felt in all the pockets. He crouched and moved aside a variety of shoes. There was a shoe box shoved right to the back. His heart fluttered. He pulled it out and sat on the floor, put the box on his lap. He opened it and saw bundles of cash.

"Yes!"

It was all fifties and twenties, little wads held together with pale tan elastic bands. He started counting it. He hadn't got far before he knew it wasn't going to be enough. After a couple of minutes he sat staring at the notes on the carpet. Eleven thousand, six hundred bucks. Shit, that was a lot of money, but not even a quarter of what he needed. Though it was something. Would it be enough to buy him more time from Carter? Could he give Carter ten grand and beg for longer to get the rest? Maybe. But was it worth two lives? And did he dare take the risk that Carter would be mollified by less than a quarter of what he was owed?

Dace frowned, shook his head. No way. Definitely no way Carter would accept anything less than what he'd asked for. But if old man Nikolov had eleven grand stashed in the bottom of the wardrobe, he would surely have more stashed elsewhere, right? He needed to keep looking. He put the money he'd found in his backpack, slung it back on, and stood up.

Directly across the hall was a bathroom and Dace checked in there. The medicine cabinet, a laundry basket, he even took the lid off the cistern. Nothing. He stepped back out into the hall, pausing for a moment, dizzy with fatigue.

"Daddy?"

Dace's heart thumped.

"Hello? Daddy?"

The voice was female, plaintive and nervous. Then a light tapping from the other door on the same side as Nikolov's bedroom. Dace saw it had a sliding bolt on it, locked closed. On the outside. Locking someone in.

"What the fuck?" he breathed.

Pictures hung on the wall between the two rooms. Old, faded black and whites, they showed a handsome young couple, no doubt Nikolov and Elena. Several shots, different locations, but just the two of them. There had been no photos in the lounge that he recalled. Just the two of them lived here, he had thought. Daddy?

"Don't be angry, Daddy, but are you there?" *Tap tap tap.* "Is everything okay?"

No, Dace thought. Everything is most definitely not okay. He had eleven thousand, six hundred in his pack. Maybe he should quit while he was ahead, just leave, try somewhere else for the rest. He looked at the locked door. Nikolov and Elena wouldn't be letting her out any time soon, that was certain. She might starve to death in there. But what the hell was he supposed to do with her? Maybe just let her out and run? But he needed more money and he was *sure* Nikolov had more hidden somewhere. Maybe she would know.

He went to the door and slid the bolt open. He sensed the person on the other side still themselves. He turned the handle and gently pushed the door in. A young girl stood there, maybe fifteen or sixteen, wearing a long, white cotton nightdress, barefoot. Her hair was sandy brown and straight, long to her waist. She smiled widely, too wide, guileless. Her eyes were a little too open, shifting hectically as she looked him over with strange intensity. As Dace realised with a pulse of adrenaline that he hadn't put his mask back on first, she said, "Hello! Are you a friend of Mummy and Daddy? What was all the noise about? I like your jumper."

"Who are you?" Dace asked.

The room beyond her was less than simple. It was

empty but for a single bed mattress on the floor, a ratty, stained doona piled on top of it and a thin pillow. Everything else was bare walls and floorboards. The light was off and Dace saw the fitting had no shade or bulb.

"I'm Baby."

"Your name is Baby?"

"That's what Daddy calls me."

How could that ancient old relic out there – *dead now, you killed him!* – possibly have fathered this teenager? Even if he could, the woman was certainly decades past child-bearing age.

"The Nikolovs are your parents?"

"They are now. They have been for... well, for such a long time. I remember... others... a different Mummy and Daddy... sometimes... when I'm sleeping. Maybe a *before* family? Daddy says it's nightmares, that's all. I'm always so confused, but I take my medicine like Daddy asks."

Dace stared, horrified. Was this simple-minded child kidnapped and brainwashed? Why? Her pupils were large, he noticed, even in the brightness of the hall light he'd turned on. She was drugged, obviously. He remembered all the bottles in the fridge. "What do you do here?" he asked, and it sounded like a stupid question.

"Do? Nothing. Try to please Daddy. Mummy sometimes sings to me. They give me the medicine, insist I sleep enough. I have to be... ready, yes. Daddy says I have to be ready."

"For what?"

"I don't know!" She giggled like a child a fraction of her age and turned a slow circle on the balls of her feet, arms out to the sides. "I like it in the between times. I feel tingly!"

"Between times?"

She stopped and turned to look at him, head tipped to one side. "Between my medicines. When my head tingles and my body feels... stronger."

"Why do you need the medicine?"

"Daddy says it's so I sleep properly. And sleep is how I get ready. I have to watch it every time." Her voice turned both stern and singsong. "Don't look away, Baby! Watch it closely, let it in!"

"Watch what?"

She smiled. "The fall, silly. When the sky splits, dark red like blood, and the broken things tumble down. Look into the abyss, Daddy says. Look and let it in. It prepares me, he says. Daddy's drugs make my dreams so much clearer. I feel the... the abyss, he calls it. I feel... beyond." She burst out a tiny bubble of giggles again and started turning circles.

When the sky splits and the broken things tumble down. Dace had vague memories of a dream like that from time to time. What the fuck was this poor kid on about?

"You need anything right now?" he asked.

"Not really. Are you going to lock the door again?"

He licked his lips, concerned. He couldn't let her out, not yet at least. "Just for a while."

"I'm hungry."

She was so thin under the billowing nightdress. "Wait there."

He closed the door and slid the bolt then hurried back to the kitchen. He grabbed two of the roasted guinea pigs off the rack and took them back to her. Her eyes widened when he opened the door and she saw them. He paused, held them back a moment.

"I have a question for you first, okay?"

She nodded, not taking her eyes from the tiny, cooked bodies.

"Where does your Daddy keep his money? Do you know?"

"Daddy's money is running out. Not much left, I heard him telling Mummy. I hear more than they realise through my door, when the medicine isn't so new inside me."

"Running out?"

"He said so. Sometime... before. I don't know... time." She frowned, looked down a moment, then back at the food. "But the other girls will be taken soon. The ready girls. Money!" She giggled. "It's all so strange."

"The ready girls?" Fatigue pulled on Dace's mind and, combined with the horrors of the night so far, and the bizarre situation before him, it was all becoming too much.

"Daddy says there's no need to worry. Money comes when the girls provide. And two are ready now!"

"Ready for what?"

"I don't know!" She sighed and giggled at the same time. "But Daddy told Mummy more money soon. He said so last time he came back down."

"Back down?"

Baby pointed at the ceiling of the hallway. Dace turned and saw the access hatch to the attic. The attic! He hadn't thought of checking in there. Maybe that's where the bigger stash of cash was.

"Thank you!" he said and handed her the two roast rodents.

She snatched them from him and sat directly on the floor. She dropped one into her lap and expertly pulled the metal cross wire out of the other. She dropped the little frame and bit into the animal, crunching up the tiny bones along with the meagre meat.

Dace grimaced and slowly closed the door. As he slid the lock back into place he heard her biting and chewing, a soft noise of desperate appreciation in her throat as she ate. He turned again and looked up at the attic hatch. How to get up there? He went back into the lounge, planning to head through to the kitchen, but paused at the sight of the Nikolovs, pale and still in death. He'd killed them both!

He dragged the coffee table off the rug, which he noticed had caught most of the blood from Nikolov's toes. He pushed Nikolov straight and rolled him up in the rug, then half-carried, half-dragged it to the old man's bedroom. He dumped the corpse alongside the bed, then went back and picked up Elena. She couldn't weigh more than forty kilos, he thought, like a loose bag of bones. He didn't look as her head flopped back off her neck. He put her on the bed and quickly left, closing the door. There was a bit of blood left on the floorboards and sprayed over the surface of the coffee table, but that was all. Otherwise no evidence of the double murder. More importantly, he didn't have to look at the victims of his crimes any more.

He went into the kitchen and took one of the chairs from the table, carried it back to the hallway. Standing on it, he was just able to reach the high ceiling and unlatch the attic door. A folding ladder was tucked up inside, a rope swinging down as the door opened. He hopped off the chair and moved it, then pulled the ladder down. It rattled open and sat against the hallway runner rug.

"Please keep your money up here!" he said softly as he climbed. If he could find what he needed, he'd take it and run. Leave Baby where she was. Then tomorrow he'd make an anonymous call to the cops, say he'd heard terrible noises from this address. Let them find everything once he was long gone.

The attic was pitch dark. He felt around the edges of the hatch and sure enough his thinly gloved fingers found a plastic switch casing. He flicked it on. A bare bulb in the apex of the rafters flooded everything in harsh yellow light. Dace began to shake from head to toes.

Along both long sides were shelves of books and papers, a desk with a reading lamp, a filing cabinet. In the centre, evenly spaced, were four long, low tables, made of dark wood. The short legs of the tables were carved into twisted and disconcerting shapes, like bodily organs piled atop one another. The tabletops had similar looping, twisting designs around their thick edges, and on two of the four tables was a body.

Two young girls, of an age with Baby locked downstairs, similar in appearance. Naked, their skin so white it seemed made of chalk, and looked dry as paper. They were emaciated, hip bones poking up higher than their hollow stomachs, their ribs made rippled ridges on both sides. There were things written on their too-white skin.

He climbed into the attic and cautiously approached the two girls. The designs on them were almost identical. Strange symbols, some that looked almost like writing, but no language he'd ever seen before. The positioning seemed to match the girls anatomy in some way he couldn't quite put his finger on. If he looked too hard at any one design, nausea began to stir in his gut. The sight of desiccated, preserved corpses made him feel sick, but he realised with some dismay the effect of the things drawn on them made his nausea deeper. The designs seemed to push against his eyes, make his head swim.

He leaned a little closer. No. Not drawn. Cut into their alabaster skin with expert strokes of what must be the finest scalpel. And then something had been pressed or rubbed into the written wounds, to blacken them. Maybe a kind of ink. Bile rose as he looked, and he turned his face away.

"Fuck me dead," Dace whispered, stepping away from the bodies.

Were these two the ones Nikolov had declared ready? And Baby next in line? How were they not rotting?

This was how the old man made his money? *Money comes when the girls provide. And two are ready now!* Dace swallowed. Was the eleven grand he'd found all Nikolov had left until these two were... what? Sold? Who the fuck bought bodies done like this? And why?

But no. Maybe downstairs was just a store of ready

cash. There had to be more, and this was the obvious place to keep it, Nikolov's hideous attic study or laboratory or whatever the fuck it was. Dace started searching.

It took more than an hour, doing all he could to ignore the bodies behind him. Two teenage girls, murdered after who knew how long trapped in that room downstairs. Another there being tortured and medicated now. How many before them? Where did he get them? They were somebody's children.

He stopped thinking about it, kept looking. He found a large jar of black ink, presumably what the old man used to stain the wounds in the bodies of the girls. There was a small label on the jar, a stylised design of an octopus drawn, perhaps, with the ink the jar contained. Dace glanced back at the girls, the black designs on them, imagined underwater denizens off the coast of The Gulp. He saw the sky, open and red, creatures tumbling. He rocked on his feet, staggered a little, and gasped. He put down the ink, blinked hard a few times. He was so tired.

Keep looking.

He found nothing. Not a single dollar.

All the paperwork was in Macedonian, or some other language like the designs on the girls. Some of the books on the shelves were clearly very old, leatherbound, their pages thin, almost translucent parchment of some kind. In some the ink was a deep brown, almost red. He stopped looking too closely, just shook all the books out in case money was stashed inside. Some fell apart as he did so. By the time he'd finished it looked like a hurricane had blown through the attic.

Close to tears with tiredness and need, he clambered back down. No sound came from Baby's room. His stomach clenched. He realised he was starving. As he went back through to the kitchen, he saw the pale pink of dawn smudging the windows.

So hungry.

He looked at the guinea pigs, roasted and stretched out on their rack, and shuddered. He wasn't that hungry yet. He searched the kitchen and found half a loaf of Wonder White bread. He opened it, sniffed. It seemed fresh. Then again, this stuff never seemed to go off. He grabbed several slices, forced himself to go slowly and ate them dry, one after another. He'd devoured almost the entire half-loaf before he felt as though he'd had enough. He put his head under the tap of the kitchen sink and drank water. He felt better. Still dog-tired, but clearer headed. He went into the lounge room and sat down on the couch, as far from where Nikolov had died as he could get.

What the hell to do? He was fast running out of time. His eyes grew heavy. He began to doze off then jerked awake, adrenaline coursing through him again. There was a room he hadn't checked. The one opposite Baby's room, the third bedroom. Distracted by the attic, he hadn't been in there.

He ran to it and opened the door, images of piles of cash swimming through his mind in the worst case ever of wishful thinking. He pictured Scrooge McDuck diving into a pile of gold, doing backstrokes through it.

Inside were piles of plywood sheeting, power tools, a toolbox and another box full of screws and nails. Leaning against one wall were two long, rectangular wooden boxes, neatly made. They looked like simple coffins. But they were more than that, of course. Delivery cases for the girls upstairs who were ready now.

Dace sagged. "Fuck!"

Had Baby overheard more? Would she know a way to contact whoever bought the girls once they were ready? What the hell was such a thing worth anyway? He was sure the poor girl had no idea beyond what she'd already said, but he had to ask. His options were running out. If she didn't know, maybe he needed to take the eleven grand and go, come up with a new plan. His time was nearly a quarter gone already.

He slid the bolt and opened Baby's door. She lay on her back on the floor, blood all around her head, the wire from the roast guinea pig jammed deep into her eye. Her mouth was open, the other eye staring blankly at the bulbless light fitting.

"Oh, for fuck's sake!" Dace wailed. His knees knocked and he sank down onto them before he could fall on his face in a dead faint. He sank his head into his hands and sobbed, the dam finally bursting. Crying he fell over onto his side and gave in for a while to all his despair. After some time, he drifted into a restless, fitful sleep.

He dreamed of the sky opening red, of thunder and roiling clouds, of things falling.

Something drilled into his sleep, dragged him awake. Dace sat up gasping, he couldn't sleep! He didn't have time. He noticed the window of the room was boarded up, covered with the same plywood used to make the boxes.

The telephone was ringing.

He stood, staggered out into the hallway and saw sunshine streaming through the frosted glass of the front door. How long had he slept? He went through into the lounge, looked at a clock on the wall. It said 1.20pm. He'd slept for hours.

"Shit shit shit!"

The telephone rang on, but he couldn't find it. Following the sound, he finally tracked it to the kitchen wall, an old plastic landline with black rubber buttons. As he reached it, it stopped ringing.

What was he planning to do anyway? Answer it?

He jumped when it rang again. He stared at it for three rings, then snatched up the receiver. In his best impersonation of Nikolov's Macedonian accent he said, "Yes, hello?"

"Mr Nikolov?" A man's voice, a little gravelly.

"Yes."

"You didn't answer the first time."

"I vas... in ze garden, feeding ze animals. Sorry, old and slow." Dace grimaced. He was hamming the accent up far too much.

"Well, I'm sorry to bother you. I'm calling on behalf of Mrs Ingrid Blumenthal. Just checking that all is ready for the order we placed?"

Dace licked his lips, grinned. "Yes, yes. All ready."

"Good. Well, we'll come along to collect the item next Sunday as agreed. Around eleven okay?"

Next Sunday? Dace would be dead by then. His mind raced. "I'm glad you called," he said, trying to maintain the accent. "I was going to call you, in fact. All is ready with your order, but there is a slight problem with timing."

"Oh?"

"Yes, we haf a family situation. Small emergency. I haf to leave very soon, can't be here next weekend. You can come today, yes?"

"What? Oh. I don't think so. This isn't much notice at all, Mr Nikolov."

"I know, I'm very sorry."

"Well, maybe we could wait one more week. When do you expect to be back?"

"Ah, not for several weeks. Maybe months. Very bad situation."

The man on the other end was silent but for breathing. Dace could hear the frustration in it. "This is most irregular, Mr Nikolov. We need the item."

"Yes, yes, I understand. I'm very sorry. So you haf to come today."

"I can't get forty thousand in cash today."

Forty thousand? Dace's mind raced again. He had eleven, he needed sixty. Another forty would get him close, but still nine short. So close, but close wasn't good enough for Carter. An idea bloomed. "Sir, I am truly sorry for this irregular situation, and you are of course a valued client. I make you a special offer. Instead of forty, how about *two* for sixty? To make up for the inconvenience. But it must be this weekend, yes?"

"Two?"

"They will keep indefinitely," Dace said, grimacing. What were the bodies even for? Would anyone need more than one?

The caller was silent again for a moment, then he said, "I'll have to call you back."

He hung up without waiting for a reply and Dace held the inert phone for several seconds, breathing hard. Eventually he hung it up and went into the lounge, sat heavily on the couch, and waited.

It was an hour later when the phone rang again. Dace jumped up to answer it. "Hello?" In his excitement, he forgot to use the Macedonian accent.

"Mr Nikolov?" That same gravelly voice again.

Dace sucked in a breath. Don't blow it. He could use this. "Just a sec."

He took the phone away from his ear, half-covered it with a palm and called out, "Grandpa! Phone."

He paused another few seconds, rubbed the handset like one person was passing it to another, then put it back to his ear. "Hello, is Nikolov here," he said in his terrible accent. He thought he sounded like an Arnold Schwarzenegger parody, more like bad German than anything. He needed it to dial it back.

"Mrs Blumenthal has considered your offer. You say it'll keep? After all, it's potentially a long time between rituals."

"Of course. Stay in the box, keep somewhere cool and dry, no problem."

"*How* long will it keep?"

"Indefinitely."

"And sixty for both, you say?"

"Yes, yes. Special, for your inconvenience. To show I'm so sorry."

"Very well," the man said. "I will come at noon tomorrow."

"Thank you for your understanding. One other thing."

"Another thing?"

"A small thing, nothing to worry about. The young man who answered the phone, my grandson. He will be here to complete the transaction. I will be organising trip, for our emergency. So sorry, but everything will be ready for you to collect. You give him the money, he gives you both, yes? All okay?"

"What's your grandson's name?"

"D... David."

"David Nikolov?"

"In English, yes. He prefers David. That's it. He's a good boy. Well, a man now, I always think of the boy he vas." *Jesus, keep it simple, dickhead!*

"Very well. We'll see David tomorrow."

Dace went and sat back in the lounge, almost vibrating. He'd done it! He would have sixty grand by noon tomorrow, nine hours before Carter's deadline. No, better than that. He'd found eleven grand already and he'd get to keep that. He would be out of trouble with Carter and eleven grand up on the whole debacle. That made it all worthwhile.

Killing two people? Was it worth that?

And Baby, driving that wire through her eye in suicide. Was it worth that?

He took a deep breath. He couldn't change anything that had already happened. He could only keep moving forward. He needed to pay Carter to save himself and his family, simple as that. And he had a little less than twenty-four hours to get organised. He needed to get those bodies down from the attic and put them in the boxes Nikolov had prepared. He looked down at his baggy Freddie Kruger jumper, saw it had brown stains on it, no doubt Nikolov's blood. He needed to change. But he also couldn't risk being seen coming and going from this place. He would need to stay until everything was taken care of, then slip away with the money, never to return. Let anyone find it later, or not. He didn't care.

Bracing himself, he went back into Nikolov's room. Already the stink of death was beginning to rise from the two bodies he'd stashed there. He lifted the old man, still rolled in the rug, up onto the bed next to his wife. Then he dragged the doona out from under them and laid it on top, then added a blanket he found in the wardrobe, covering them both as thoroughly as possible. He only needed to mask the smell of their decay until after the pick-up had been made the next day, then he'd be gone.

"You two got what you fucking deserved," he said to the lumpen bed, and turned away.

Nikolov was taller than him, but not by much. His pants and boots were okay, and if there was blood on either, he couldn't see it. He pulled off the Freddie jumper and stuffed it into his backpack with the rubber mask, then rummaged in Nikolov's stuff until he found a black woollen pullover. He put it on. It was a little long in the body and the sleeves, but not ridiculous. It made him look smart enough.

He went to the bathroom, stripped everything off and had a hot shower, trying to feel vaguely normal again, then redressed. In the spare room, he lay the two boxes on the floor side by side and found their matching lids. Then he put aside a drill and screws to secure the lids on. He looked at his hands as he moved these things around and realised he'd need to take off the gloves when the buyer arrived, or he'd look suspicious. He'd have to be careful not to touch anything, or remember what he touched, when that time came.

He went back up into the attic and stood beside the corpses. He didn't want to handle them but had no choice. He glanced back at the attic hatch and wondered how the hell to get them down. The hatch was large, but not huge. Maybe a fireman's carry over his shoulder? They were young, and rail thin. Swallowing, he slipped his hands under the first one and carefully lifted her. She weighed very little and seemed stiff, rising in his arms like a plank of wood. As he turned, she sloshed gently. Dace froze, bile rising in his throat. He tipped the body left and right and felt some liquid shifting back and forth inside her.

"What the fuck?" he muttered, but tried not to think too hard on it.

She was too stiff to lay over his shoulder, but he managed to hold around the hips with one arm, pressing her against his body, and use his free hand to carefully descend the ladder. He kept his face away, though her cold, white flesh pressed against his cheek. She smelled musty, but spicy. Some almost enticing odour. He hurried to the spare room, laid her in a box, then returned for the other. In a few minutes he had them both down, the ladder folded back up and the attic hatch closed.

He stood with the drill in his hand, about to secure the lids, when he imagined the buyer asking to see the merchandise. It wouldn't be an unreasonable request. He put the lids on loosely, and left, closed the door behind him. Now there were bodies in all three bedrooms of the house. What an absolute fucking nightmare.

It was a little after three in the afternoon and he was finished. All he could do was wait until noon the next day, in a house with five corpses. He desperately wanted to leave, go home, go anywhere. But he didn't dare. So he went into the kitchen, found cleaning products and took care of the last bit of Nikolov's blood on the floor and coffee table. He saw his kitchen knife just under the edge of the couch, forgotten where it must have been knocked in his struggle with the old man. He took it to the kitchen and put it on the table with his backpack, so he wouldn't forget to take it when he left by the back door again after all this was over. He thought about going outside to feed the numerous guinea pigs, just for something to do, but even being spotted in the garden was too much of a risk.

He watched TV instead. As his hunger grew, he searched the kitchen again. He found some frozen fish fingers in the freezer compartment of the old Crosley Shelvador and grilled them, ate them with the last of the Wonder White bread. Time rolled on and he watched more TV. He discovered some half-decent whiskey, a Glenlivet 15, that was a little more than half full and he made the most of that. By a little after ten he was asleep on the couch.

He dreamed of the fall again, bodies twisting as they tumbled down, some thrashing their many limbs, some inert, seemingly already dead. He stood on a slick beach, watched the red hole in the sky vomit forth multitudes. He turned, saw more falling over the thick vegetation of gum trees. He saw a large curved back rise and fall in the trees, like a whale cruising the ocean. *Sasha*, his dream-self cried weakly.

He woke with a hangover a little after eight. The dream was gossamer, fleeting as consciousness returned. How could Baby have the same dream? Why did Nikolov want her to open herself to it? He shook his head. Some questions didn't need answers. Maybe the answers would be more disturbing.

He found coffee grounds and a stove-top percolator in the kitchen and made strong coffee. He drank the whole pot, felt jittery but better for it. He was hungry again, but there was nothing else in the house except the guinea pigs. He didn't feel like boiling up vegetables for breakfast, the only other option. He stood before the rack of roasted rodents, grimacing. They ate these in South America, didn't they? Was it really so weird?

He reached out and plucked a chunk of meat from one small, rounded thigh. It was a little grey in colour, more oily than he had anticipated. The skin and the texture of the meat reminded him of Cantonese duck dishes he'd had on a trip to Sydney years ago. The taste wasn't dissimilar to duck either, rich and slick, but chewy. So little meat to the thing, all close to the small bones. Despite his distaste, he ate about half of one, left its denuded bones on the rack and turned away. Appallingly, it had settled his stomach from the previous night's excess of whisky. He supposed any greasy breakfast sufficed as a good hangover cure.

He killed more time watching television, made another pot of coffee. As the time drifted around towards noon, he became more agitated, more nervous. At twelve on the button, there was a rapid knock at the door.

Dace sucked in a breath and jumped up, turned off the TV. A mirror on the wall in the hall showed his pale, stressed face as he glanced at it in passing. He took another moment, composed himself, forced his shoulders and jaw to relax. A shadow outside the frosted glass remained motionless. Broad shouldered, similar in height to Dace.

He slipped off his gloves and opened the door and smiled. The man was maybe in his fifties, close-cropped grey hair, receding a little from a high forehead. He had a square face, strong jaw, brown eyes. He wore a neat suit, shirt but no tie, shiny shoes, and carried a smart leather attaché case. He smiled and seemed immediately harmless and friendly. "David Nikolov?"

"That's right. Grandpa said to expect you. Everything's in order." Dace stepped back, gestured inside, eager to close the door.

"I'm Talbot, Mrs Blumenthal's representative."

"Nice to meet you, Mr Talbot."

"Just Talbot, thanks."

"Sure, okay." Dace closed the door and stood a little awkwardly.

"Nikolov has never mentioned you before," Talbot said, the smile fading.

"No, he wouldn't have. He keeps his business entirely to himself, even though me and my father are always around to help out. These are unusual circumstances for us."

"The family emergency."

"Yes. Grandpa asked me to offer his heartfelt apologies."

"Your father is here too?"

"No, just me." *Don't say too much*, Dace told himself. The best lies were simple. If you loaded a lie with details, you made obstacles that were liable to trip you up.

Talbot stared, unblinking. Dace became uncomfortable again.

He swallowed. "Grandpa said you'd agreed on two for sixty?"

"That's right."

"Okay, cool. You want to see them? I didn't seal the lids yet."

"Of course."

Dace nodded, forced a smile. He gestured into the spare room and followed Talbot in. The man crouched, put his case on the floor beside himself, and looked carefully at each girl's body. Appallingly, he reached between their legs, forced his hand in and leaned close to look. Dace grimaced but held his tongue. Who knew what the fuck the man was checking for.

Talbot nodded, picked up his case again and stood. "Your grandfather is offering us a very good price here."

"He feels terrible about the change of plans and the position he's put you in. He's a proud man, values professionalism, and wants to make it up to you."

"Hmm." Talbot stepped aside and gestured at the boxes.

Dace took up the drill, reminding himself to take it with him when he left, as he'd removed his gloves. He set the lids, quickly drilled screws into each corner, a couple more evenly spaced along each long side. Then he stood and smiled. "I'll help you out with them?" This was the part he'd dreaded, where he might be seen outside, even recognised.

"Not necessary, thank you. My driver will help me."

Dace nodded, tried to keep the smile from his face. He could stay indoors, after all.

"But in a moment," Talbot said. "The paperwork first."

Dace paused. "The... paperwork."

"Yes. They're useless without the incantations."

Dace laughed, heart hammering. His mind raced. "Of course, sorry. Grandpa left that stuff in the kitchen. This way."

Talbot frowned, but followed him from the room. Dace's head spun, the jitteriness from the coffee redoubled, he was lightheaded, dizzy. What the hell could he do? This close, there was no other choice. He had mentioned the kitchen before his conscious mind even registered the plan.

He walked directly up to the kitchen table and closed his hand around the handle of the knife. Without pausing to think further, he turned. Talbot was a few paces behind, paused in the doorway.

Talbot frowned, looked down at the knife in Dace's hand and said, "What–" then Dace slammed the blade into his chest, right to the hilt.

Talbot managed to get one hand half up to block the blow, but it wasn't enough. He cried out, blood bubbling over his lips, but his eyes went wild, his expression feral. He thrashed Dace with both hands, the blows battering into Dace's face and head. A whistling whine curled in through Dace's left ear and his vision crossed, darkening from the edges, as one of Talbot's hands cracked into his jaw.

"Fuck!" Dace yelled, and his voice was slurred.

Talbot pushed away from him, the knife sliding free with a wet suck. Dace staggered back as Talbot made a burbling cough then came at him again. The man swung large, strong arms, raining blows again.

"Fucken die already!" Dace screamed, raising the knife and plunging it down again and again. He felt it hit Talbot's arms, the blade grate along bone. The man roared in pain and anger, but still fought.

Dace backed into a chair and it folded the back of his knees. He went over, the chair tipping with him, grinding painfully into his arse and the back of one thigh. Talbot fell on him, slamming elbow strikes with one blood-soaked arm into the side of Dace's head. Something cracked like a gunshot near his eye. Consciousness was fleeing, the blackness closing in on Dace's vision like twin tunnels of night. The man's blood was hot all over his face, his hands were slick with it. But he still held the knife. He raised it and stabbed it down into Talbot's back. The man arched away with a roar and Dace stabbed again and again.

Finally, Talbot fell still, collapsed limp on top of Dace as he lay bent awkwardly over the chair. He gasped for breath, desperately trying to stay conscious. His head rang from Talbot's blows, from the exertion.

He heaved, the chair grinding into his lower back as he forced the dead man off him.

"Fucking hell!" Dace said, though the words were mostly sobs.

He was soaked in Talbot's blood, and more spread in a rapidly widening pool across the black and white kitchen floor.

Dace staggered to the sink and ran the taps hard, washed his face and hands. He pulled off the jumper and shirt, left them in the sink as he rinsed his neck and shoulders. His head ached, all around one eye and cheekbone hurt like hell, made him hiss at the slightest pressure. His vision was blurred that side.

"Broke my fucken face," he said. He wondered if it was his cheekbone or the orbit of his eye that had fractured. It felt like both. But a kind of elation coursed through him. That was some fight, and he'd won. It felt good.

He found a black plastic bin liner under the sink and put his blood-soaked clothes in it. He'd worn them, there might be DNA evidence, so he had to take everything with him. He rolled the kitchen knife up in them too, then stripped naked right there at the sink. He put all the clothes in the bin liner, left it on the kitchen table.

Talbot had dropped his attaché case in the kitchen doorway during the fight. Dace crouched, grimacing at a stab of pain in his butt and upper leg from the bruises the chair had left, and popped open the clasps. It was crammed with neat wads of bright green one hundred dollar bills. A quick count confirmed there was exactly sixty thousand dollars. He whooped. "I fucking did it!" he yelled, then winced at his throbbing face.

An icy pulse in his chest accompanied a sudden memory.

Not necessary, thank you, my driver will help me.

Dace licked his lips, mind racing once more. He hadn't noticed a car or anything when he'd let Talbot in. He took the case with him and limped into Nikolov's bedroom, found shirt, trousers and shoes. They were all a little too big, but they'd do. He jammed Nikolov's drill into his backpack, took out the eleven grand he'd found and stuffed that into his pockets. He pulled out the Freddie mask and striped jumper, put them aside. Then he jammed the pack into the bin liner. He put his gloves back on and wiped the front door handle, the bedroom door, the wooden caskets, then the taps in the kitchen. Sure he'd covered all his tracks, he went into the bedroom with the caskets and cautiously lifted the edge of the curtain, peeking out into the bright daylight.

A large white van was parked at the kerb right outside. In the driver's seat was a tall, thin man, skin white as toothpaste. His face was long, his toothless mouth slack as he stared directly ahead. He wore overalls with a huge baggy jumper underneath. The sleeves stopped before his thin wrists, his strangely long-fingered hands resting on the steering wheel. He sat stock still, waiting.

"You have to be kidding me," Dace whispered.

Sasha's story, in the boat before everything turned to shit.

The water is black, the young boy had said about the creek at the McFarland place.

Fucked up his mind too, he's not all there, so they say, Sasha had said. *I wouldn't know, I won't go near the freak.*

Dace smiled. He wouldn't need to go near the freak either. From the position of the van, the weird bastard wouldn't have been able to see into the front door. He hadn't seen anything. All that mattered was keeping it that way.

Dace headed back to the kitchen, slipped on the Freddie mask and jumper. Making sure he had everything he'd brought with him or touched in the bin liner, he left the house by the back door, bin liner in one hand, Talbot's case in the other.

As he came down the side of the house he paused, checking the street outside. No pedestrians, but a few cars. He leaned forward, caught a glimpse of the white van, the pale weirdo still motionless inside. He ducked back, dragged over a battered metal bucket as quietly as he could, and put it up against the side fence. He stood on it, dropped the bin liner over into the shadow of the house next door. Keeping the attaché case in one hand, he awkwardly clambered over and dropped to the ground, then froze in place. After a moment he crept forward, staying low as he moved into the shade of the large frangipani tree in their front yard.

He glanced to the house, saw nothing but the front window reflecting sky. He hoped no one was home, or at least, hoped they weren't looking. Concealing Talbot's case with the bin liner, he moved along behind the tree, then stood and strolled confidently down the garden path to the front gate, like he was simply heading out from the house next door. Dressed like Freddie Kruger. He stifled a giggle at the absurdity of it.

From the corner of his eye, as much as the mask would allow, he glanced sidelong at the van as he made the footpath. The thin, pale man's eye's widened at the sight of him, but he otherwise didn't move. Dace turned his back and walked down the hill as quickly as his battered arse and leg would allow. When he'd put a couple of hundred yards between himself and the van, he crossed the street and quickly pulled off the mask and jumper, stuffed them into the black bin bag. His face and head throbbed in time with the rapid beat of his heart, but he was out. Elation churned inside him.

He went home, showered again, and changed into his own clothes. He stashed the eleven grand in his bedroom then put Nikolov's clean clothes in the bin liner with everything else. He crammed the bagged stuff into a plastic storage tub like the one that had been stolen at the start of this whole debacle, only bigger. He added a couple of five-kilogram weight plates from a dumbbell set. Then he drilled holes in the tub with Nikolov's drill, put the drill inside the tub, put the lid on and tied the thing securely shut with strong nylon rope, looping it around and around, knot after knot. He drove to the harbour, carried the tub to Carter's boat, and motored out to sea.

The wind in his hair, the fresh briny breeze, was like a benediction. His face throbbed painfully and his butt ached, but some ibuprofen seemed to take the edge off. He went around the heads, well out from shore into bigger swell. When he was a good kilometre offshore, he leaned over the side and held the tub in the water while the holes he'd drilled let the ocean in. As it became too heavy to hold onto he let go and watched it sink away, trailing bubbles back up to the surface. He went back home for the attaché case.

When he drove up to Carter's place he saw Rich

working on something in the car port. The young man had come to work for Carter a few months ago. He always seemed a little distracted, Dace thought, acting like he was trying to remember something. But he was a nice guy, fitted in well with Carter's operation.

"Hey, mate" Dace said, getting out of his old Mitsubishi.

"What happened to you?" Rich asked.

Dace's eye had swollen almost shut, black and yellow bruising spread from his chin to his forehead on that side. It hurt like hell. "Walked into a door."

Rich gave a laugh, shook his head. "Sure you did."

"Not even five o'clock yet," Carter said from his doorstep. "I knew I kept you in my employ for a reason. Assuming you're here to settle your little problem, of course. If you're after more time, I'll be mad as a cut snake about it, son."

"No, all good," Dace said with a smile. He walked over and handed Carter the case.

Carter took it with one raised eyebrow. "So what the fuck really happened to your face?"

"Walked into a cupboard door."

"Looks like a cupboard jumped off the wall and beat the shit out of you, mate." Carter turned, carried the case back inside. He put it on the kitchen bench and counted the money. "Well, fuck me dead with a rusty crowbar," he said, closing the case again. "You did it."

"I'm really sorry for everything, Mr Carter."

"I know you are, mate. I know. But business is business."

"Yes, sir."

Carter handed him five hundred dollars. "Remember I said we'd allow your fee. A deal's a deal. How the fuck did you raise sixty grand in less than forty-eight hours?"

Seventy-one grand actually, Dace thought, but wasn't about to admit that. With the money in his bank and this five hundred, which he had forgotten about, he had over twelve grand of his own now. More than he'd ever had at once. He drew breath to make some excuse then Carter raised one palm.

"Actually, maybe I don't need to know. Is it better if I don't?"

Dace nodded. "Probably, yeah. Maybe burn that case too."

"Right-o." Carter looked hard at him, his gaze seeming to dig beneath Dace's skin. "You're not the same."

Dace smiled. "No. I'm not." He felt stronger, more accomplished than ever before. He'd been a mess of nerves and panic through the whole debacle, but he had done it. He'd faced things he would never have imagined and he'd triumphed. Damn right he wasn't the same. "In truth, Mr Carter, perhaps you've under-utilised me in the past. I'm capable of a lot more than you might think."

Carter laughed. "Good on you, mate. I do like to see a man realise his potential. All things happen for a reason, hey? You'll go far, you keep up this level of work."

Dace smiled, thinking about two dead elderly Macedonians. Fuck those twisted freaks, he'd done a service ending them. And a young girl with a wire through her eye, maybe that had been a mercy. There was nothing he could have done for the two dead teenagers that sloshed, with disconcerting symbols carved into their flesh. He thought about the blood flooding from Talbot as he thrashed in his death throes and enjoyed a tingle of victory. There was a thrill in winning a life or death scrap like that.

"Thanks, Mr Carter."

"I have a job for you, but I'll need to organise some stuff first. I'll call you tomorrow."

"Okay, cool." Dace turned and headed back for his car, trying not to limp. He wondered what the job might be. And if he didn't like it, well, maybe twelve grand was Get Out of Gulp money.

Rock
Fisher

Rock Fisher

Troy Mackay was pissed off. All the effort, all the time put in, and she runs off with Albert fucking Chang. Al was a great guy, Troy didn't hold it against the man. Al didn't know Troy and Cindy were on-again-off-again, he didn't know how much energy and money Troy had sunk into proving his love for Cindy, and Troy had seen the way she fawned all over Al in Clooney's the previous weekend. The bitch knew exactly what she was doing, playing him, stringing him along, then swanning off with Al right in front of him last night.

With a sigh, Troy trudged past the bank and the roundabout, carrying his rod and tackle box. When he'd awoken to his alarm, still angry, he'd thought to blow off the fishing. Which was spiting himself because it was his solace. But something had drawn him to the window, looking out into the pre-dawn darkness. Like gamblers, fishers always thought the *next* time they'd get the big score, it kept them motivated. Troy was self-aware enough to recognise the addiction of it. But something else seemed to nag at him this day, something indefinable.

It was barely dawn and already hot as hell, the late-January heat lingering right through the night. It would only get worse once the sun came up properly. He walked along the cement footpath by the grass, then past the lighthouse and its surrounding car park. He took his own private route over the rocks just south of the lighthouse and zig-zagged down the steep decline to the rock shelf on the furthest south-east corner of Spiny Point. He had tried several times to learn why it had that name, but no one seemed to know. An aerial view of the small peninsula where the lighthouse stood did show a spit of rocky land with several small points along its north side and a wide, shallow shelf along the south. It looked sort of like an echidna if you squinted and didn't think about it too hard. But that was a stretch as far as Troy was concerned. Regardless, this spot, at this time, was prime for bream and blackfish. He had his 8-foot rod and Alvey Combo reel and planned to cut some cunjevoi off the rocks for bait. Usually he'd bring more gear but couldn't be bothered right now. He was too upset about Cindy Panko.

Well, they were welcome to each other. Al would no doubt learn pretty quickly that Cindy was a weird and vindictive person. A 'malicious fucker', as Chrissy at the pub had called her once, and Chrissy was smart as hell. He should have listened to her in the first place. But Cindy was hot, and Troy loved exploring every inch of her creamy skin and dreamed of doing it again. Maybe the chance would come around, when she got bored of Al. But one thing was certain, she would never be his true love. All his ideas of settling down, having someone to care for, to care for him, were wasted on Cindy. If that ever happened, as he desperately hoped it would, it wouldn't be with Cindy Panko.

He felt like one of the old boys in Clooney's. He'd always refused to become like them, complaining about everything. Nothing but whinging about fisheries inspectors and fishing rules, all the bloody amateurs taking undersize fish, never any bait, and all the damn leatherjackets. Troy wondered why they kept fishing when everything about it was apparently so miserable. Droughts are no good for fish, rainy weather sucks, the wind is a pain in the arse. The fishing is always awful, it was better when they were kids before the bloody council ruined everything. They even moaned about things like the streetlights being too bright or chips not tasting like they used to or craft beer taking up too much space in the bottle shop. It seemed that to be a keen fisher, you had to whinge about everything. Troy didn't want to be that way. But maybe just for today he'd stare sullenly out at the ocean, grey in the dawn light, and let his inner cantankerous old bastard have dominion.

He loved to get up early and fish, it was his meditation. Maybe it would make him feel better. One thing he and his dad and his older brother had always enjoyed was the fishing. Never his sister, the middle child. Rose always screwed up her face at the very thought of it. That was okay. The Mackay boys enjoyed their thing. But his dad had given it up, too early, too late, too cold, too hot. Any excuse for the passion he'd lost. Same as the way the passion had drained from his marriage. Troy's brother still fished occasionally, but said he had no time any more, now he was manager of the wood yard and a qualified tree surgeon. Always busy, and about two minutes from married with kids, Simon had done okay. His girlfriend, Laura, was the right stuff. A bit ordinary in the looks department, but solid, fun, honest, kind. They would have staying power. Si was a lucky bastard. He would get his family.

Troy reached his spot and stood staring at the ocean for several minutes, checking the swell, feeling the breeze. Nerves tickled over him, a strange sensation of expectancy. Why was he nervous? The thing his dad had instilled in him and Simon right from the start, when he and his brother were both wide-eyed little boys, was respect for the environment. Always keep a good sense of your surroundings, never turn your back on the ocean, and save yourself from wave knockdowns and subsequent lacerations, or even drowning. When it came to participant deaths, rock fishing was the most dangerous sport in Australia, Troy had been told. Unexpected waves or slipped footing off a platform into the churning waves with no lifejacket claimed a lot of lives every year. His dad had made him and Simon well aware of the risks, had always insisted they wear lifejackets as boys. Of course, he didn't any more. He didn't want to look like an idiot out here.

But today the sea was calm, just on the turn of the tide, perfect conditions. The sky was slowly brightening ahead over the ocean, soft orange pushing away the pink and grey. It might stay a little overcast, but that would only trap the summer heat in.

Thinking about his dad's old lessons, thinking about his family, made Troy melancholy. But he was only twenty-five. Plenty of time to find a wife. Make a home and a family of his own. His home wasn't *bad* growing up. It was perfectly normal, except his parents didn't love each other. They stayed together for the kids then, and they stayed together because they didn't know any better now. All three Mackay siblings were out of the family home, though all still in The Gulp, and Mum and Dad Mackay orbited each other in the big house at the top of Thomas Street in blissful apathy. They were good friends, they had their own hobbies as well as shared interests. They both worked, they had pals around town they socialised with, it was all normal. But it was so fucking *empty*. Cardboard cut-out people living cardboard cut-out lives. No aspirations for anything bigger or better, just treading water until they died. Not what a real family *should* be.

Staring at the ocean he remembered his dad out here back in the old days, vibrant and enthusiastic. So different to the blank sheet of paper the man had become. Troy wanted more than that. He wanted someone he genuinely loved. Someone who fired up his heart every time he saw her, even after thirty-five years of marriage. Or more. He wanted kids who grew up happy and *wanted* to visit after they'd moved out, instead of the way he and his brother and sister only forced themselves back to the family nest for special events. Birthdays, Christmas, anniversaries, the occasional Sunday lunch when Mum got downhearted that all her little babies were grown and flown. They'd recently endured the fake frivolity of Christmas so at least that was done with for another year. He would have his perfect family one day, but it wouldn't be with Cindy Panko. He needed someone better. He had time.

The ocean swell matched his breathing and his nerves rose again. He sensed an insistence from the water, an urgency, and frowned, but a smile tugged at his lips. He set up his rod, fingers a little clumsy with haste. Something's out there, he thought. All these years had given him a sixth sense for the right spot, the right time. All fishers either claimed to have that second sight or claimed it was bullshit. He'd always been in the latter camp, but not today. Now, inexplicably, he was a believer. He crouched, sharp knife sliding into the wet crevices at the water line as he carved away chunks of cunjevoi for bait.

Ready to cast, he checked his watch and sighed. He only had a couple of hours. Would it be enough? Another day making dental instruments lay ahead of him, eight hours of knurling scalers and sickle probes. Something else he needed to change, that was no lifetime career. The thought of it made him feel hollow inside. Maybe if he got a better job, he'd get a better girlfriend, but there was precious little work going in The Gulp. Precious little with any real prestige anyway. And getting out of The Gulp was harder than finding good work.

Fuck it all. Fish and forget, that was his mantra. It was how he stayed sane among the drudgery of life. He let the meditation sink over him, watched the swell, watched the clouds, cast and recast. Today he would make a grand catch. He didn't know how he knew, didn't question it. Just believed.

As the sun rose, the overcast sky cleared and the heat rose. It was going to be a scorcher after all. He'd pulled in a couple of decent sized bream after a bit more than an hour, which was disappointing. It wasn't anything like the inner feeling had made him expect. They'd feed him for a couple of days, along with the stock of vegies he had in his flat from his mother's garden. Whatever other faults she might have, no one could say she wasn't a green thumb. Vegie beds took up nearly half the large back yard on Thomas Street and she kept herself, all her kids, and several friends and neighbours well-stocked with fresh produce.

Troy checked his watch. He was due at work in just over an hour. It would take about twenty minutes to walk back to his flat on Freemantle Street on the south side of The Gulp, then it was only another five minute walk to Turner's Manufacturing in the little industrial park on the very southern edge of town, where the bush rose steep and thick behind the large metal warehouses and workshops. So he had about half an hour in hand.

"Come on," he muttered. "Today's supposed to be special."

He baited up and sent the line sailing out. The sun was well above the horizon now, shining gold and glittering across the water. Some of the locals were saying they were in for a long, harsh summer, but didn't they always say that? Summer was always long, usually too hot, and getting increasingly humid even this far south. Thanks, climate change.

His line snagged suddenly. He flicked back, felt the hook catch and smiled. This felt bigger than a bream. Much bigger. He let the line go a little and it raced away fast. Frowning he tried to pull it back, but whatever he'd hooked was strong. His relaxed fishing became a sudden battle as he wound up, hauled in, let it run, wound up again. Whatever he had, he needed to tire it out before it broke his line. Or bit through it, some distant voice in his mind suggested.

"This is it," he said. "Come on, in you come!"

For ten minutes they battled, the whole while Troy's mind swam with possibilities of what he might have snagged. Then sudden slack and he staggered back.

"Fuck it!"

Another rock fisher, about a hundred metres away around the shelf, glanced over at Troy's outburst. "Lost another one, hey?" he shouted across with a laugh in his voice.

Troy realised it was Trevor Clancy, one of the middle-aged whingers he drank with at Clooney's, iron grey hair and hard eyes. Troy flipped the bird and Trev laughed, turned his attention back to his own line. With a sigh, Troy began reeling in. That fisher's sense was bullshit after all. Wishful thinking. He felt a drag here and there and realised his hook must still be in place. He'd thought the line had snapped, but it didn't feel that way now. Whatever it was got lucky and slipped the hook.

The line snagged again and Troy spat curses. Definitely caught up on something inanimate this time. He tugged and wound the reel, but it wouldn't give. He slipped the knife from his belt, about to cut the line and his losses, but thoughts of sea life tangled in discarded fishing line passed by his mind's eye. A lot of the old boys didn't care, they thought themselves above the welfare of the ocean, but Troy had a respect for it. He fished for sport, certainly, but he fished for his dinner too. There was purpose to it, man in nature, sustaining himself. He didn't believe in that process causing unnecessary suffering. He slipped the knife back and decided to try a little longer to reel in.

He wound and leaned the rod up and back. The rod bent, the line seemed to stretch, then as he was about to quit, a little movement. He hauled again. And again. Little by little, the line came back to him, but reluctantly. It seemed to be dragging something heavy along with it.

"Fucking kelp," Troy muttered, picturing a great wad of the thick plant being drawn along the seabed. But he didn't want to leave line in the water if he could help it, so he kept up the effort.

He flicked a glance over his shoulder and saw Trevor watching. "Fucken cut it, ya drongo!" Trev yelled.

"Worry about your own self," Troy called back.

He heard the man's guttural laughing as Trev lit a

cigarette and crouched by his tackle box, baiting up.

It took ten minutes and with every passing second, the urge to keep pulling in grew stronger. Maybe his earlier sense hadn't been wishful thinking. A deep yearning ached in his chest, a strangely primal need to see whatever this was caught on his line. With every wind, he thought less and less that it was anything as simple as kelp. On some deep level, it called to him. Troy had a sensation that whatever he'd hooked badly needed to come ashore. It needed his help.

It was a strange and slightly disconcerting train of thought, but he couldn't help picturing whatever it was as though it had limbs that reached, stretched for him like a child asking for a hug.

Finally, he saw something causing a shallow wake at the end of his line and he took a couple of steps down the rock, careful not to get too close to the wet and slippery edge. His father's lessons were burned in. As the bundle of whatever it was got closer, Troy realised it was incredibly heavy for its size. It wasn't kelp, but some dark, slick seaweed of a kind he didn't recognise. Thin, flat leaves with blisters all over that seemed like bubbles, pressing out in translucent bulges. Each blister was fluid-filled, seawater he presumed, but it seemed thicker the way it moved. Troy reached down and grabbed hold of the mass, hauled it up onto the rock beside his feet. It was warm despite the cool water sluicing off it. Too warm, like a living thing. A warm-blooded thing. A sensation of need rose from it and Troy stopped, stood back a pace or two in discomfort. The feeling was strong, too much.

"No, no," he whispered to himself. "This isn't..." What? His face was twisted in involuntary concern, almost disgust.

Despite his concern, he was drawn back to it. He dropped his rod beside himself and stood looking down. "The fuck is it?"

He crouched again, slipping his knife out, planning

to cut the line and kick the weird, hot seaweed ball back into the water. But as he got closer again he saw the weed wasn't a solid ball, but wrapped around something else. He used the razor-sharp edge of his green-handled knife to slice away some of the suppurating weed, and revealed a hard, leathery, but transparent curve of some mass inside. This was generating the heat and Troy immediately felt an overwhelming urge to take care of it. Nurture it. Some part of his mind rebelled at the thought, but that was buried by the urgency with which his heartbeat and his breath shallowed. This was something special, something unique and valuable and *necessary*.

A shadow seemed to shift slightly inside it. He pressed at it with one forefinger and the surface gave, but only a little, like pushing against the arm of a leather couch. Except this thing was thicker-skinned, harder. And hot. His fingertip tingled.

He sliced away more of the blistered weed and revealed the entirety of it. About twenty-five, maybe thirty centimetres long, two-thirds as wide, a rough lozenge shape, tapering to edges with short hooks and curls of the same clear, thick, tough substance. His hook had slipped through the bubbled weed and caught in one of these, and he carefully worked it free. Where the point had punctured the small frond, a viscous clear liquid leaked. Frowning, he gently pressed the pad of his index finger against the wound, and held it there for a moment, unable to resist the urge to salve its hurt. When he took his finger away, the wound had stuck together and stopped leaking, barely noticeable any more. His fingertip tingled more, almost burned, where the stuff had touched his skin.

He picked the thing up, marvelling at its weight. It had to be at least five kilos, which given its size seemed incongruous, tricky to hold in one hand as he carried his rod in the other. As the early sun lanced across it, he saw inside. A tight mass of some kind, hundreds, maybe thousands of intertwined pili or flagellum that shifted slightly, languidly. This was a living thing. No, he corrected himself. This *would be* a living thing. It was an egg, surely. But a massive one. Even the biggest sharks laid eggs a fraction of this size, and this wasn't a shark egg, though it had similarities to some he'd seen. And even egg wasn't quite description enough, the way it yearned. It was in part a child too, an infant in desperate need.

Troy looked around, suddenly anxious that no one see him. This was his, and his alone. His to care for. A couple of steps down the rocks had taken him out of Trev's eyeline, so that was good. No one else around. Time was getting on, he would be late for work, but this was worth it.

He hurried back up to his gear and slipped the egg into his large, plastic catch bag with the two bream. "Sorry, it's not a very dignified way to carry you," he whispered to it. It occurred to him briefly that talking to the thing was kind of crazy, but it didn't feel wrong. His urge to take care of it, to be there for it, was overwhelming. He paused, looking at the lumpen catch bag. He should throw it back, it was too much. An image of launching a surprised and terrified child out into the waves washed over his mind and he balked.

"No, no, I won't," he told it. "It's okay. You're okay."

The nerves returned, but they were excitement now, a need to do the right thing.

He wiped his hand on his jeans, his palm tingling where he'd held the egg. The finger he'd pressed to the small hook wound still burned slightly. He looked, but saw nothing on his skin, no marks.

He packed quickly and started back up the rocks.

"Quitting time?" Trevor called.

"Gotta go to work. You?"

"Nah, day off. Catch anything?"

"Couple of bream. You?"

Trevor shrugged. "Not really. But there's time. Clooney's tonight?"

Troy nodded. "See you there."

He clambered back up the rocks, rod in one hand, tackle box in the other, catch bag heavy over his shoulder.

When he got home, he had a plan. Not much of one, but enough for the moment. He had a 95-litre fish tank on the dresser in his lounge room. His flat was small, one-bedroom, bathroom, open space for kitchen and lounge, but it was his. One good thing about The Gulp, rent was low because no one wanted to live there. His parents had fronted him the bond and his job at Turner's paid enough to live on his own.

The dresser next to the TV along one wall held a bunch of junk but was mainly a place for his tank. He kept a simple community aquarium of tropical fish, mostly guppies, platys, and tetras and a few Corydoras catfish. It was a simple pleasure, a pretty, watery ecosystem in his tiny house. It was freshwater, not salt, but he knew somehow that would be okay. The egg needed to stay wet and warm, that was all.

He put his gear down in the hallway by the front door, went to the kitchen corner and put the two bream in the fridge. He'd clean them later. Then he carried the catch bag over to the fish tank. He slid aside one half of the glass covering under the bright LED light bar and carefully slipped the egg from the bag into the water.

The fish started zooming around, expecting food as they always did whenever the lid was moved. Proof, as far as Troy was concerned, that the whole three second memory thing was bullshit. Fish, even little tropical ones like this, were smarter than people gave them credit for.

The egg sank to the bottom and sat on the variegated tan, brown and black gravel, leaning back against a curve of driftwood that decorated that end of the tank. He had a small stand of vallisneria along the back of the tank, a tall thin, flat-leaved plant. The aquarium store in Enden always labelled it 'vallis/eel grass'. It was excellent in tropical tanks, hardy, easy to keep, pretty to look at. It was pressed back a little as the egg settled against the driftwood, but otherwise the introduction of the large, unusual item seemed to have no adverse effects. Any salt on it would hopefully get cleaned up by the filter without hurting his fish. The egg seemed to glow slightly, no doubt the thick translucency of its skin catching and reflecting the aquarium light. It was beautiful. The fish circled it, searched it, then moved quickly away. They gathered up the other end of the tank, all seeming to agree at once to keep their distance. Troy smiled. More proof they were smart, being cautious about a new introduction to the tank. Although they were usually more curious than that.

He glanced at his watch. 8.28am. "Shit!" He had two minutes to get to work. He was going to be late. He closed up the fish tank and ran out the door.

He got a stern talking to for being late as he stood sweating on the factory floor, but no official warning. Troy was, after all, a diligent and reliable employee. He was rarely late, always did good work, was always polite and agreeable. But despite the lack of reprimand, he was distracted all day. He did his work, went to the fish and chip takeaway just down the road for lunch and mechanically ate a basic serve. The whole time all he could think about was the egg in his tank back home. What was it? Why did it fill him with such... longing? He had a hard time pinning down exactly how he felt other than the overwhelming need to nurture it. At one point he found himself thinking of Cindy Panko again, or more specifically what he'd hoped for with Cindy. Family. *Real* family.

When he got home, he went straight to the tank. Things had changed a bit. All his fish, some fifteen or so, were still up the far end away from the egg. The vallis growing behind it had twisted a little and small marks marred the smooth surface of the long flat leaves.

Looking closer he saw the marks were tiny bumps, like pinprick blisters. He remembered the weed the egg had been wrapped up in when he caught it. Was this tropical plant going the same way? No matter, as long as the egg was safe.

And it was. Smooth, gently glowing with reflected light, the myriad tendrils inside languidly writhing. The pinkie finger-sized hooks and curls of the outer edges of the egg lay relaxed in the water, shifting ever so slightly in the soft current from the filter. Waves of rainbow iridescence rippled across it, mesmerising in their beauty.

He glanced at his right hand, the one he'd held the egg in. It still itched, the index fingertip still burned. He saw tiny marks on the pad of his finger, minuscule bumps like gooseflesh. He pressed at it with his thumb, but there was no pain. The itch across his palm was distant, not really much to worry about. He dropped his hands and stared at the hypnotic beauty of the thing he'd caught, glistening under the aquarium light.

Troy startled when his phone rang. As he pulled it from his pocket to answer he caught sight of the time. Just after 9pm. He'd sat for nearly four hours staring into his tank, but it only felt like minutes. His stomach rumbled with hunger. The call was from his mother.

"Hey, Mum."

"How are you, darling?"

"Just fine, thanks. You?"

"Oh, you know. I'm still alive, ha ha." She did that a lot. Not a laugh but saying the words "ha ha" like they were punctuation.

Troy didn't have anything to say, just stared at the egg with the phone pressed to his ear.

"Anyway," his mum said after a moment. "Lunch on Sunday, your brother and sister are both coming, Dad'll be there, of course. Can you come?"

Far out, Christmas had only been a few weeks ago, and she was gathering the family again already? "Yeah, sure. What's the occasion?"

"Oh, Troy, does there need to be a reason? We're a family."

Family. He smiled at his egg. "Yeah, of course. Okay. I'll see you about noon on Sunday."

She was saying something else as he took the phone from his ear and hit the End Call button. Absently, knowing he was likely to forget, he tapped 'Lunch noon' into his calendar for Sunday and set an alarm for 1 Hour Before Event.

His stomach roiled again and he realised he still hadn't eaten. His phone was still in his hand. The time said 11.15pm.

"What the fuck?"

Troy tore his gaze form the tank and turned his back. A sensation of loss and longing gusted through him, but his mind also cleared a little. Hunger dragged at him. Refusing to look back at the fish tank, he walked into the kitchen corner and put together a cheese and ham jaffle. Quick and easy. He stood at the counter and ate it with his back still to the egg.

He desperately wanted to look again, but a sense of disquiet tugged at him. He resisted the urge and went into the bathroom, showered, brushed his teeth, and then crossed the hall to his bedroom, all the time ignoring the lounge room behind him. He fell into bed, scratching absently at his right palm, and exhaustion swept over him.

He had the dream again. The one with the slippery, black beach, the red, gaping sky, the things falling. He'd had it on and off his whole life. He felt like it meant something, but he wasn't sure what. He always mostly forgot the details on waking. His phone alarm went off at 4.30am, still set from the day before. He rolled over, looked at it for a moment, then ended it. Reset it for 7.30. He'd skip fishing for today.

It seemed only moments later that it went off again, and he sat up in bed with a groan.

"At least it's Friday," he muttered.

He staggered into the front room and went to the kitchenette in the corner, started coffee. He realised he was avoiding looking at his tank, but that was okay. He needed coffee first, and more food. He crunched Vegemite toast as the percolator coughed and spluttered on the stovetop, then he poured the coffee and finally turned to look at the egg.

Immediately the sense of wonder filled him again, the urge to nurture. Mug cupped in both hands, he went and sat on the arm of the armchair beside the tank, the closest he could get and still sit down. The egg glowed, it seemed to exude contentment. The vallis plant all along the back still had those small blisters, only larger. The normally tall, flat leaves seemed to sag and curl slightly. He noticed the fish were still gathered up the other end and they all looked... odd. The guppies and tetras were humped, like their spines had arched upwards. The swam a little listlessly, gills wide, mouths working harder than usual. The small catfish, usually industrious little creatures always vacuuming at the gravel with their bristly noses, drifted a little lacklustre. Their usual colour was muted, pale.

Was the egg poisoning them somehow? Troy pulled out all his test kits, adding drops of the relevant chemicals to small glass vials of water from the tank. pH level, ammonia, nitrite, nitrate. It all came up good. He was as diligent with his fishkeeping as he was with everything else in life and prided himself on the health of his pets.

He frowned. Why were they so... affected?

He did a twenty-five per cent or so water change just in case and added a little conditioner to the new water he put in to avoid any pH shock. Then he did a dose of Melafix, a general antibacterial. He did a maintenance dose once a week on Mondays anyway, but another one wouldn't hurt. He usually dosed the tank for three straight days whenever he put new fish in, so he supposed the addition of the beautiful egg counted the same.

Satisfied he'd done all he could, he sat watching again. His phone rang. As he tapped to answer, his eye caught the display. 9.30am and Boyd calling. His boss, and he was an hour late.

He quickly put some gravel into his voice. "Hello?"

"You planning on coming to work today? I was generous yesterday, but you were only ten minutes late then."

"I'm really sorry, Boyd. I'm sick as a dog today. I meant to call you earlier, but must have passed out again."

Boyd's voice softened immediately. "You okay? I mean, you need help?"

"No, thanks. Maybe something I ate? I've been up all night. I'm really sorry, man. I'll be there Monday."

"Okay, well take care. Go to the doctor if you don't improve."

"I will."

"Call if you need a lift or something."

Troy smiled. Boyd Turner was a good guy. He'd taken over the factory when his father retired, keeping it in the family. The man was only about forty-five but managed that rare combination of being one of the lads and a respectable elder. Troy hated to let him down. "I can walk to Tanning Street Medical Centre in a few minutes if I need to. Thanks though."

"Okay," Boyd said. "Well, you take care and I'll see you on Monday."

"See you then."

He hung up and saw his phone battery was low. He moved to the couch where a charger cable lay along the arm, always ready, and plugged it in. His palm itched and he looked at it, saw the same bumpy flesh across it as he'd noticed on the fingertip before. The finger had become more misshapen, the bumps pressing together to make his fingertip appear swollen and irregular. The burning had intensified, his hand stiff and tingly when he clenched it. Weird, he thought, as he watched the egg.

It was his phone that distracted him again a few minutes later, this time Brendan Testa calling. Troy's best friend since high school and an all-around good guy. "Yo, Bren. What's up? You not working?"

"Working? I finished an hour ago."

Troy pulled the phone from his ear, looked at the display. 6.02 pm. What the actual fuck? How did this keep happening? "Oh yeah, right," he said. "Lost track of time."

"Pub tonight? Missed you last night."

Troy decided to play along with the lie he'd used earlier. "Yeah, must have eaten something bad, I was sick all night. Slept it off today though. See you about seven." His stomach grumbled. He'd gone hours without eating again. "Might grab a bistro dinner, actually."

Brendan laughed. "Friday night treat, eh? Why not. I'll join you."

"Cool." Troy hung up and pulled himself off the couch, determinedly refusing to look at the tank. He caught a glimpse of a couple of his fish anyway as he turned. They seemed bloated, misshapen and awkward in the water. He made a small sound of despair, but kept his back to them by pure force of will. He went to the bathroom and washed, went to his bedroom and changed, then left the flat without a backward glance.

He walked slowly to the pub, enjoying the fresh air and exercise, but the summer heat was cloying. He walked everywhere, given his lack of car, but didn't mind that. He'd taken lessons from his dad as a teenager and got his licence like everyone else. He took his test in Enden, not bothering to engage in the permanent debate about whether Enden or Monkton was the easier place to pass. But he'd never bought a car. The expense of one bothered him, and while he'd like the freedom, he lived and worked so locally it seemed unnecessary. Brendan had a car and was always happy to drive when they went further afield. Maybe Troy should get one soon. For some reason The Gulp suddenly felt a little claustrophobic. Some deep part of him had become agitated. He pushed the thoughts away, scratching at his palm, flexing his fingers. The whole hand felt swollen and stiff. The bumps across his palm stood a little higher, hard like tiny pebbles. His index finger throbbed, the last joint so swollen it wouldn't bend at all.

It was only just after 6.30 so he walked past the pub and down to the harbourside, a need to see the ocean dragging him along. He stood on the cement path that curved around the bay, the squared-off harbour for boats to tie up off to his right, the lighthouse beyond that. The water shifted gently, lapped against the low wall in front of him. It was still light, would be for another hour or two yet, but the sun had dropped below the swell of land off to the west making everything soft and pastel. The brine smell and cry of gulls comforted him.

"Something lingers about you."

Troy jumped at the scratchy sound of the old woman's voice. He turned, the sea witch only a metre away, staring up at him with her face scrunched in... what? Disgust? She was tiny, barely four and half feet tall, older than the Bible, wrinkled like a ball sack. Her hair was white and thick, in wild disarray about her head as usual. She wore layer after layer of woollen clothes despite the heat. Troy was hot in shorts and t-shirt. He imagined she was stick-thin beneath all her clothes. She had three teeth, one top centre and two evenly spaced in the bottom of her wet, gummy jaw. No one knew her name or where she lived, and they all called her the sea witch, though not to her face. Troy assumed she was homeless, but she'd been around The Gulp forever. His dad said she was just as old and hanging around the harbour when *he* was a boy, but surely that wasn't possible. Troy liked her well enough, saw her often when he came to fish, always said hello. He didn't believe the stories about her, she was just a crazy old lady. He felt sorry for her more than anything.

"Lingers?" he said.

She stepped forward and grabbed his right wrist, turned his palm up before he could resist. One glimpse and she dropped it, danced a couple of steps backwards. "Put it back!"

He frowned. "What? Put what back?"

"Whatever it is you took from the sea. It needs to go back, right now. Take a boat, go out as far as you can. Weigh it down so it stays down!" Her voice rose in volume as she spoke, her rheumy grey eyes widening.

How did she know he'd taken something from the sea? "What are you talking about?"

"You know!" she said, narrowing her eyes and wagging one finger at him. "You know very well. Put it back!"

"No," he said, and turned away.

As he walked back towards the pub, he heard her sigh. "So it begins," she said. When he looked around she already had her back to him, shuffling away towards the lighthouse.

He ordered a chicken schnitty with chips and salad in Clooney's, his hunger clawing with a vengeance. He took the table number then moved around to the bar and ordered a beer from Chrissy.

"You okay?" she asked as she poured. "You look pale."

He shrugged. "Had a bit of a stomach bug last night. Maybe that's it."

"Nothing a few beers can't cure, hey?" She had one eyebrow raised, sarcasm heavy in her voice.

She was so beautiful, Troy was among many who admired her. But none would ever suggest anything, knowing her thing with her dad. She certainly wasn't the type of family he wanted. Family made him think of the egg again. He smiled softly. "We'll see, I guess," he said, and went to find a table.

He said hello to Mark on the way past, the man's facial scars slowly turning from pink to white as the months passed. They would always be visible though, giving him a permanently fierce expression. Chicks might dig scars, Troy thought, but not that level of disfigurement, poor bastard. Barry wasn't in it yet, but probably would be soon. Troy glanced around for Barry's mum, but couldn't spot her. It always paid to keep an eye on that violent bitch and her friends. Trev and a couple of others stood chatting nearby.

"Missed you last night," Trev said with a grin. "Too embarrassed by your terrible catch to come in?"

"Get fucked," Troy said, trying to be humorous, but his heart wasn't in it.

"Touchy fucker," Trev said, then turned back to his friends.

Troy found a table and sat down. Brendan arrived a moment later. He was tall and skinny, a good-looking guy, but didn't spare a glimpse for Chrissy while she poured his beer. He'd never been with a girl to Troy's knowledge, and they'd been mates a long time. But it was also something Brendan seemed entirely unconcerned about. Troy could never decide if Bren was gay and ignoring it, or asexual, or what. And it didn't seem to bother Brendan so Troy didn't worry about it either. His mate was happy, that's all that mattered.

"You order food?" Brendan asked, putting his beer on the table.

"Yeah. Schnitty." Troy pointed at the table number.

"Cool. Reckon I'll have one too." He went to turn away, then paused, frowned. "You okay?"

"Yeah, why?"

"You look pale. Bit drawn or something."

"I'm fine. Had a bug, remember?"

Brendan nodded, went to order his food.

Troy sat trying to ignore his roaring stomach. A few sips of beer had made him lightheaded, he was so hungry. Brendan returned, put his order number in its little stand on the table next to Troy's.

"So, what's new?"

"Same old shit," Troy said with a grin. He felt distracted, found himself thinking of the egg in his tank at home. A powerful urge to return to it pulled at him.

They made small talk, but Troy was preoccupied. Brendan was going on about some work thing. Troy's hand throbbed. He kept it on his lap under the table but glanced down and saw it had swollen even further. The whole thing looked like a rubber glove someone had blown up like a balloon. It itched interminably.

His food arrived and he downed his beer, then said, "You wanna get a round in as my dinner's here? I'll get the next one."

"Sure."

When Bren got up and went to the bar, Troy quickly used both hands to cut his schnitzel into bite-sized pieces, fumbling awkwardly with the knife in his fat fingers. By the time Brendan returned, Troy's swollen hand was back under the table and he ate with just a fork. Brendan frowned when he put the beers down, but said nothing. His chicken schnitzel with mash and vegies arrived and they sat quietly, enjoying each other's company and their food.

Some sense of normalcy returned as the meal hit Troy's stomach, but the itch in his hand didn't ease, nor the drag at his chest that seemed to draw him back towards home. He imagined it felt like this when parents had a new baby and went out, leaving the child with a babysitter. An anxiety of abdicated responsibility.

"You know what, mate," he said to Brendan. "I think that bug knocked me about more than I realised. I thought a good feed would fix me up, but I don't think it did."

"You do look a bit peaky." Brendan's eyes were narrow in concern.

"Sorry, man, I owe you a beer. But next time, yeah?"

"Sure. You gonna be okay?"

Troy smiled, but it felt fake even to him. "Yeah. I reckon I just need to sleep it off."

He passed a couple of his Turner's colleagues coming in as he went out.

"Thought you were off sick?" one said.

"I was. Thought I was better, but I'm not. Going home again."

"See you Monday?"

"Hope so!"

He hurried away up Tanning Street. Besides the burning itch in his swollen hand, and the discomfort of the tightened skin, he did actually feel much better for the feed and the couple of beers. He just needed to get back to his egg.

As he reached the opposite corner of the block, where the Victorian pub stood, he saw Cindy Panko heading towards him. On her own. He wondered where Al Chang was. Maybe she was going to meet him. He felt a lurch of longing in his gut, remembered the many times they'd enjoyed each other's bodies. But she was no good, certainly no good for him. She wasn't made of family stuff. The egg at home exerted a greater pull on him than Cindy's body now. Some distant part of his mind suggested maybe that wasn't right. Maybe that was fucking weird. But he didn't care.

"Hey, Troyyy," she said, dragging out the sound of his name.

She had a great figure, long shiny brown hair and big eyes. Her skin was always creamy. "Hey," he said cautiously, pausing. The urge to get back to his egg intensified.

"Where you going?" she asked.

"Heading home."

"It's not even 8 o'clock."

He shrugged. He didn't owe her an explanation.

"Wanna have a drink with me?" she asked. She pointed to the Vic. "We could go in there if you don't want to be in Clooney's tonight."

"What about Al?"

Her face twisted into something nasty. "What about him?"

"Like that is it?"

"Al Chang can get fucked. But by someone else from now on."

"So you come crawling back to me, that it?" The words were harsh and out before he realised he was going to say them.

Instead of being hurt, she grinned impishly. "I like it when you're angry."

"I'm going home." He stepped around her and started to walk away, but she fell into step beside him.

"How about I come too?"

"What?"

"Let's fuck, Troy. Come on. And you've got some grog at home, I'm sure. Let's get pissed and fuck."

He couldn't ignore the stir in his groin at her words, but the drag in him intensified again. His egg needed him. Family first. "No. Fuck off, Cindy."

She stopped, eyes wide. "Well fuck you too, shitcunt!" she spat.

He heard her Dunlop Volleys slapping the pavement as she marched away from him. He didn't look back, kept walking.

When he got back to his flat, he went straight to the tank. The plants were all swollen with numerous blisters and darkening towards black. They looked oily. The fish were unrecognisable. Bloated and contorted, yet somehow alive, here a gasping mouth, there a gaping gill. Eyes bulged from strange positions on the crooked scales, fins were feathered or gathered into bizarre points, protruding at random from their confused bodies. They bobbed and rolled in the water, tumbled occasionally by the current from the filter pushing cleaned water back into the tank from the top. They no longer avoided the egg, either through disinclination or inability he wasn't sure. They drifted and flexed feebly in the water, seemingly blind and lost to their fate. He didn't mind.

But the egg, oh, that was magnificent. It had grown, now filling a little over half the length of the tank, about the size of a rectangular couch cushion. Its surface glowed, more than a reflection of the LED light bar, definitely some internal iridescence, rainbowing its surface. The myriad tendrils inside writhed lazily.

Troy's sense of urgency, of longing, eased immediately. He was where he needed to be, caring for this. His hand itched and pulsed, but despite that warning, maybe even invited by it, he desperately wanted to touch the egg again. To hold it.

He suddenly felt encumbered by his clothes. Hurrying to the bedroom, he stripped off, left his clothes in a pile on the floor, and returned to his tank. Naked, he slid the glass covering aside and reached in. The warm water was a balm to his swollen, itching skin. He couldn't lift the egg easily in one hand, but he got his puffy palm under it and hoisted it up out of the water, then pressed it against his chest, cradled in the crook of his elbow. He kept his left hand away from it, some part of him realising he might need better use of that hand, despite being right-handed.

The egg was warm, almost hot, and pulsed with life. It emanated a kind of peace and a kind of vibrancy simultaneously. It felt right, pressed against his flesh. He would protect this thing. Nothing else mattered.

He hugged the egg to him for a long time, unaware of exactly how long, but eventually the weight became too much, pulling at him. His breathing had turned to shallow gasps, his heart raced, and the egg itself yearned for water.

He quickly returned it to the tank. All inside his arm

and across his chest was stippled with little bumps, already the skin stretching to a translucence that showed liquid inside. Troy felt as if he'd had the best sex of his life, spent and exhausted and exhilarated. All this time wanting a family and he had it all in this one beautiful thing. Paradoxically, both child and lover, something to care for and something to be with, a family in rainbow beauty. It transcended family, made a mockery of the concept of a couple producing offspring. It was all things combined into one and it wanted him.

He stumbled backwards to the couch and sat, staring at the thing he loved, unaware and unconcerned as hours drifted by.

At some later point, hunger roused him. He staggered into the kitchen and tried to find something to eat, but he hadn't shopped in a while, and nothing was especially obvious. He found a pack of bacon in the fridge and tore it open, ate the fatty strips of meat raw and cold. Some potatoes sat in the vegetable crisper and he took one, crunched it like an apple. Taste, texture didn't matter, he simply needed sustenance.

With his back to his beloved family in the tank he realised he was exhausted. He knew self-care was an important part of any relationship. He needed sleep. The egg was safe in the water, so he went through into the bedroom. He saw himself in the mirrored sliding door of his wardrobe. Naked and lean, a handsome enough man. But his arm and torso distracted him. Across the upper right side of his chest and shoulder, and all along his right arm, his skin was rippled like a burn scar. He moved closer. Not rippled but stippled. A mass of liquid-filled blisters, each about the size of half a grape, pushing up from this skin, blurring together in places. They itched, the skin over them both semi-translucent and darkening to an off brown colour against his usual pale pink. Not brown, he thought, something deeper. Maybe a shade towards purple, like a stormy sky. He pressed gingerly at one of the lumps with the index finger of his left hand. It felt hardened, but still flexible. A strange gift from the egg, but family changed a person, after all. Family meant becoming something bigger than oneself, greater than the sum of parts.

He crawled into bed and slept.

He dreamed again of the rent sky, glowing red, the creatures falling. They rained over the ocean and over the bush behind the slick, black beach. The heavy clouds rolled and swelled, lightning crackled. He heard an unearthly siren sound that seemed to echo across the entire sky. And he sensed something beyond the sky, beyond the mammoth red celestial wound. Some presence outside his comprehension, older, vaster than he could imagine. It was pleased with him.

He woke to his phone ringing.

He untangled himself from the bedclothes and realised it wasn't a call, but the alarm tone. Was it time for work? What day was it? The phone was in his pants pocket on the floor, and he fumbled it out with his left hand, his right arm stiff and unresponsive.

Mum lunch noon

It all came back. It was Sunday. Wait, hadn't he gone to the pub on Friday night? Then come home? Cindy telling him to fuck off. What happened to Saturday? He rolled onto the floor and sat up, looked at himself in the mirrored sliding door.

His entire right arm and shoulder, and down to his hand, was swollen and lumpen, almost one thickened mass. The purpling of the skin had deepened, the fluid-filled blisters larger, like half golf balls now. More had pushed into each other and merged, occasionally making a kind of swollen number eight shape where two were partially combined, some in strings of four or five.

The itching continued but had a delicious heat underneath it. He daren't scratch for fear of bursting a pustule, but gently slapping at the skin with his left hand felt almost orgasmic. He tried to flex his right arm and though it was stiff it moved a little, the shift of the muscles under the corrupted flesh was a deeply satisfying discomfort. Troy smiled at himself.

Then he remembered the phone. One hour. If he didn't show up for the family lunch, they would ask questions, they might even come around. It would be far easier to go along, then not have to see them again for weeks, than try to wriggle out of it now. He glanced towards the door, imagining his egg beyond. If he went to see it, he would never drag himself away. Family meant responsibility. Get dressed and slip out, see the egg after lunch.

For one wild moment he imagined taking it with him, introducing his old family to his new one. But no, the egg needed water. He would return to it.

He dressed and pulled on a baggy hoodie despite the summer warmth, aware he needed to conceal his swollen right side. Sweating already, he stared at his right hand. His fingers had thickened, pressed close together like fat sausages, but purple-black, the skin tight and irregular. His hand itself was swollen almost to a ball. In truth, it barely looked like a hand any longer, more like some strange coral growth.

Troy went into the bathroom and found a small first aid kit, and in it a large triangular bandage for making a sling. He'd had to do a first aid course as part of his job safety protocols and remembered how. He made a sling, big enough to conceal his hand if he tucked the leading edge over it. It was tricky, working it into position left-handed, but he finally managed. It did the job. He'd think of a reason for it on the way there.

It was a long walk to his parent's house, right across the south side of town and up the steep hill. He was sweating profusely by the time he arrived, ten minutes late, but knew he'd have to suffer that as he couldn't take the hoodie off.

"Troy! What happened to you?" His mother's face

was shocked as she opened the door.

"It's nothing, Mum. I fell and dislocated my shoulder. The sling is just a precaution."

"Oh, darling!"

"Really, don't fuss, Mum. It's been put back. It doesn't even hurt."

"Troy broke his arm!" his mother yelled into the house as she headed back down the hall.

"Ya fucking nong," Simon said. "How'd you do that?" His brother grinned from the doorway into the dining room, leaning laconically against the frame. "And take the hoodie off, idiot. How hot are ya?"

"Slipped and dislocated my shoulder. Really, it's fine." He wanted so badly to be back with his egg.

Laura stepped up behind Simon, wrapped her arms around him. "You okay?"

"Yeah, I'm fine."

"You're very red in the face."

"I'm fine!"

Simon patted the air with both hands. "Okay, weirdo, calm ya farm."

Rose was sitting at the dining room table, a glass of wine in hand. His sister was always more relaxed than the rest of the family. She smiled and shook her head, rolled her eyes good-naturedly.

"Let's eat!" his mother said. "Everyone sit down. We can all catch up."

They moved into the dining room and took their seats around the large, dark mango wood table. Troy's father poured the wine, stoic as usual. He smiled and nodded as Troy sat down. "How long does the sling stay on?"

"Just a few days, until the shoulder has rested."

"Doesn't sound too bad." His dad frowned. It was clear he wanted to say more, probably about the hoodie. Troy was sweltering in it, but thankfully his parents had air-conditioning on in the dining room, and that helped.

"What a dickhead," Simon said with a laugh. "How do you dislocate a shoulder by slipping?"

Troy sighed. "Let it go, mate."

"I will, actually," Simon said. "Now all the glasses are filled. Mum, come back." Their mother paused on her way through to the kitchen and looked back, eyebrows high. "Show them, Laura," Simon said.

Laura grinned like she'd won the lottery and held up her left hand, fingers fluttering. A diamond ring glittered on her finger. "He popped the question!"

Troy's mother squealed, Rose rolled her eyes again, Simon beamed like the proverbial cat with the cream.

"And what was your answer?" Troy's dad said, a dumb half-smile stretching his cheek.

"Dad, come on!" Simon said, but he laughed anyway.

Their mother danced around the table, grabbing Laura in a hug, then Simon. Troy's dad looked puffed up with pride and stood to shake his son's hand. Even Rose, usually cynical, had a warmth in her eyes despite the earlier roll. Troy trembled, a mild panic rising in him. It was all so normal, so fucking domestic. How could they be so excited about something so bloody mundane? In thirty years Simon and Laura would be two more husks like his parents, their lives dribbled away on nothing.

"... okay, mate?"

Troy jumped, caught his brother's eye. "What?"

"I said, are you okay, mate? You look ill."

"I'm... I don't know..."

"Can't you just be happy for me or something? Why are you always the bloody weird one, Troy?"

Troy stood, knocking over his chair. He was lightheaded, his entire right side and arm burned with an intensity that made him grit his teeth. Despite the air-con he was hot as hell.

His father stood, brow furrowed. "What's happening, son? Take the top off, you're overheating.

Here, let me help."

The rest of the family stilled, all celebration drained away.

"Fucken hell, Troy, pick your moment!" Simon said.

"Wait, don't be mean," their mother said. "Troy?"

He heard that unearthly siren, like the one he'd dreamed. He felt the pounding wind and rain, the storm as the sky split red and purple. He couldn't breathe. The vastness cajoled him.

"My egg!"

"Your what?" Rose asked.

"I have to go!"

His mother reached for him, her eyes wide. "Troy, what's happening. Let me call the doctor."

He pushed past her and headed for the door. "No, I'm fine. Really. Maybe the fall affected me more than I realised." *The fall. Everyone in The Gulp dreams of the fall.* Whose voice was that in his head? A scratchy old woman's tone. "I just need to go home. I'm sorry. Congrats, Si. Well done, mate. Laura."

"The fuck?" Simon said, scowling.

Troy half-ran, half-fell along the hallway and pulled open the front door.

"Let me drive you, son," his dad said, hurrying along behind.

"No, I want the walk. The fresh air."

"It's a scorcher out there, the car has AC–"

"I'm fine! Thanks though. I'll see you soon. Sorry!" He pulled the door closed and strode off along the path towards the street. As soon as he knew he was heading back to his egg, his head cleared a little.

The front door opened again, his family crammed in it, looking out.

"Troy?" his mother called.

"Honestly, I'm fine," he shouted, without looking back. "I'm really sorry. I'll call you later."

He turned onto the footpath and walked as quickly as he could without breaking into a run. He needed to be home, simple as that.

Standing back in front of his tank half an hour later, he stared in wonder. The egg had grown again, almost filling the tank. The fish and plants had become a part of it, multi-coloured appendages to the mass. The finger-like growths all around its edge had also begun to blur together, making a thick skirt that rippled softly in the current.

Troy tore away his clothes, left them piled on the floor, and lifted his family from the water. He held it tight against his chest, both arms wrapped around it. It was so hot, and so heavy. Orgasmic waves of satisfaction pulsed through him. He sank to the floor under the weight of it, nestled one end into his lap as he sat cross-legged. Hugging it tightly, he rocked gently, murmuring words of love, promises of protection, soft gasps at the pleasurable sensations it sent through him.

Time passed, hours or even days he didn't know. Or care. His phone rang repeatedly, but he ignored it. Eventually it stopped. He assumed the battery had quit. On several occasions, he heard banging on his door. People called his name. He recognised his mother's voice, then his father, more stern. A female voice at one point that might have been Rose, might have been Cindy.

The skirt of clear flesh around the egg spread over his shoulders and merged into his skin. The thickening, purple, blistered flesh of his arms and chest spread to cover his whole upper body, burning with a delicious, insatiable itch. He felt it creep up his neck, spread across his face where he kept his cheek pressed to his beloved.

His vision began to blur, everything tinged purple. His bones grew, spreading up and outward. Over time irrelevant, his spine arched back, his ribs flowered open. His legs shifted and reformed beneath him as his face tipped back. The egg was heavier than ever, more than a metre across, maybe almost as deep, nestled in the cradle of his reforming flesh.

There was purpose to his transformation, he knew. It was the next stage his family required. First the water, now this. Next? It didn't matter, he would do whatever it needed. He would *be* whatever it needed. He exulted in the twisting of his flesh and bones. His arms had merged with it and with each other, wrapped protectively around. His torso had become a basket of blistered, purple flesh atop the thick short stumps of his legs. His head and neck had swollen and become one, pressing out somewhere from the edge of the new entity he had evolved into. Purple sheened his vision, a sound of distant waves constantly filled his ears.

Something called to him, some presence beyond normal hearing. An urge irresistible. On stocky limbs he shifted awkwardly towards the door of his flat and heard them gathered on the other side. He realised he had known they were coming. Or the egg knew, which was the same thing really. They knocked, and he tried to tell them he had no hands to open the door. Instead his voice was a thick slurry of noise, his tongue five times its normal size twisted up inside his contorted face, letting out only strangled coughs and barks. He leaned, tipped one purpled eye towards the door as the knocking became pounding.

"Yeeessssstthhhh," he called, as loudly as he could. "YEEESSSSTTHHHH!"

The door burst inwards, the lock splitting from the wooden frame.

Four people stood there, all pale as chalk. An incredibly old man, a young woman in her late teens, a middle-aged woman in jeans and a red jumper, long hair tied back, and a middle-aged man who had kicked in the door.

"It's time," all four said together in voices that resonated with vibrations he felt right through his new self. A fungal aroma hung around them.

"Tiiimme," Troy slurred, staggering on his crooked

legs, the swollen, blistered bulk of his egg-cradle body ungainly on top.

"For so many months we bided our time," the four said as one. "Prepared. Waiting. We knew you were coming."

They helped him through the door and supported him down the stairs, out into the night air. It was hot, redolent with scents of night jasmine and the sea. The egg buzzed and trembled in the nest of his flesh.

"Whhheerrre?" Troy managed to say as they surrounded him and hurried along the footpath.

"A place is arranged," they said in unison. "Not far. The re-emergence is imminent. The return is upon us."

"Yeessss," Troy slurred as he trundled between them. "I ffeeeeelll itttt. Sssoooonnnn."

In Clooney's, Carter leaned on the bar talking to Chrissy. He didn't often come into the pub, but now and then he liked to get a taste of life down in town. And it was his pub, after all, named after his great-grandfather Clooney P. Carter. A colonial settler, Clooney had built the place by hand, so the story went, and though he named it The Gulpepper Inn, everyone then called it Clooney's, and the habit had stuck. He suspected few people knew that story any more. Time marched on.

Chrissy said something, but Carter shivered, then looked up, instantly forgetting whatever she'd been talking about.

"You okay?" Chrissy asked.

"Something's changed."

"Changed?"

"The energies around us just rippled."

Chrissy nodded. "It's starting?"

"Yes. We knew something was coming. Well, I hope Ingrid Blumenthal got the vessel for the ritual. She was dealing with the Macedonian." Carter frowned, lips pursed. "Come to think of it, I should have heard from her by now. It's been weeks."

"She's a strange one," Chrissy said with a shrug. "She'll come through, right?"

"I hope so. I wonder why she's been so... absent. Normally Talbot keeps me up to speed, but I haven't heard from him in ages either."

"Her husband?"

"And her brother," Carter said distractedly.

Chrissy frowned, opened her mouth to say more, but he turned away. He went to the door of the pub and looked out into the night, sniffed the hot air.

The old woman who was always at the harbour stood on the low wall surrounding the water, staring up into the stars. The sea witch, the locals called her. Carter thought maybe it was a fair moniker.

She felt him looking and met his eye. Even from this distance, he saw her old face was twisted in concern. Carter lifted his chin in a question, and she nodded, resigned. She climbed down and shuffled away towards the lighthouse.

"You okay, boss?" Dace Claringbold asked, strolling up to the pub.

"Yeah, son, I think so. But gird your loins, we might have work to do soon."

"You know me, Mr Carter. I was born ready." He slipped past, heading in towards the bar.

"Time marches on," Carter said to himself. "A new time is coming."

He wondered what might be required of him soon. And he wondered why it felt like Ingrid Blumenthal wasn't in town anymore.

Maddy Taylor sat in Clooney's with Dylan, chatting to Rich, one of Carter's newer goons. He'd only been around a year or so, she thought. Nice guy, but anyone who worked for Carter needed to be kept at arm's length. He'd been telling her how he wasn't from around The Gulp, but had found himself a place here. He seemed a little preoccupied as he talked about it, like he was trying to remember something else. Despite her concerns about having anything to do with Carter or any of his people, she had to talk to someone because all four members of Blind Eye Moon were sitting right there at the next table, drinking beer and chatting quietly. Dylan was mesmerised by their proximity. She was in danger of fangirling if she didn't distract herself. Wait until she told Zack the band had just been hanging out in Clooney's like regular people, in full make-up and everything. They weren't playing a gig that night, but another local band was due to take the stage in an hour or so. Maybe they'd come for them. Imagine being a regular pub band, Maddy thought, and have Blind Eye Moon show up to your gig.

She noticed Rich and all four members of BEM were distracted, looking towards the front of the pub. She followed their gaze and saw Carter standing in the open doorway, looking out into the night, still as a statue. The man gave her the creeps. She didn't want to think too much about what he was doing, but he looked weird framed by the doorway like that. The tableau looked, she thought, like a Blind Eye Moon album cover.

"He can feel it too," Howard said.

Edgar nodded. "Of course. How could he not?"

"You think he's got it in hand?" Shirley asked.

Edgar turned to the drummer. "We'll see, I guess. He takes care of stuff usually, and leaves us alone. So I'm happy to return the courtesy. There's something about him I don't like, anyway. Let's continue to enjoy the truce, shall we?"

"Do you think he'll ask us for help if he needs it?" Clarke asked. "Or too proud?"

Edgar shook his head, took a gulp from his beer. "Not sure. Powers shift in this place all the time. For now, let's get drunk and see if this band is any good."

"Yeah, but this is bigger," Shirley said. "Something major is unstable. Or changing. You can feel it, same as us. And if we all feel it, if Carter is concerned about it, we shouldn't ignore it."

"True," Edgar said. "But let's wait and see, yeah? If it needs our attention, so be it. If not, we let it be." He grinned, shrugged. "Weird shit happens all the time in The Gulp."

The End..?

Read more from Alan Baxter
https://www.alanbaxteronline.com/my-books/

Afterword

I hope you enjoyed this selection of dark weirdness. I've always been fascinated by life in country towns, especially Australian ones. And I've always loved harbour towns. I live in one, after all. The Gulp is not the town I live in, though its geography may seem familiar. The Gulp is a gestalt of many country towns, set in something that's a version of many coastal regions. It's a concept more than a place. Let's all enjoy it from a distance and hope we never find ourselves there. Unless, of course, you enjoy this book enough that you'd like to revisit The Gulp through more stories like these. There are certainly more tales to tell...

Glossary

Throughout this book, I've used Australian English spelling, and a bit of Aussie slang. Hopefully this will help you decipher some of it.

Akubra – Akubra is an Australian hat manufacturer. The company is associated with bush hats made of rabbit fur felt with wide brims that are worn in rural Australia. The term 'Akubra' is sometimes used to refer to any hat of this kind, however the company manufactures a wide range of hat styles including fedora, homburg, bowler, pork pie, and trilby. The name is claimed to derive from an Aboriginal (possibly Birpai) word for a head covering.

arvo – slang for afternoon.

bumbag – fanny pack.

cunjevoi – the aboriginal name for a sea squirt that lives around the edge of the low-tide mark, and often forms mats over the rocks.

doona – duvet, continental quilt.

esky – an Australian brand (Esky) of portable cool box, but the word is commonly used generically for all portable coolers or ice boxes.

flannie – flannel shirt, usually red or blue checks.

grog – booze, any form of alcohol.

jaffle – a toasted sandwich.

parma – parmigiana, a way to prepare chicken with a tomato sauce, ham and cheese covered schnitzel. Regional arguments over chicken parma versus chicken parmi will never be settled in Australia.

RBT – Random Breath Test – roadside sobriety check.

schnitty – schnitzel, usually chicken or veal.

servo – service station. Petrol pumps and usually a small shop.

shag – a fuck.

tucker – food.

Woollies – common slang for Woolworths, a national supermarket chain.

Devouring Dark

Finalist for the Aurealis Award, Ditmar Award, and Australian Shadows Award!

"Devouring Dark is a powerful tale of crime and death, cleverly crafted and flawlessly executed. I'm a fan of Alan Baxter and Devouring Dark is a perfect example of why. Do yourself a favor and join me for some shivers."
– James A. Moore, author of *Seven Forges* .

Hidden City

"A grim and gritty fantasy noir with razor-sharp humor. I loved it!" – Tim Waggoner, author of TEETH OF THE SEA.

Steven Hines listened to the city and the city spoke. Cleveport told him she was sick. With his unnatural connection to her, that meant Hines was sick too.

Bound
Alex Caine #1

Finalist for the 2014 Ditmar Award for Best Novel!

Alex Caine, a fighter by trade, is drawn into a world he never knew existed — a world he wishes he'd never found.

The Roo

Something is wrong in the small outback town of Morgan Creek.

A farmer goes missing after a blue in the pub. A teenage couple fail to show up for work. When Patrick and Sheila McDonough investigate, they discover the missing persons list is growing. Before they realise what's happening, the residents of the remote town find themselves in a fight for their lives against a foe they would never have suspected. And the dry red earth will run with blood.

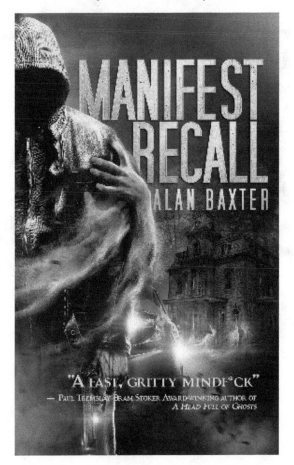

Manifest Recall

"If you like crime/noir horror hybrids do check out Alan Baxter's MANIFEST RECALL. It's a fast, gritty, mind-f*ck." – Paul Tremblay, author of A Head Full of Ghosts and The Cabin at the End of the World.

Following a psychotic break, Eli Carver finds himself on the run, behind the wheel of a car that's not his own, in the company of a terrified woman he doesn't know.

Served Cold

2019 AUSTRALIAN SHADOWS AWARDS WINNER

16 provocative and intensely chilling tales blending horror, fantasy, and the weird.

"At turns creepy and visceral, Baxter delivers the horror goods." – Paul Tremblay, author of A Head Full of Ghosts and The Cabin at the End of the World

Crow Shine

Winner of the 2016 Australian Shadows Award for Best Collected Work; Finalist for the 2016 Aurealis Award for Best Collection; Finalist for the 2016 Ditmar Award for Best Collected Work.

"Alan Baxter is an accomplished storyteller who ably evokes magic and menace. Whether it's stories of ghost-liquor and soul-draining blues, night club magicians, sinister western pastoral landscapes, or a suburban suicide–Crow Shine has a mean bite."—Laird Barron, author of Swift to Chase.

The Book Club

Finalist for the 2017 Aurealis Award for Best Fantasy Novella.
Honorable Mention, Best Horror of the Year, Vol. 10, ed. Ellen Datlow.

Jason Wilkes's life takes a turn for the worse when his wife fails to come home from her book club. Jason calls Kate's 'book buddy', Dave, who assures him she left hours ago. Contacting the police, Jason finds them equal parts sympathetic and suspicious. He tells them almost everything, except that he's been hearing Kate's voice, calling as if from far away. He certainly doesn't mention that he's seeing shadows that reach for him.

Primordial
Sam Aston 1

"PRIMORDIAL has everything you'd want from a
monster story—great characters, a remote location and
a creature with bite!" – Jeremy Robinson,

Sometimes, the legends are true. When eccentric
billionaire Ellis Holloway hires renegade marine
biologist Sam Aston to investigate the legend of a
monster in a remote Finnish lake, Aston envisions an
easy paycheck and a chance to clear his gambling debts.
But he gets much more. Something terrible lives beneath
the dark waters of Lake Kaarme, and it's hungry.

Overlord
Sam Aston 2

What lurks beneath the ice?

Marine biologist Sam Aston is hired to explore a series of subterranean caverns deep beneath the Antarctic. Somewhere within this lost world of magnificent caverns and underground seas lies a source of limitless clean energy, but something guards this treasure. As enemies bent on obtaining this world-changing resource for themselves close in from above, Aston and his team plunge further into the depths, and discover they are not the first to come this way...and they are not alone.

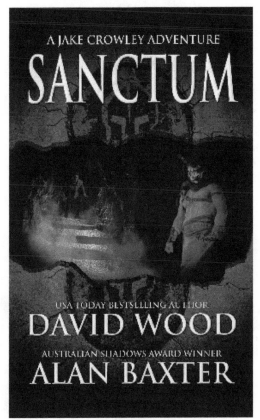

Sanctum
Jake Crowley Prequel

A quiet English village harbors a dark secret.

Trying to escape his past, veteran Jake Crowley takes a teaching position in the village of Market Scarston. But his slow rehabilitation is interrupted when a group of students are apparently attacked by Black Shuck, the legendary demon dog, and Crowley attracts the attention of a secret society dating back to the days of the Roman Empire.

Blood Codex
Jake Crowley 1

An ancient order. A deadly conspiracy. A race against
time. When Jake Crowley rescues Rose Black from
assailants on the streets of London, the two find
themselves embroiled in a mystery that could cost them
their lives. People are dying, and all the victims have
one thing in common with Rose: a birthmark in the
shape of an eagle. From beneath the streets of London,
to castle dungeons, to the heart of Christendom and
beyond, Jake and Rose must race to stay alive as they
seek to unlock the secrets of the Blood Codex.

Anubis Key
Jake Crowley 2

Some doors should never be opened.

When Rose Black's sister goes missing, she once again calls upon Jake Crowley for help, but the two get more than they bargained for. The search takes them on a twisting journey, where danger lies at every turn. From ancient pyramids to lost cities, deadly cultists and conspirators lie in wait as Jake and Rose navigate depths few have dared on a pulse-pounding search for the ANUBIS KEY!

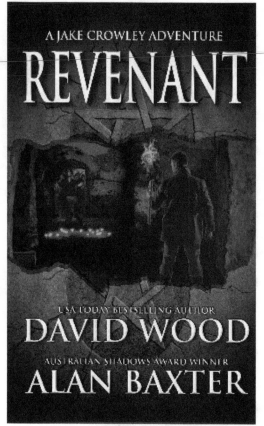

Revenant
Jake Crowley 3

Archaeologists excavating a mass grave in a historic
New York City cemetery make a gruesome discovery:
stacked like cordwood are skeletal remains going back
decades, but all have one thing in common. Each skull
bears a hole in the exact same location. When their
friend is murdered investigating this bizarre discovery,
Jake Crowley and Rose Black set off in search of the
killer. Their path will take them to abandoned hospitals,
hidden chambers, and into the depths of the strange
world that lies beneath New York City in search of
Edgar Allan Poe's secret journal

RealmShift
The Balance 1

Isiah is having a tough time. The Devil is making his job very difficult.

Samuel Harrigan is a murdering lowlife. He used ancient blood magic to escape a deal with the Devil and now he's on the trail of a crystal skull that he believes will complete his efforts to evade Lucifer. But Lucifer wants Samuel's soul for eternity and refuses to wait a second longer for it. Isiah needs Samuel to keep looking for the crystal skull, so he has to protect Sam and keep the Devil at bay. Not for Samuel's sake, but for all of humanity.

MageSign
The Balance 2

Three years have passed since Isiah's run in with Samuel
Harrigan and the Devil. He has some time on his hands
– a perfect opportunity to track down the evil Sorcerer,
Harrigan's mentor. It should have been a simple enough
task, but the Sorcerer has more followers than Isiah ever
imagined, and a plan bigger than anyone could have
dreamed.

With the help of some powerful new friends Isiah
desperately tries to track down the Sorcerer and his cult
of blood before they manage to change the world
forever..

About Alan Baxter

Alan Baxter is a multi-award-winning British-Australian author of horror, supernatural thrillers, and dark fantasy. He's also a martial arts expert, a whisky-soaked swear monkey, and dog lover. He creates dark, weird stories among dairy paddocks on the beautiful south coast of NSW, Australia, where he lives with his wife, son, and hound. The author of over twenty books including novels, novellas, and two short story collections – so far – you can find him online at www.alanbaxter.com.au or on Twitter @AlanBaxter and Facebook. Feel free to tell him what you think. About anything.